The Daysman

The Daysman

STANLEY MIDDLETON

Hutchinson
London Melbourne Sydney Auckland Johannesburg

Hutchinson & Co. (Publishers) Ltd

An imprint of the Hutchinson Publishing Group

17–21 Conway Street, London W1P 6JD

Hutchinson Group (Australia) Pty Ltd
30–32 Cremorne Street, Richmond South, Victoria 3121
PO Box 151, Broadway, New South Wales 2007

Hutchinson Group (NZ) Ltd
32–34 View Road, PO Box 40–086, Glenfield, Auckland 10

Hutchinson Group (SA) Pty Ltd
PO Box 337, Bergvlei 2012, South Africa

First published 1984
© Stanley Middleton 1984

Set in VIP Plantin by
D. P. Media Limited, Hitchin, Hertfordshire

Printed and bound in Great Britain by
Anchor Brendon Ltd, Tiptree, Essex

British Library Cataloguing in Publication Data

Middleton, Stanley
The daysman.
I. Title
823'.914[F]   PR6063.I25

ISBN 0 09 154850 0

To Keith and Edna Train

Neither is there any daysman betwixt us
that might lay his hand upon us both.

(JOB, ix, 33)

And he said, Who made thee a prince and
judge over us?

(EXODUS, ii, 14)

1

Downstairs the children were talking, shrilly, and the sounds dulled the blare of television noise. John Richardson in his study, the small area of recovered space under the roof, sat at his desk and listened, trying to discover whether his three daughters quarrelled or merely raised their voices to make themselves heard over *Crossroads* or whatever it was they were paying no attention to on the screen. From the top of the house the altercation hammered like pandemonium, but if he clattered down the aluminium ladder to the bedroom, and then the stairs, he would find in the living-room a scene of cheerful order.

First the television would not be so strident as it seemed from two floors above, and his eldest, sixteen-year-old Marguerite, would be in an armchair with a folder on her knees, scribbling happily away at her mathematics homework, smiling, one eye half cocked towards soap opera, the right hand dashing down the lines of equations with their scrolls of integral signs. The second, Virginia, eleven, would be at the table also engaged on homework but frowning, sighing, fiddling with her hair, perhaps even snapping at her sisters to turn the sound down or off; she took those matters seriously, and liked to make her attitude plain. She would have no trouble with her work, would be progressing through it with all the fluency of her elder sister, but needed to demonstrate the outward and visible signs of a struggle that did not exist. Fay, the youngest, six years old, would be flat out on the carpet with a book, chin in hand, her only signs of concentration the occasional drumming of her toes. All three would look up at their father, Virginia with a spasm of exaggerated annoyance, the other two with indifference, and then resume their pursuits unless he spoke. Their mother, Joanna, he guessed, would be in the kitchen proving to them all that her work, like theirs, was continuous, but without

9

the comfort of intellectual content. The preparation of tomorrow's meals or sandwiches for those who would not eat school dinners involved a clashing of tins and pans, and when this was complete she would advance into the living-room with her ironing board and a red-faced expression not unlike that of her second daughter.

Richardson grinned to himself, and concentrated on the exercise-book in front of him.

> 'Love looks not with the eye but with the mind
> And therefore is wing'd Cupid painted blind.'

He inserted a tick in the margin, and read the carefully spaced-out words of the sentences following. The earnest miss was explaining to him here why Shakespeare's clichés were of interest, in that they were based on common observation but would suddenly sparkle into a delicacy of words that could not fail to dazzle the listener. 'In this case?' he wrote in the margin. A pound to a penny he had made some such assertion in his lesson, and this girl had taken the sentence down, and now served it back to him, stone cold. He flicked shut the cover to make sure of the writer's name. She was clever, and therefore it was possible that this couplet, brand-new to her, did what she said it did, conjuring up a Renaissance painting or tapestry. He did not erase his remark. She could find fitter examples; she had better if she wanted to impress university examiners. This couplet represented perhaps the rest of the speech, but it was most likely that the girl had recently discovered the truth of the statement in her own experience, and to find it so exactly paralleled in verse seemed a confirmation rarely achieved, a confluence of literature and life. Richardson pursed his lips and pressed on.

The phone chirruped. His eyrie up here under the roof, meant to protect him from noise, seemed a sounding board, a collecting post. When his wife used the vacuum cleaner, it howled as if at his ear; the washing machine quietly thumped its way across his desk whereas in the kitchen it worked in silence; footsteps and speech two floors below echoed about his head. He looked away, hoping to be called, when he'd descend complaining about interruptions. Nothing. Marguerite's easy tones

10

reached him, incomprehensibly; his daughters took to the phone at every opportunity so that he sarcastically offered to fix a system of intercommunicating wires between their bedrooms. Now Margot would be explaining to a friend some problem set for homework and that would inevitably lead to psychoanalysis of the music mistress or a discussion of Dryden's, the new chemistry master's, appalling suits. He heard steps which blotted out the talk; his wife entered the bedroom below.

'Hello, there,' he called down cheerfully.

'Hello.'

'Are you busy?'

'What do you think? I'm putting the ironing away.' Joanna trotted out, it sounded more like stamping, to the airing cupboard, blundered back, slapping drawers open and shut.

'Who's Margot talking to?'

'Steve. Who else?'

'Won't be long before all three of 'em have their boyfriends.' That made him feel jovial, above the conflict, shouting down the trap-door, but Joanna had gone without waiting for his ruminations. He returned to the *Midsummer Night's Dream*, read a page or two of the essay, pained and pleasured, awarded it a reduced alpha mark, scribbled a complimentary comment. The girl was good; the essay much more thorough than anything he could put together. Marguerite below replaced the telephone, turned up the television sound.

At least it was warm up here in the study, and bright, with shelves of books, one bright-red wall, a white false-ceiling, carpets, an armchair. The top of one bookcase was decorated with photographs: two of Joanna, one recent, the three girls together at the seaside two years ago, all looking small, lost, smiling and innocent, one of Fay in her pram, Marguerite and Virginia together in the garden, aged twelve and seven then, in riding hats, breeches and hacking jackets, with crops in hand. At this end the final snap showed Richardson and his elder brother under a gothic arch. It had been taken some while ago, probably before Fay was born, though he couldn't remember, so, say seven years, which would make him thirty-two at the time and Eric forty-one. They looked isolated, the pair of them, though the occasion was a reunion of their school, and the yard

11

in front of them had been full of Old Broughtonians, hatted wives, sober children, in solemn groups, hand shaking, laughing, seriously greeting masters, pointing their cameras at Victorian gargoyles or leaded stained-glass or towards the new, concrete hall, the sixth-form complex. The brothers appeared young, might in fact with different ties have been prefects about their daily duty, in the same sub-fusc suits they had worn as boys, the same slightly pinched, smug expressions, the same neatly parted hair, though at that time John had been for three years headmaster of a comprehensive school in Surrey and Eric had held a chair of Indian studies for four at Yale.

Eric had been over for a conference and had insisted that he and his brother attend the reunion. This had been typical; it is what a decent man would want, and yet not to be expected of Eric. He had taken a brilliant scholarship to Oxford from Broughton in classics, gained an outstanding first in Classical Mods, but then, for no reason, had changed to a course in Sanskrit and Hindi.

John Richardson remembered the announcement at home.

His father, a schoolteacher, had been shocked, incapable of grasping how one who was scoring such success should wish to change.

'I had a letter,' the old man said, 'from your tutor.' He had indeed; he took it to his bedroom, to the lavatory, the far end of the garden to fetch out and read three, four, seven times a day. 'He said he looked forward to an equally satisfactory and deserved result in Greats.'

Eric had seen the missive.

'I might do as well in . . .' he began.

'You might not. That's what worries me. You are due to start on what is regarded as the foremost course in humanities in Europe, if not the world, and you choose to throw it all in.'

'I'm a linguist, not a philosopher or a historian.'

'Your pastors and masters don't agree.'

Eric patiently explained how he had come to be interested in Sanskrit through his philological studies, how he had consulted the professor, why he considered it a rational extension of his progress so far, but his father gruffly interrupted.

12

'You might just as logically have decided on Chinese or Hebrew.'

'Exactly, but . . .'

'But you'll be up against those who have already started the course, have a decided advantage over you.'

Eric began to consider out loud, with extreme lucidity, why he did not think there was much force in the argument; already he sounded like a full-blown professor.

The dispute lasted for days, well after the father had given up, but he had continued believing this to be the equivalent of the university education he never had, which he envied to the end of his life. Eric showed no passion, spoke drily, completely sure of himself, treating his father as a promising if awkward pupil.

Their mother had intervened with exasperation.

'For goodness' sake,' she cried, 'won't you ever stop? You're not doing one ha'porth of good. You're like squabbling children.'

Father would have liked to have killed her with a word, but no such spell existed. His wife frightened him with a bustle of common sense, as his eldest son silenced his arguments with cold, intelligent authority. At present he could bully John, but he'd soon lose that advantage. The old man had lived to see Eric gain a fellowship at Oxford, transfer to Cambridge and to win his chair at Yale; then he'd talked about the boldness of scholarship, the necessity to move, the irrelatedness of disciplines, and one would have gathered that he had counselled his son, against the boy's will, to abandon Greek for Sanskrit. He often sat with the professor's books on his knee, two in Devanagari script, or his learned articles with references to Hittite or Gothic or Lithuanian or Old Irish, as he had sat with Eric's tutor's letter, uplifted. He had taught himself the Sanskrit alphabet but shook his head over the convolutions of grammar, delighted by his son's prowess, glad that he himself was one-up academically on his colleagues, for example, but basically afraid to go further, to test his limitations. 'I'm too old,' he'd say, puckering his face, but with what pleasure he'd basked in his son's achievements. And there, in the first volume, stood his name: To my father, Bernard Thomas Richardson.

Marguerite had ceased, then, to talk into the telephone, and John returned to his essays. He had always said that when he became a headmaster he would not give up teaching, and had not done so; he put in at least one or two classroom periods each day. Though this was unusual, and he argued that it kept him in touch with the bread-and-butter of school life, it was popular neither with administrators, who invited him in to conferences, symposia, consultations which interrupted the steady continuity necessary, nor with his subordinates, who regarded it as just another attempted demonstration of his superior pedagogic powers, with everything weighted in his favour – for when he'd done his short stint he could sidle off to read *The Times* or if he felt energetic to mark the few exercises, or stroll round the campus laying down the law to secretaries or caretakers or passing postmen, while they had to go headlong into the lower school to hold down thirty roistering vandals.

'A headmaster can please nobody,' he told his father, on his appointment, at thirty-four the youngest secondary school principal in the county.

'Will you try?' B.T. asked. This surprised John; irony did not feature largely in his father's defences, and now, though neither knew it, the old man was within a month of death.

The telephone rang again. Since Margot had communed with Stephen, no one downstairs seemed in any hurry to answer. Selfishly they had decided it was for their parents.

Virginia called upstairs.

'For you, Daddy. Phone.'

'Who is it?' he grumbled, passing through. Virginia, already frowning at her books, did not even lift her head.

The voice which answered the bark of his surname into the mouthpiece was clear, much at ease.

'This is Felicity Brooks, Stephen's mother. I'd like to ask a favour of you.'

'Surely.'

'It's about my daughter, Veronica, that I'd like to ask your advice.'

Mrs Brooks outlined the difficulty. Veronica had refused to take up a university place after 'A' levels, had done a year abroad, taken a secretarial course, and now held down a dead-

14

end job answering the telephone and typing letters in an architect's office, bored out of her mind. Now, 'at long, long last,' the clear voice breathed, sense seemed to begin to prevail, and Veronica just considered, no more, a university application, or at least had not demurred when her mother suggested that she consult someone about it. She'd drawn the line at her old headmistress, 'a stupid fat cow' (Mrs Brooks did not report this), but had offered no objections to her brother's girlfriend's father.

Richardson did not know the Brooks family socially, though he had bumped occasionally into Stephen below paying court to Margot. He was a tall, good-looking young man, in jeans and fancy shirt, well spoken, very polite, with a slightly nervous smile which bared the bottom part of his upper front teeth. He was preparing for 'A' levels, then to sit a history scholarship at Cambridge where he hoped to read law. The Brookses (real name Caulfield-Brooks) lived, according to Marguerite, in a large house backing on to the golf-course in Wentworth Park, and the father, an engineer, spent a great deal of time abroad, in the Middle East, and for this reason Richardson, perhaps wrongly, connected him with oil. The mother was said to write.

'I'd be very grateful, because it's so difficult. Vernie's a grown woman, she's twenty, and yet doesn't know her mind. We don't want to push her into anything, but I can't help feeling that she'll be missing something if she doesn't go. Her father grumbles, but he'd do that in any case.' A well-delivered scale of laughter.

The daughter had no idea what she wanted to study, that was half the trouble; she'd 'A' levels in English, French and Maths. Perhaps if he'd talk to her, etc., etc. He asked her to name a time.

'Will you come to us, or would it be more convenient if Vernie drove over to you? We ought to have invited you and Mrs Richardson over before, now that Stephen and Marguerite are so friendly, but Conrad has been abroad since the beginning of August, and looks like staying there.' He knew how it was, didn't he?

Curiosity made him say he'd call on them.

Felicity Brooks fluttered through sentences of thanks, causing him to think of an aviary of small dun birds, flapping

15

wings, tail feathers, crests, all a-quiver, alive, nothing out of the ordinary, but unstill, restlessly doing little.

When on his way back upstairs he reported on the nature of the call and asked how Marguerite found Mrs Brooks, the girl said, 'She talks a lot. Bossy, y'know.'

'And Veronica?'

'Oh, all right."

2

Outside, as John Richardson stared from the windows of his study at the Penrose Comprehensive, trees were white and beautiful with frozen fog. Starlings miserably strutted on the cleared paths behind the kitchen, the paved paths up to the impressive front steps and the main doors were dry, but elsewhere on the playgrounds, the tennis courts, the roofs, the playing fields, the small yards, the car parks two inches of frozen snow congealed greyly.

At three-fifteen the place was clear of its students. In the bitter winter weather, he had cut down the lunch-hour, he'd held two staff meetings about doing this permanently, and had learnt nothing except that three of his staff in quite different ways had seemed fit for certification as lunatics. This did not surprise him, except that one of these men was an excellent teacher, a good father, a city councillor in the Labour interest and a Methodist local preacher. And yet his impassioned set-speech, his intervention had conveyed the impression that, if the headmaster removed an hour from the lunch-break, the cultural societies would disappear and with that the normal order of the universe, and the subsequent descent of the incurred wrath of God. Perhaps the man always spoke with these fiery metaphors; certainly the rest of the staff, or its representatives, the number was too great for a meeting of the lot, had sat through the jeremiad with expressions of boredom and consultation of wristwatches.

Stanley Smith, head of the department of science, crunched across the main yard towards his car. He opened the boot, put in his small leathern attaché case, a museum specimen from the thirties, adjusted its position to his satisfaction and then knocked together his green wellington boots, which had picked up little of the packed, hard-frozen snow, before he removed his trilby hat, of the same age as the case, an heirloom, and sat in the driving seat, his car door wide-open to the calm ferocity of the weather. From this distance the man's movements would have suggested that he was in his sixties if not seventies, and yet Dr Smith would not be thirty-four for another eight months, was a martinet to pupils and subordinate staff alike and in the three years of his tenure had revolutionized the teaching of science in the place. He brooked no opposition, but his success had been so spectacular (no one expects quick results in institutions of learning) that he reigned unopposed over his empire. The head expected him to leave; he knew one university education department which, even in those times of cut-back, was ready to make a place for him. The man had produced one excellent book on the teaching of science, and was halfway through another, sat on one national committee and had appeared on television programmes dealing with the training of scientists and technologists.

Smith banged his car door to, edged across the wrinkled snow into the drive and out on to the street, presumably to his wife, quietly beautiful but more ambitious for him than he was, and his small children. It was a privilege to know, to deal with such men, Richardson thought, idly enough; youngsters would win scholarships to Oxford and Cambridge; others would gain university places because of what that man did and said; those who, in others' hands, might have ended up as foremen electricians in the mines would become doctors of philosophy. People of the energy, the skills, the beliefs of Stanley Smith made it powerfully clear that teachers could alter lives dramatically, made it blatantly plain to those shabby mediocrities who occupied space and passed time at the front of most of the classrooms. Richardson did not want to lose Smith; he represented success; but just as surely his wife would winkle him out so that he would end his career as a headmaster, a professor

17

of education, the principal of a college of higher learning, a director, an administrator wishing to God he could get his hands off the piles of paper and round a test-tube or on a balance, at a bench, well-to-do, less happy.

Corners of the school were minutely alive with, Richardson noticed, odd little black figures, some sliding, others picking a hazardous, mincing way. By this time the place ought to be empty; the line of special buses, their times changed after a wrangle with bureaucrats as idiotic and colourful as a stage revolution, had disappeared, the staff car parks, the students', were almost bare, and yet from crannies, and for the next half-hour small children would emerge, collars up or down, some coatless even in this bitter weather, all with valid excuses for their presence, making solemn or ludicrous tracks for home. Miss Taylor brought in the final letters for signature, each unimportant, before she replaced her typewriter cover (the other secretaries had dispersed five minutes after final bell) and donning furry boots and overcoat, left the campus, the oddities, the wide-spread buildings, labs and blackboards to him and the dust and the caretakers.

'Good night, Mr Richardson,' Miss Taylor called.

'Good night. Drive carefully.'

Enid Taylor dropped her catch, and left for domestic worries. She lived with an elderly mother, a much admired woman, lively and demanding, who had lately begun to lose her grip on reality so that it was touch and go whether the daughter would arrive home to an admirably cooked and served dinner or to a cold house with Mrs Taylor sitting dazed and distressed by a cold hearth in a litter of biscuit crumbs. There seemed neither rhyme nor reason for the changes in behaviour; they happened without pattern, but the Taylor took it cheerfully, glad she could cope. She drove her six-year-old car across the yard with élan. A brave woman.

Richardson sat down at his desk, began to read an interim report on 'Examinations at Sixteen Plus', found after ten minutes that he was wasting time, that the little he was taking in he knew already, and filed the document away, smiling thinly to himself. He turned off the electric fire, drew his coat from the modern, ugly, elaborate hanger, a product of one of the workshops, and wondered if it would ever be possible to grade by written and practical examinations the sixteen-year group, and if it were managed what good might accrue, and to whom. Such discussion of human endeavour – and most of his time here was spent on such intractables – seemed this January to be unimportant, frozen into proportion by the fiercely cold weather outside. The shuddering damp, the ice-packed pavements, the flu epidemic, the misery of existence knocked or wrung all life out of humanity. With the return of spring, bird-song, temperatures in the fifties fahrenheit, it would be proper to consider examinations and careers and love, but for the present nature warred against warmth, so that ambition, analysis, prognosis died with it.

'Is it going to last for ever?' The head caretaker, overalled, marching a broom along the corridors.

'I hope not.'

'They say on the radio we're going to have winters like this for the next ten years.'

'Conjecture.'

'Good night, then, sir.'

'Good night.'

At home Mrs Richardson's kitchen shone, the air delicious with the smell of cooking. Fay sat on a stool reading a book of fairy tales.

'Has the telly broken down, then?' her father enquired, jovially.

'I shall help Mummy if she needs me.'

'And that's put me in my place.'

The other two banged in later, complaining about the cold; their schools worked on to usual hours, making no concessions to climate. This evening they ate in the kitchen, off available flat surfaces, two large toads-in-the-hole, a dish Richardson did not much care for, but a favourite with all three girls.

'It must be fattening,' he suggested to Marguerite, handing her a huge second helping.

'Of course, but I see to it that I work it off.'

'And Mum's batter . . .' said Virginia.

'And the size of the sausages.' Fay.

19

'You sound more and more like television commercials,' he chided.

'At least they're appreciative.' Joanna.

'It's delicious, really delicious.'

'Too late.' Margot and Ginny, crowing. Fay clapped the performance, in delight, and while her father shook a finger in mock anger, her mother ordered her to get on with the meal. As he washed the dishes, this evening with the help of Virginia, Joanna, who would not sit down but marched round them, clearing up, opening and shutting cupboard doors, asked, 'Are you out tonight?'

He reminded her of his appointment with Veronica Brooks.

'Is Mr Brooks abroad?' she demanded, of either.

'Don't ask me.' Ginny. 'I don't love lovely Stephen.'

'Don't you wish you did?' he wanted to know.

'He's quite good-looking. I'll give you that.'

'She's a fair picker is our Margot, then?'

'They go after her.' The child spoke with the certainty of her eleven years.

Joanna began to grumble about his chasing out on so inclement a night. The radio had forecast freezing fog, and when he said he'd walk, she described an accident to a near neighbour who had fallen on the ice at the path at the end of her garden and found herself incapable of making her way back to the house. She had been ridiculously rescued, after shrieking for help, by the dustmen.

'I shall be careful,' he said.

'Are you always careful?' Ginny.

'I expect that's how it seems to you.'

'Yes. In a way. We ought to have a washing-up machine; it would be worth it with five of us.'

'What's that to do with care?'

'You're careful with money.'

'I see.' He could hear Joanna laughing, though she had set her face against such mechanical help, but she did not like to see him having his own way, even if it complemented hers.

'You tell your mother.'

He wrapped up against the night and wore wellington boots to keep his footing on the ice-packed, uneven pavements.

20

Barely a soul passed in the streets which had lost all semblance of comfort, made up of houses not homes, after the darkening of the lying, frozen, bumpy snow.

The Brooks family lived in a tree-lined cul-de-sac, with one edifice divided into two villas on either side. The divisions were huge enough to be called mansions, with the two wide brick-built Norman doorways in the middle and a spacious square of shrub-filled garden behind the low, forbidding street-wall from which, during the war, the iron railings had been cut, leaving ugly stumps. Why houses of this size had been built in twos he could not imagine, unless some Victorian entrepreneur had designed and constructed the four dwellings for his family use. Three-storeyed, double-fronted, with wide bay-windows, outbuildings and stables in the rear reached by a broad drive, the places preached enormous weight in the poorly lit street, tall, spacious, solid, both threatening and homely, provincial, the back-street striking it rich, and glorying in it. He wished there were enough light to examine the decoration which he guessed to be elaborate, but now he carefully climbed the six uncleared steps which led to the paved area before the front door. Inside, through stained-glass he could see the glow of reddish bulbs.

Mrs Brooks answered the bell.

The hall with its straight flight of stairs, carved wood, heavily gothic, turning at the top at an undisguised right angle to a balcony, was impressive and, thank God, warm. Brass-hung globes with red, dimpled glass, artfully, randomly scattered, half concealed in shadow the table with flowers, the chairs, a gold-framed picture of – he could not see – chaos and old night.

Mrs Brooks allowed him to change boots for slippers before ushering him into a great drawing-room where they sat before a gas-fire, their armchairs protected oddly by tapestry screens. She waved a hand at these.

'Victorian builders seemed incapable of stopping draughts,' she said.

'Perhaps they did not want to.'

'Why not?' Sharply, suspiciously.

'Discomfort is what made England great.'

She wrinkled her face into a brief, acknowledging smile, a

21

handsome woman, but unprepared for paradoxes, conceits of this nature.

'What would you like to drink?' She pointed down at a dark oak table; he chose whisky; she poured an inch into a thick tumbler from a square cut-glass decanter, added water at his instruction. These preparations seemed formal, hieratical, for she stood, manipulating glassware decorously, looking always towards him; her own quick splashing of gin, from a bottle, tonic, ice-cubes was perfunctory, as if she begrudged time not spent in his service.

'It's very kind of you,' she began. He listened to the woman's polite sentences, watching her carefully made-up face. It appeared remarkable that one so well dressed, at ease, articulate should need an intermediary in negotiation with her daughter. 'I can't say,' she was warning now, 'how Veronica will co-operate with you. She agreed to see you, but that was more than a week ago.' She briefly reviewed Veronica's schooling; the girl had been expelled from two boarding establishments, and had done best in the two years of sixth-form work at the local public day school. 'We thought she'd really settled down at last. Until we came here, of course, we'd been moving about; I lived abroad with my husband. Stephen throve at his prep and we were very uncertain what to do about him when we bought this house seven years ago. We sent him to the high school in the end, and he's done really well, so presumably we took the right decision.'

'I take it you chose this place because of your husband's work?' he said, politely.

'Partly. And this was my grandfather's house.' She said no more about that, but talked on, quickly, almost coldly, like a newsreader instructed to leave no gaps lest an enemy broadcaster seize the chance to insert satirical ribaldries. She had plenty to say, was never short of well-chosen phraseology, but he wondered if she spoke to enlighten him or disburden herself. She did not seem to expect him to question her, bridled, if that were not too strong a word, at his interruptions.

She invited him to take more whisky, and when he refused, raised her eyebrows, sucked breath in, dashed herself another gin.

22

Now she outlined the plans she and her husband had put to Veronica, all of which, unreasonably, had been rejected out of hand.

'What does she want to do?' he asked.

'Nothing, as far as we can make out. She'd be content to sit here all day and read and play records. She has this job, of course.' Dismissive.

'Will she help in the house?'

'Not really. Not that there's any need.' Mrs Caulfield-Brooks drew a finger down her cheek, checking perhaps that flesh existed still, under its cosmetic layer. He could see that she had once been beautiful in a thin style, with large eyes, high cheek-bones, a small but imperiously held nose, good teeth; she was still, as she knew, an attractive woman. Before she spoke again she put her left hand to her left breast, killing some pain. It seemed a tender, self-revealing gesture, unremarked by the woman. 'We do not know what she wants. She does not know herself.' The voice, hard and small, contradicted the clasped breast.

'Men?' he asked.

'She seems normal. Had her share. Her father bluntly told her that that was one of the advantages of university. She'd meet a better selection of males.'

'There's been nothing serious?'

'Not that we know of recently. She wouldn't say anything to us, anyway.' Mrs Brooks seemed not quite open.

'Has she always been like that? Secretive?'

'I can't say. She was a normal, cheerful little girl, but then again there were periods when we saw very little of her. But she was cheerful. It wasn't until later that she became rebellious, was expelled from school.'

'For what reason?'

'Disobedience. I realize these places have old-fashioned pettifogging rules and regulations, so we weren't too distressed. We were a little surprised, I must admit, because most girls put up with it. I know I did, and things were stricter by far, then. But, anyhow, when we came here she seemed to settle down at once, got her "A" levels, even played hockey and netball in her own time. She didn't want university, she said, so went off to

23

France for a year, and worked in a factory owned by a colleague of my husband. Manufactured furniture. She swept the shavings up, as far as I can make out. Then she came back, and signed on for a secretarial course, off her own bat. Quite pleasantly. No hassle. We didn't object; they're qualifications which are always useful, and she found herself this office job, with Plumb, Cheadle and Wilkins, the architects. Derek Cheadle is a friend. But she's bored. She says so. And it worries me.'

'You think university is the answer?'

'What else is there? It's difficult enough to find employment. I suppose Conrad could get her a place with his firm, but it's a step sideways, into the same mechanical routine.'

'Even abroad?'

'When you've lived abroad as much as we have, and that includes the children, it loses some of its attraction.' That put him in his provincial place. 'Perhaps we should go up now.' She had lost interest. He drank off his whisky, and unbuttoned his jacket. With no ceremony, no words even, she led the way.

Felicity Brooks knocked at her daughter's room, waited, and at an indistinct invitation thrust the door open and said coolly, 'Here's Mr Richardson, Vernie.'

She signalled him forward, did not enter herself, clicked the door to after him.

The room, much smaller than he expected, closed in behind the shut door, a chaotic jungle: the window, curtains undrawn, not to be reached, was thicketed, blotted out with plants which thrust upwards from pots on the floor, gilded and bronzed receptacles, a Roman holiday; the table was crowded with a music centre, paper, haphazard piles of records, two guitars; no drawer was closed; every cupboard door bulged open, revealing crazy lines of books or record sleeves; a crimson frock with black lace was flung over the back of one of half a dozen unmatched, littered chairs; magazines, newspapers, cardboard boxes of inexplicables – in one case Christmas tree baubles, in another felt hats stacked crown over crown – barely allowed corridors of passage along a shabby, reddish carpet of excellent quality; the walls, quadri-coloured, staring white, by the windows, ultramarine, biscuit and ruby were hung with posters, mistily focused girls with crimped hair, a pop group, two advertisements for jeans, a theatre bill of the nineties, two Toulouse-Lautrecs, three Phil Mays, a staggering lightning-stroke staircase of a collage in red and black, a Modigliani nude, a Salvador Dali print, a blow-up photograph of Michelangelo's David, and wall-lamps amateurishly spotted with red paint, while above a bare bulb under a plain china shade, coolie-hat fashion, hung as over the editor's desk.

In the one armchair, by a powerfully burning gas-fire, colourful as the rest of the clutter, Veronica sat.

'Come on,' she said. Her voice was deep contralto, posher than mother's, not unfriendly. 'Come on in. What do you think?'

'No horse brasses,' he said. 'No joss sticks. No Paddington Bear.'

'In my bedroom. Sit down.'

He took the one unencumbered seat, an uncomfortable circular thing with a rail that prodded the back, perhaps an art deco piano stool. The fire bit into his trouser legs.

Veronica was plump, pretty with darkened eyelids, but rounded unlike her mother and brother. Her knuckles were dimpled. She wore a wide, shapeless full-length dress of wine-red, banded in black and cream at sleeves, waist, neck and hem.

'Mummy's given you a drink, I imagine.' She snatched up from amongst the debris an electric kettle, brandishing it. 'I can offer you tea or coffee. From bags. Both.' She spoke as if she were chewing some utterly delicious titbit. He thanked her, and refused. She smiled again, without reference to him, and said, 'Go on, then. Give me your advice.'

'I'll need to know just what you think.'

She nodded, as if that seemed sensible.

'You're wasting your time,' she said. 'I'm quite content, really. I have a job, and it occupies me, and a place here. It's my mother who thinks I'm bored.'

'Why?'

'There are some things she classes as interesting. Going to university is one of them. Even if it will do me no good employment-wise, she still thinks it's worthwhile. Typing business letters, taking down shorthand, answering the

25

telephone, fetching in the boss's cup of coffee, that's boring. Now, I admit that to a certain extent it is, but no more let's say than a teacher's job, or a doctor's. You go through the same routine performances.'

'I can tell you've not been in a school for some time.'

'I'm talking about schools, not blackboard jungles.'

He let that go.

'Your mother means that you're not extended, doesn't she? A university would open your eyes in a way that the lower reaches of commerce wouldn't.'

'Lower reaches?' She mused on that.

'You're not going to live with your parents all your life? They'll die, and you'll have to depend on your own resources. So your standard of living, inflated at present by your father's earning capacity, will fall because it's very unusual for secretarial staff, especially women, to be promoted to managerial or executive positions in industry. Whereas, if you have a degree, you'll be in a stronger bargaining position, even if you want to go back into business. Paper qualifications are . . .'

'Yes,' she said, stopping him. 'I know. They all tell me.'

'Moreover, I agree with your mother that three years at a university are three years well spent.'

'Only if that's what you're trained for, or have been led to believe it's what you want.'

'You'll meet a more interesting range of men.'

'You make it sound like a supermarket,' she said.

'And none the worse for that. It's a hard world. We could do with a few bargains, best buys. It's heartbreaking for a schoolmaster like me to have to send decent young people out to live on social security.'

'They're parasites on the state; I on my parents.'

'It's not their fault. They'd work if they could.'

'I work, Mr Richardson, may I remind you?'

'I'm sorry. I headed myself off the subject. What I'm saying, and your mother, is that you're excluding interesting possibilities, limiting yourself needlessly. You're clever, I'm told, but have never quite accepted schools, for one reason or another. You'll find university different. Besides you've been out in the hard world.'

'I've seen people made redundant.' She smiled still.

'And learning is worth something in its own right.'

'You don't need to go to university to learn.'

'No, but it's easier there. You do it more quickly, painlessly.'

'Doesn't that contradict your puritan ethic? We used to write essays on "The fascination of what's difficult" in the sixth form.'

'Yeats,' he said.

'Yes. He wanted to be a poet. I know, I know. He also wanted to be a man of action, a successful lover, a public figure. What if I want to be a secretary?'

They talked for twenty minutes, without rancour, without direction, he thought, so that she'd begin to trust him, take an interest in him. At the end of it he asked for a cup of coffee and she rose to fill the kettle from a sink he had not noticed. Plugged in, it hummed comfortably. Two spotlessly clean mugs were lifted down.

'Milk substitute,' she said. 'There's no fridge here.'

'You surprise me.'

She laughed.

'You're not altogether solemn, are you?' she said, not looking at him.

'You should hear me in school assembly.'

'You're just an actor.'

'In other words a hypocrite, you mean.'

'Same Greek original,' she said, surprising him, 'isn't it?'

She poured out the coffee, handed his over, said she dared not keep biscuits in the room. As they sipped, she asked him his first names.

'John Bernard Neil.'

'What's your wife call you?'

'John.'

'Like it?' He nodded. ' "The pious monks of St Bernard". Can I call you Bernard?'

'Why?' Sharp, suspicious.

'I like it.' She answered innocently, but clasping her mug added, 'It's the sort of thing you'd expect of a twee family like ours, isn't it?'

He produced his brochures; his pile seemed lost in the room.

27

When he asked her if she would read them, she said suddenly, directly, 'Imagine you knew nothing of me. That I was one of your sixth-formers. What courses would you suggest?'

'I'm ready for that.' He took a list he had prepared from an inner pocket.

'Efficient,' she said, glanced at it, laid it down.

Again they talked as they sipped; Veronica asked the right questions, but without much show of interest. She consulted his list again, smiled cat-like.

'There we are then,' he said, setting down his mug. 'Shall I rinse these?'

'No, thank you. I don't like domesticated men.'

'I see. I think it's all straightforward, then.'

'Yes. I filled in UCCA forms when I was at school. Only I didn't send them off.'

He stood; so did she. She was taller than he expected. When he said goodbye she dropped him a small mock-curtsey.

'I'll come again if I'm needed,' he said.

'You're always that, I'm sure.' She smiled. 'Bernard.'

He made his way along the richly red carpet of balcony-corridor and staircase to find Mrs Brooks waiting for him.

'How did it go?' she asked.

'At least she listened to me. I've left her with relevant information.'

'Will she . . . do you think?'

'I've no idea.'

Mrs Brooks to his amazement was stroking his upper arm, strongly, not gripping, but positively. He had guessed her as a non-toucher.

'It's hard,' she said, 'when the father is at home so rarely.'

'Yes.' He held himself stock-still.

'Sometimes I'm at my wits' end.' She looked upward to where Stephen came down the stairs. She ceased to stroke but did not relinquish her hold on Richardson's arm.

'Here's mother's pride and joy,' Stephen said. He'd never spoken facetiously like that before in Richardson's hearing, had been serious, intense, on the edge of discovery.

'Mr Richardson has been talking to Vernie.'

'But did she talk to him?'

28

'Stephen! Can I offer you another drink?' to Richardson, who refused.

'Did you come by car?' The boy.

'I walked.'

'Super. I've given up my scooter so conditions must be bad. Bye. Be seeing you, then.'

He waved, disappeared somewhere into the back of the house. Mrs Brooks still had a hand on the visitor's arm, but she made no attempt to detain him when he said he must go, merely asking in a low voice to call in on them again.

He left wondering how she would occupy the next quarter of an hour. It was ten minutes to nine.

3

Richardson sat in his office a week later. The forecast thaw distantly dallied in the West Country. Here snow and skies and mist froze greyer.

He rose to shake hands with the parents Miss Taylor ushered in. They took their seats grudgingly, unbuttoning their coats with red fingers, unwinding scarves. The mother wore an ugly beret pulled down to her eyebrows.

'Now,' he said, smiling. 'I think I understand the problem, but I'd like you to tell me for yourselves.' He crossed his legs; behind the desk his shoes shone.

'Well,' the father cleared his throat, growling.

'Yes, Mr Miller.'

'It's our Samantha.'

He nodded, concentrating on the woman, his fingertips together.

'She's goin' about with this black lad.'

'Yes.'

'What do you think we feel about it?' burst from the mother. 'She's a clever girl, well we think she is, she got ten "O" levels, and me an' her dad was ever so pleased to let her stay on. And she got good marks in the Christmas exams, and now what do we find? She's got this, this 'ere West Indian youth.'

'I see.' He put his left thumbnail to his teeth. 'Let us try to look at this as rationally as we can, Mrs Miller. One thing we all have in common is concern for Sammy's welfare. Now, I'll cut a few corners, if you don't mind. What exactly is your problem? Is it that Leroy is black, or is it that he's stopping Sam from working properly?'

'Both,' the mother said. 'She's out three times a week, even in this weather. She comes back very late. She'd be in at all hours if we'd let her.'

'You've talked to her about this, I take it?'

'We have.' Mrs Miller belched a snort of exasperation.

'Every mealtime till I'm sick of it.' The father.

'And what line does she take?'

'She says we 'ate blacks, that we're racialists,' Mrs Miller snapped. ' "You know nothing about him; you won't let me bring him home; you won't see or say anything in his favour just because he's West Indian." That's what she says. I mean, I tell her, "You're young," I say. "You don't know your mind yet. We want you to get on with your schoolwork. That's what we're bothered about." But it's no use reasoning with her.'

'Do you think, Mr Miller, there's any truth in what Samantha says?'

'Eh? Um, um, a . . .' The father staggered from some daydream. 'Oh, I don't know. Well. I mean. It wouldn't be our choice, now, would it?'

Mrs Miller flew at it again. They wanted the best for the girl. They were prepared to sacrifice. Both went out to work. It was a struggle sometimes, but they thought of her future. The sentences thumped like darts into a board, but crooked, poisoned barbs. Moral indignation flushed the woman's face as easily as his electric fire. She was, he guessed, selfish, and domineering, earning so that she could drive down, dressed to the nines, to Bingo three nights a week, leaving the daughter to get her young brother to bed. The sentences crashed on. 'I said to 'er dad . . .' 'I told 'er to 'er face . . .' 'Once you let 'em think they can 'ave their way . . .' 'Stubborn she is, an' always 'as been . . .'

The telephone interrupted her rapid fire. A fellow head-master boringly outlined his plans for an in-service course. He wondered why Miss Taylor had allowed the call, and guessed that she had been listening to Mrs Miller's flow from next door and had decided to relieve him. He nodded, murmuring pacifically, said he must cut himself off, did so, and apologized to the fidgeting Millers. The woman catapulted herself into speech.

'I said to 'er, "I'm goin' down that there school to see that there Miss Macauley. And if I don't get no satisfaction there, I'm going in to tell the 'eadmaster just what's going on." '

He allowed her time to work herself into a temper in the hope that she'd clear her system. Certainly she seemed incapable of stopping, flinging sentences at him like half-bricks and cobble-stones from the hands of a rioter. He hummed peaceably, and she took the sounds as encouragement, repeating herself, appealing to her husband, stressing the value of education. Only when she spoke disparagingly of the discipline of the school did he interrupt.

'Mrs Miller.'

She disregarded him, tumbling into the rapids of invective.

'Mrs Miller.'

His voice slapped her face. She stopped, mouth agape.

'Are you suggesting that I am in some way to blame for your daughter's predicament?'

She wasn't; she wasn't. He allowed her half a dozen trailing passionate non-sequiturs.

'Do you in any way hold yourself culpable?'

She cocked her head, like a comical bird, but bravely pitched herself in at him again.

'We've always done our best for that girl. We've grudged her nothing. She's got a nice bedroom there, for study. A stove as well as the radiator. She went on a trip to Paris with the school. She's going to them Playhouse evenings.'

'She pays for them herself,' her husband said. 'She works as a waitress on Saturdays.'

Richardson allowed Mrs Miller a further self-defensive outburst.

'Do you love your daughter, Mrs Miller?'

She regarded him with hostility, speechless, incredulous.

'Yes. And don't let nobody tell you otherwise.'

'Who would?'

'She might.'

'I see. If I asked Samantha how she thought you showed this love for her, what would she say?' That was unfair, and stupid; there was no sense in making an enemy of the woman because he judged her selfish, garrulous and unintelligent. She was not answering; tears stood in her eyes; she trembled, perhaps with anger.

The husband looked at his feet.

'I sympathize with you,' Richardson began. 'I have three daughters. But I cannot see any advantage in antagonizing the girl. Out three times a week, as well as the Saturday job, does seem excessive, but I shall make a close enquiry into the progress of her schoolwork. You must try to be patient, and if you cannot hide your anxiety, at least don't let it express itself in exasperation. She thinks she is grown up, knows her mind. We may judge it otherwise.' He handed out calm sentences.

'What sort of lad is he, this 'ere Leroy?' Miller asked. 'Is he decent?'

'Very. He's not as clever as Samantha. Though he's older, he's still struggling with "O" levels.'

'Will he get them?'

'Perhaps. One or two.'

'He'll never get a job, then,' Mrs Miller flew in. 'Blacks here have to do even better than we do.'

'That's so.'

'So . . .'

'Mrs Miller.' This time she stopped. 'I am not saying that Leroy will make a suitable husband for your daughter. But she must discover that for herself.'

'What if she ends up with a black baby?' The father, surprisingly.

'She's on the pill,' the mother said. 'I found the box. And a prescription from the doctor.'

'Perhaps she left them to be found.'

'Oh, no, she didn't. Tucked away. Wrapped up, thc sly bitch.'

32

'You never told me.' Miller. His eyebrows met, cruelly.

'Did you speak to her about it?' the headmaster asked.

'Yes, I did. She asked me not to tell her dad.'

The woman's anger petered out, and when he had promised to interview the girl, to send the parents a full report on her academic work, Richardson shooed them out easily. They shambled off, half satisfied, an unattractive couple, not obviously from appearance the parents of the comely Samantha. He sighed as he made a careful note; he intended to keep his word to them, but before he had finished writing Miss Taylor sidled in with his black coffee, and an announcement of the arrival of the next three people to be interviewed. He saw himself a poor social worker, without the time or staff to cope adequately, but he pushed on cheerfully enough. After break, when Miss Macauley would frown and worry and drop her papers all over him, he had a teaching period with the lower-sixth arts, on Spenser's Sir Guyon, the Knight of Temperance. Thank God for learning. He wondered how many of the dozen sixteen-year-old girls in the set were on the pill. Temperance and abstinence. He shook his head, pressed his bell-push.

In the lunch-hour his wife, Joanna, telephoned that she had fetched Fay home from her school with a high temperature.

'I asked Dr Brinkley to call. She wasn't pleased, but she's coming. The reason I rang was to see if you're out tonight. There's nothing in the main diary. Now if you are, I'll have to cancel my WEA class.' Joanna sounded angry, as if they were deliberately bent on crossing her.

He reassured her, told her he would come out to collect the prescriptions once the doctor had called.

'And neglect your precious duty?' she said. He hoped the sarcasm eased her anxiety. Joanna needed to be kept occupied, as he did, but he at least was prepared to wait. To sit by Fay's bed until the doctor had turned up and had made a diagnosis would stretch her beyond her endurance, so that by the time the family polled in for tea her nerves would be taut; fur would fly. He imagined it, told Miss Taylor to have the letters done in good time, so that they could leave early.

He heard no more from home that afternoon and took it that the doctor had actually issued the medicine; it sometimes happened. Five minutes after the final bell he was pulling on his overcoat, when there was a sharp knock, and his door was pushed open without invitation, a practice he discouraged. Macauley, he guessed in boredom, knickers in daily distracted twist.

To his surprise a young man from the chemistry department, Anthony Moore, stepped in.

'Could I have a word with you, sir?'

'I'm in rather a hurry.'

Moore's face sagged; he, at twenty-five, suddenly looked fifty. He turned to go, a sharp, incisive movement, out of character.

'No, no,' Richardson ordered. 'What is it?'

Moore came back. His hair, though greased, was untidy; tobacco-stained, nail-bitten fingers dragged at his lapel. His thin lips were nicotine yellow.

'It's personal.'

Richardson sat on the edge of his desk, looked at Moore's old-fashioned trousers, sports coat, collar and tie. Stanley Smith allowed no ravers in his department

'Yes?' Making the word sympathetic.

'It's something that's happened. In my private life.'

'Do you want to sit down?'

'No.' A subdued shout, as if he resisted an immoral suggestion.

'You'd better tell me about it, Mr Moore.'

The man took a curious step to the right, as if practising for a dance, then looked over his shoulder towards the outer office, making sure he was not overheard.

'They've all gone home,' Richardson said.

'It's my wife, sir. She's left me.'

The headmaster waited, forcing nothing, quite still, ready when the young man committed himself. He nodded, trying to recall Mrs Moore's appearance; with so large a staff, it was difficult. She was perhaps the fair-haired girl with the thin legs. He wondered if he'd ever spoken to her.

'I'm sorry,' he said, as Moore seemed disinclined to speak. 'When did this happen?'

'On Monday. There was a note.'

'I see. Had there been, any, er, warning signs?'

'No.'

'Let me see. I don't remember. Did she go to work?'

'She had a part-time job in the library in Wilford.'

'Yes.'

Moore shifted uneasily; his shoes needed cleaning. This smart, respectably dressed young man looked unattractive, unsavoury, mean.

'She was having driving lessons. She's gone off to live with the driving instructor.'

'And you'd no idea?'

Moore shook his head, took a wallet from his pocket, extracted a folded sheet of paper.

'Dear Tony, I'm going to live with Wallace. There's nothing you can do about it. I shan't change my mind. Don't try and get in touch with me. I'll let you know about my things. I'm sorry, but this has just happened. Sandra.'

Richardson passed it back to Moore, who grimly scrutinized it for a moment, then refolded it, returned it to his wallet.

'You don't know where she is, then?'

'No.'

'You don't know this man's address?'

'I don't. I suppose I could write to him at the driving school. He's married, I think, has children.'

Moore groaned aloud, suddenly, seemed not to know he had done so.

'Are you eating well?' Richardson asked.

'Enough. I get lunch here.' He'd noticed the young man on the next table in the dining-room that day, or was it the day before? Nothing had marked him off from his colleagues.

'What do you do in the evenings?'

'I have a night-school class on Tuesdays.'

'Did you go this week?'

'Yes.'

'That's wise. If you can keep on at your job it helps. Have you talked to anybody? Dr Smith?'

'No. I didn't feel . . .'

'I'm glad you've come to see me. Now. Let's think. I have to go soon. We've a bit of trouble. Fay, our youngest, is ill.

Nothing serious, but . . . Nothing like yours. I'll tell you what. Would you like to come home with me for tea? You'll be welcome.'

'No, thank you, sir.'

'I'd be glad if you'd come. It would pass an hour. I know it seems harsh to say, but the world's still going on. I can guess how this has affected you. It's dreadful. But you'll have to stagger by. Life can't stop.'

'I can't understand it. We, we were happy. We used to laugh about things. Only last week . . .' His voice, exploding on the first words, died. 'I'd no idea. I mean it doesn't seem possible. Just like that.'

'Did she talk about the man?'

'Well, yes. He told her to do this, or that. Driving becomes a bit of an obsession, doesn't it? When you're beginning . . . He'd advised something, or praised her.'

'How often did she see him?'

'Once a week. But I think he's been calling at the house. Something a neighbour said. Thought I'd changed my car. It never crossed my mind that . . . that anything was wrong.'

'No. It's awful. Look, do come home with me for a meal. My wife will be glad to have you.' She wouldn't; that was for certain.

'No, sir. Thank you. It's kind. I've things I have to do.'

'Now, are you sure?'

'Yes, sir.'

'Will you come in again and see me tomorrow? Are you free at all?' He scuttled round his desk, opened his diary.

'Last period in the morning.'

'Eleven-thirty, then.'

'Would you like me to have a word with Dr Smith about this?'

Moore thought, the skin of his young forehead creased; an ineffective hand tried to wipe trouble from his face; he ended with two fingers ferociously whitening his chin.

'No, thanks. I'll tell him some time. He'll have to know.' The face was vague. 'He's more interested in success.'

'Perhaps you're right.'

Richardson pushed his diary back into the drawer.

'Eleven-thirty tomorrow, then. I'm sorry, Tony. I really am.'

36

He put out a hand, which Moore took sheepishly. The young man's eyes swam. 'We'll think again. But keep yourself warm, and busy.' He sighed, for Moore's benefit. 'Just before you go. If there's anything I can do, you must let me know.' He talked on, encouraging, sympathizing, letting his voice dredge into the man's misery, convincing him that he'd told somebody, that he was no longer floundering on his own. 'What's your programme, now?'

'I have to do some shopping. Then cook my tea.'

'Good. And then?'

'I've work to prepare. And some marking to be finished.'

'Of course.'

Richardson slapped his arm, and Moore smiled, then made his way along the corridor with something of a swagger.

Joanna waited, not patiently, with a prescription; he decided to walk, and on his way passed a girl, presumably one of his pupils, who half smiled at him. It was only rarely he ran across one of his charges in this desirable residential district; perhaps this was one of Marguerite's friends, or Virginia's. He found it increasingly difficult to put an age on young ladies.

'Keeping warm?' he asked. The girl stopped.

'Yes, sir.' One of his.

'Do you live hereabouts?'

'No, sir.'

'Have you been home yet?'

'No, sir. I've been to see about a second-hand bicycle that was advertised.'

'Successful?'

She shook her head, old before her time.

'No. They'd sold it.'

'Bad luck. Still, it's hardly cycling weather.'

'I don't mind. There'll be others.' The girl picked with a toe-end at a heap of frozen snow, scattering a small, reluctant pay-dirt. That demonstrated her embarrassment perhaps, but she smiled bravely.

'Let's see. Whose set are you in?'

'Mr Moore's.' A portent?

'A good man. I like Mr Moore.'

'He's all right.' Unenthusiastic.

He wished her goodbye, and they teetered off in opposite directions along the ice. Cold bruised his cheekbones, pained his shoulderblades, gored sinuses.

In their few private minutes he told Joanna about Anthony Moore, and though she listened – not always the case – she was barely interested and immediately switched the conversation to Fay's fever.

'I feel such relief when I've spooned that penicillin into her,' she said. 'God knows how they went on in the bad old days.'

'Waiting, you mean?'

'What else?' Snappy; she'd expected him home earlier, but now she took to her heaviest coat, left her car in the garage, patronized the infrequent buses quite cheerfully. 'You can't carry the sorrows of the whole world, y'know,' she warned him as he saw her out of the front door.

'It feels like it, sometimes.'

She punched his biceps, very friendly, excited to be going out.

He sat for a time in the half-light of the bedroom with Fay, but most of the time she slept, restlessly and sweating, crying now and then for a drink. It was too dark to read and his occupying thoughts only disturbed, distracted, came to nothing, sorted nothing out. He had no bent for abstract thought, needed problems which could be handled, pragmatically settled.

When his wife returned, rather more quietly than usual, and had inspected the patient, dosed and settled her for the night, she sat in the kitchen with her husband.

'Is this Moore man going to be all right?' she asked. That gladdened him.

'I hardly know him. I don't know what the effect will be.' He explained that he'd promised to talk to him again.

'Invite him up here, if you like. Won't do much good. These young men love to hate the headmaster, I expect. Still, it's all you can do.'

'Yes. It's a relief, I hope, to put it into words to somebody. I ought to tell Stanley Smith about it, or he ought.'

'Oh, he's a bloody fool.'

'Why do you say that?'

'They used to talk about muscular Christians. He's a muscular scientist. If his wife deserted him, it'd be three days before he noticed.'

'Oh, come, come . . .'

'I don't like him. Nobody should be as sure of himself as he makes out he is. He's not a human being. He's a walking textbook.'

'What's his wife like?' Richardson asked. He enjoyed his wife's militancy.

'Interesting. A lot about her. She's lumbered with the family all the time while he writes his books and formulates his projects and impresses educational pundits at conferences, but she's quite funny about it, and pretty, and ambitious for him, and hasn't lost her spirit yet.'

'Will she?'

'Quite likely.'

'She won't leave him?'

'God knows. I haven't left you yet, have I?'

'Why did she marry him?'

'He's a good catch for anyone capable of looking after herself.'

'Like you.'

'You said it. Come on,' she ordered, whipping up the mugs, 'let's go to bed. Madam's likely to disturb us.'

4

The interview next morning with Anthony Moore proved dull.

Richardson was uncertain what he expected, but the young man appeared both more certain and more sullen. For a start he arrived nearly ten minutes late, at a time when he knew the head was likely to be busy, offered no adequate excuse, and thereafter made little attempt to talk, as if he resented last night's confession. He could cope, he claimed; he'd have to, wouldn't he? He appeared angry, and yet incapable of orally expressing his anger. Richardson felt down, disappointed, but talked on.

'You must remember, Tony, that you are not on your own. You have friends. And I hope you count me amongst them. If ever you need help, you'll come in to see me at any time.' No answer, not even a glance. 'I mean this. You will, won't you? I'm no miracle worker, but what I can do, I will.' Nothing. 'I think I understand how you feel.' No disagreement. 'There are days when I feel utterly pessimistic, alone, beaten down.' Moore sat like a reprimanded fourth-former, guilty and putting up a half-show of defiance, a miserable bundle of clothes as the headmaster pressed his claim. In the end, Richardson gave in, stood up and curtly said, 'Don't be afraid to come back.' Moore shambled to his feet as Richardson rounded his desk. 'If your colleagues want to know why I asked to see you, tell them it was about that 4–C chemistry set.'

'That would be a lie.' The first sign of animation.

'Are they settling down now?' Two doting mothers had complained that their sons spent three or four baffled hours each night Moore set them chem homework.

'Yes. All right.'

'No more complaints?'

'No.'

'Well there you are, then. That's made it the truth.' He palmed Moore out into the corridor as his phone rang. That bit of foolery would not commend him to the young man's favour. He reached out a hand. Miss Taylor announcing Mrs Brooks, who hoped he did not mind her ringing up during working hours. He soothed.

'Would you see me again?'

'About Veronica?'

'In a way, yes. But not altogether. She's decided against university. Just set her face against it. I'll tell you all about that, but there's one other matter, a personal thing.' He arranged to visit her the following evening, turned to his morning's delinquents, his letters, the heating engineer, the education officer. In a five-minute lull in the lunch-hour he rang home and learnt that Fay seemed much better, had eaten a little, was good as gold.

Joanna laughed, unexpectedly, that night at his announcement.

'You're beginning to be at that lady's beck and call,' she said.

'This is only the second visit.'

'She needs her husband back home.'

'Probably. But don't say so in front of Margot. On Stephen's account.'

'She's well able to work that out for herself. As well you know.'

He could not decide whether his wife was irritated or amused. She had once stated that, though she disliked Stephen, he'd be good for Marguerite in the long run.

'What's wrong with the boy?' He, as she knew, could not resist poking at her prejudices.

'They think they own the earth, that family.'

'You hardly know them.'

'You don't need to stare long at a piece of coal to see that it's black.'

Joanna was careful. Her family, the Calder-Clowes, treated the rest of the world as its trusted retainers, her mother, daughter of the fourth Baron Lenton of Milbourne, especially so. The father, a well-to-do consultant, ruled dictatorially over his wards, but lived quietly at home, drily, available to the devices and desires of his wife. Joanna, the only daughter, had escaped to university and marriage with all speed, but now was constantly vigilant for others, such as her mother, ready to push her around. The Hon. Mrs Calder-Clowes, now dead, lived powerfully on in her daughter's mind, so that Richardson suspected that Joanna recognized and hated equivalent leanings in herself.

His wife saw him to the door.

'Don't stay too long,' she said. 'You won't do any good.'

'She might cure herself, talking to me.'

'If there's talk to be done, home's not a bad place for it.'

'To whom?'

'Me, for a start.' He was taken aback by her tone, for Fay had been up that day, cheerfully, for the teatime meal, and Joanna on top of the world. He put an arm round her shoulder, but she shrugged him off. Outside it rained, with the temperature above freezing point, though packed snow still caked the pavements, polished and ugly and dangerous.

Mrs Brooks had led him straight inside the drawing-room, where out of deference to Joanna's ill-temper he refused a whisky.

'Coffee, then?'

'Later, perhaps, but I mustn't stay too long.' He muttered excuses; wife cooped up with sick daughter, pressure of own work.

Immediately, Mrs Brooks, glass full, abandoning the drinks-tray, dealt with Veronica, who apparently had carefully read his brochures, made one or two remarks which mildly encouraged her mother to envisage change, but had then, one day later, when questioned flatly denied all possibility of university entrance. 'I've thought about it,' the girl said, 'because you wanted me to.' She had listened to Mr Richardson ('Old Mother Richardson', *ipsissima verba*) and read his pamphlets. 'I'm not going to go. There's no sense in it.'

The mother's disappointment at the volte-face had driven her to angry questions, at which Veronica had pushed her empty plate from her – she'd finished her main course – and walked from the room. Since then they had exchanged polite trivialities, and that was all.

'So you can't give any reason for her decision?'

'No. I thought she was really considering it seriously. From the way she talked. She's very intelligent. And then suddenly, "No." It didn't, it doesn't seem rational.'

'Had something happened?'

'How am I supposed to know that?'

Mrs Brooks resisted the gin bottle no longer, tried again to tempt him, failed. She sipped, squinting at him over the glass.

'The next morning,' she said, mouth still inches only from the rim, 'a friend of mine rang, Jane Cooke.' She waited for him to admit to acquaintance, but he could not. 'She wanted me round at once. It was very inconvenient, I can tell you, but I went because she's had a great deal of trouble. For the past year or more her mother has been in and out of hospital, terminal cancer as well as other things, terrible state, they take her in, operate or treat her, and then send her back for Jane to look

42

after. It's awful, and Mrs Allegro is a dreadful patient. Always was a dragon. But now, with the pain. And she's incontinent. I can't tell you half.'

A further swig of gin fortified her.

'Well, in the end they've got her into this new hospice and I should think that's the best thing. She was due in that afternoon, and Jane wanted me to go along with them.' Felicity Brooks looked up expecting a question she did not get. 'Jane was pretty nearly incoherent, and if you knew her you'd see that was nothing like her usual style. She's a sharp, sporty type, the golf-club captain; you can't imagine.' He thought duly of tweeds and brogues. 'I suppose it was the result of all the trouble she's been through, but she said she couldn't take her mother on her own, and would I go with them? In the taxi?' Mrs Brooks lowered the level of the gin. 'Now I asked a few questions. I mean, after all, it was what she wanted, best for her mother, best for her. But do you know what the trouble was?' The question, rapped forcibly out, demanded an answer, but Richardson sat still, demurely, hands on knees. 'The hospice, a big house called Northfields in Lenton Park, was next door to the place where the Allegros had lived when Jane was a child. She hadn't realized this because it had had some other name then.' At the pause Richardson made no comment. 'She, Janey, hadn't put two and two together, and now did I think it was right to take her mother to this place where she'd overlook the house she'd lived in for twenty years, the garden, the lot? It didn't make sense to me, Mr Richardson, I can tell you. The old lady's in a mess, emotionally and physically, and what she needs are painkillers and kind words and good nursing, and it doesn't matter where she receives it as long as receive it she does. I said so, to Jane, and she seemed to accept it, but she absolutely insisted that I go with her.'

'You said you would?' At last, his calm question.

'I couldn't do otherwise, could I?'

'No.'

'I dashed home, had my lunch, such as it was, and then back. The whole thing went off well, as far as these affairs can. The old lady seemed pleased, or at least resigned, and now it had come to the push Jane was quiet and well organized, just as I

43

would have expected. Up at the hospice they were very good. They made us welcome, talked to us, and asked us to wait about until they'd put Mrs Allegro to bed. We sat by a huge bay-window and Janey pointed out their old garden and the summerhouse, absolutely calm, cheerful almost. And various people came up and spoke to us; they seemed to know who we were, but they didn't fuss, were most pleasant.'

'Did you see any of the patients?'

'One or two who were mobile. One old man in a dressing-gown came and sat with us for a little while, and we talked about how awful the weather was. It was all very natural. I don't say I felt exactly comfortable, because I knew what place it was and what it was for, but . . .'

'Is it well furnished?'

'Beautifully. It's not been opened long. But somebody has spent money on it.'

'Good.'

'And then they took us in to see Mrs Allegro. She was in a smallish sort of ward with two other old ladies, and she seemed quite at home; sleepy, if anything. I don't know if they'd given her . . . So we didn't stay long. I went back with Jane; we had a cup of tea and that was that.'

She eyed him, as if in challenge.

'But it wasn't?' he asked, lightly.

'It was not.' Back to the gin. 'I don't know what I did that evening. Nothing out of the ordinary as far as I can remember. I went to bed at much the usual time and slept as well as I normally do; not that that's very well. But next morning. Stephen's usually up first and makes a cup of tea which he brings to Vernie and me. She gets up straight away, and the two of them are out of the house by eight-thirty. They don't have elaborate breakfasts. Cereal, toast, fruit.' She reached again for the gin bottle, but immediately replaced it unopened. 'They have to be out on time, so they leave their dishes and I do them when I wash mine. That day, as far as I recall, I was perfectly all right while I drank my tea in bed, but then . . .'

He waited for her.

'I was overcome by a weakness. It was as if every ounce of strength was drawn out of my body. The feeling was purely physical. Like a massive dose of flu, except that I had no temperature.'

'Couldn't it have been that? A virus infection?'

'No. I rang the doctor straight away, and he came round that morning. Told me to stay where I was, take it easy. I did get up once to make myself a drink, and it was then I began to connect the illness with the hospice. Even then, I wasn't sure. I thought I was physically ill and this had made me feel so depressed about Mrs Allegro. Not the other way about. By the time Stephen came home I was on a crying jag. He wanted to send for Binns again, but I told him that was useless. Veronica rang him up at evening surgery and he made me up a sedative. I was ill, really ill, for three days.'

'It does sound like a bug.'

'I don't know. The reason why I think it's not is that from that first afternoon onward the whole of my weakness and pains centred on that hospice. I was tortured by the place, clean and bright as it was.'

'I see. But you're better now?'

'Yes. I've improved marvellously over the past four days. But the first three, I just cannot begin to describe them. Now that I feel fit again I wonder if they happened, they were so awful.'

'In what way?'

'Extreme weakness, some aches and pains and this over-powering feeling of disaster. It wasn't merely catastrophe; it was as if that had occurred and worse was to follow.' Mrs Brooks smiled at him, giving no pleasure. 'When I put it into words it sounds flat. I can't express the power. It was like a curse. I don't even know how to describe it.'

'It's ineffable,' he offered.

'That's a crossword word,' she said equably. 'I asked you to come so that I could tell you what had happened. Veronica and Stephen would only worry, and Dr Binns is old-fashioned.'

'But if you're feeling so much . . . ?'

'No. What I want to tell you is how bad it was. My children know I don't kick up a fuss for nothing, but they think, as you do, that I had some short-term infection. But the power, the overwhelming naked power, was quite unlike anything I'd ever experienced. It was a cataclysm, an earthquake. I didn't think

45

one human body could contain, let alone bear, anything of that proportion. You believe me, don't you? You don't think I'm mad, or feeble, or exaggerating to win sympathy, do you?'

'I take your word.'

'Thank you.'

'At the same time I don't quite see my rôle in this.' He spoke drily, matter-of-fact.

'Somebody must be made,' her voice hissed an acid intensity, 'to understand precisely what happened to me.'

'And then?'

'Then I can go on.' She spoke almost carefully. 'I feel better. I can go out shopping. I'm interested in music again. But something infinitely worse than death infested me, and I have to say so.'

'Why?' he asked.

'Because it's so much outside my experience. I exploded, imploded with depression. It's never happened before. Oh, heaven knows, I've been down in the mouth often enough with Conrad abroad. I'm a disappointed woman you could say. But I've come to terms with myself. And now this flattens me.'

'I've no means,' he objected, reasonably, 'of registering the strength of . . .'

'I don't expect you to register.' She spat the last word. 'I expect you to report, to yourself, perhaps to others or back to me what I've told you. If I said that my head had been hacked off and floated two feet above my shoulders, I'd expect you to report that back.'

'For what purpose?'

'I don't know what. To counteract madness, perhaps.'

'Wouldn't a tape-recorder be even more accurate?'

'A tape-recorder wouldn't, couldn't comment.'

'I can't think anything I've said has been of much value.'

'You say you believe me.'

'But might I not be a good liar?'

'I should know. Don't you think I wouldn't see through you?' Her hands were clasped in her lap, narrowing her shoulders. Thin as a lath, she might leap like an arrow from her chair into his face. 'But I've told you now. You understand what sort of woman it is you have to deal with.'

46

'Yes.'

'Yes? That's not much.'

'I've listened to what you've said.' He spoke slowly, not loudly, but with a schoolmaster's rudeness, checking the impertinence of a subordinate. 'I've no means of checking your account.'

'You could ask Stephen, or Veronica.'

'By your own admission they'd hardly be capable of supporting your story. But, no. I believe you. I don't see why I shouldn't.' That was a lie. 'Just tell me. If you felt this crushing sense of catastrophe, would you not be likely to feel an equally powerful sense of joy, exhilaration?'

'I don't see that's logical.'

'Never mind the rights and wrongs of the argument, would you?'

'I have not so far . . .' Each word dropped separately, like a stick of bombs. Her face screwed itself round the mouth as if to hamper speech. 'I told you. I'm a disappointed woman. My tendency would be towards sadness.'

'Why is that?'

'Too long, too complicated. I'm a writer, but I've never produced anything commensurate with my powers.'

'Powers?' he said. 'Do you mean ambitions?'

'You may well be right.' Her voice changed, rapped business-like, and she stood up. 'I'm afraid that will have to do for this evening.' She thanked him volubly, but was rid of him in no time, without mention of another meeting.

In the cold street outside, he walked carefully, puzzled by her experience, by her summons to him, the abrupt dismissal, by the odd formality of her language. 'My tendency would be towards sadness.'

When he arrived home Joanna, reading as energetically as she cooked or cleaned, asked him no questions, and he was too weary to initiate talk.

5

Two days later Richardson received by second-class post a letter from Veronica Brooks. It was brief, but explained that her mother thought she should write to thank him as well as explain and apologize for her decision not to try for university. The idea, slightly attractive while he plausibly argued it, had no appeal now, but it wasted time making her mother understand this. She was his sincerely.

He read the letter over, and its grudging terseness seemed humane, in the middle of an investigation into bullying. Richardson would have said that organized bullying did not exist in his school; careless clouts on the head or sporadic grabbing of smaller boys' pens or penises he admitted, but the extent of this had shaken him. Confessions extracted by the deputy in charge of discipline had revealed a web, a conspiracy almost, a mafia. Six boys had been sent home, a dozen parents written to; already an irate father had contacted the director complaining about his son's suspension in an important examination year and just before mocks. Richardson, who had himself made the first discovery when a couple of small boys had played truant, felt that his staff had let him down, had dashed without proper vigilance out of lessons to the staffroom or the home-fire, had failed in their duty. He had said as much, had torn a cruel strip off the first deputy, which explained the ferocity of his present inquisition. Richardson's anger was directed chiefly against himself, in that he saw himself as the head of a large, loose organization over which he had neither control nor oversight. The staff were divided: the old brigade demanded the reintroduction of flogging; the younger, more energetic teachers complained they were too busy filling in an eternal round of administrative paper to do more than teach; the majority looked down their noses in professional apathy. The headmaster did not usually see much sense in rousting his

48

subordinates, but this time half a dozen were fetched in, had their faults made clear, amongst them Moore, the cuckold. The atmosphere seethed, excitement with bitterness. Rumour flourished. Against expectation, the headmaster hoped that mock 'O' and 'A' levels would settle the place back into routine.

Richardson stood, he felt, unsupported.

Stanley Smith, for instance, took the lofty view. 'I agree, headmaster, it's an advantage that the thing's come to light. I don't want to see small children made needlessly unhappy, though God knows I'd add to the sorrow of one or two of them, give me half a chance.' The northern accent jutted through the Oxford veneer. 'You've taken action, so now let's forget it, because here it's the exception, not the rule. Twenty or thirty years ago, I don't know, there'd have been much worse official bullying by staff, by prefects and it would have been regarded as morally beneficial. Well . . .'

' "God give to men that are old and rougher
    The things that little children suffer," ' Richardson quoted at his desk top.

Smith smoothed his hair over the incipient bald patch, and – he would never sit in his superior's presence – squinted down at the headmaster. Immediately he broached the real objective of his visit: discussion of the open day at the university for science students.

Joanna seemed equally dismissive.

True, she listened each night to his account of developments, asked intelligent questions, but her final judgement had been that her husband and his staff were just a bunch of children, and she even suggested, jovially, that schools were institutions expressly built to prevent teachers from growing up. In no way did she understand how deeply this had hurt her husband. When he taxed her, she refused to talk seriously.

'You're obsessed,' she said, 'like all your profession.'

'I wish that were true.'

'All those who are any good, then. Not that that's many.'

'There were in my charge quite a large number of small children . . .'

'A dozen. Twenty at the outside.'

'. . . whose lives were being made unbearably miserable

when there was no need for it. If I, and some others, had been doing our work even moderately efficiently, it could not have happened.'

'I often think,' she strutted round in a flowing, attractive nightgown, or peered into a mirror to improve her face, 'that it's the nature of small children to be made unhappy. Even in a child-orientated society like ours. They're bound to be frustrated because they can't do as they like, even if we allowed them to try. Fay, who's not anything like neurotic, was screaming her head off this morning because she couldn't get her sledge out of the shed; it was wedged under some wood that had fallen down.'

'Why did she want it? The snow's gone.'

'God knows. To sit on it, and remember what it was like to skid down the slopes. I don't know. But she was desperately unhappy. The whole universe had pitted itself against her. You and I know better, but she didn't. And it's not a bad thing, either. Kids are very pampered these days.'

'No more so than adults.'

'Quite right,' she said. 'That's why we're taking to jogging or yoga.' She climbed magnificently into bed, took up her book and glasses. 'I expect,' she said pacifically, 'that you've dealt very adequately with this, so now all you've got to do is prepare yourself for the next crisis.'

That was it ticketed, 'the last crisis', but he remained sore, edgy, touchy; his staff, who did not credit him with humanity, showed their surprise in fear or amusement. Nobody asked for trouble, but to some he handed it out, unasked.

Early in March, with sunshine which gave promise of spring, though the cold lurked still, he arrived home early to be confronted with glum faces. He was prepared to be cheerful, for aubretia and forsythia, he had noticed, had begun to flower in sheltered places in front gardens. When Marguerite came into the room she was crying; tears rolled grotesquely.

'What's wrong?' he asked, softly. He could have done with some peace.

'Veronica Brooks has died.'

'When?'

'Yesterday. She committed suicide.' Margot's voice, which

had been low and adequately controlled, broke before she rushed from the room with a squeal of weeping. The two other children looked up, Fay already snivelling. He put his arm round his younger daughter; she clung, hung to his coat. He picked her up and, hugging her, marched out to the kitchen where Joanna, who must have heard all this, worked at the stove.

'Margot's gone upstairs,' he said. 'Will she be all right?'

His wife sighed, in ill temper, turning down the gas jets under the saucepans.

'I'll go and see,' she said. 'She jumped from the high-rise flats in Radford. They don't know how she got out to do it.'

'Is that near where she works?'

'No.' Joanna left them, impatiently, and he carted Fay back into the dining-room, where he sat with her on his knee. She hid her face in his pullover. Virginia made a poor pretence at consulting a book. The television set stood dark, silent. His only comfort was the warm body of the child snugged on his lap. Upstairs, in a house that seemed wildly alive with small sounds, he heard nothing of Marguerite or Joanna. A saucepan boiled over in the kitchen, and Virginia, mother's image, leapt to deal with it.

'Careful, now,' he called. She returned, nodded confidently in his direction. 'What was it?'

'Potatoes. I've seen to it.'

She lifted her book again, but looked up at him.

'Well done, Gin,' he said. 'Always efficient.'

Virginia smiled, and Fay lifted her face from his chest. He kissed her.

'Am I heavy?' she asked.

'You weigh a ton,' he answered. 'But I like cuddling ton-weights.'

'You must like cuddling Mummy then.'

'Don't let her hear you say that.'

They laughed, all three, but nervously, as if at the unseemliness of such behaviour, and then sat quiet.

Before too long Joanna bustled downstairs, poked her head round the half-open door, said softly, 'She's coming down. We'll eat now.'

51

'Ginny saw to the potatoes.'

'I wonder what's for tea,' Fay said, suddenly pert.

'Casserole,' Virginia answered. 'It's Tuesday.'

'Come on,' he said, putting Fay to the ground, 'we'll lay the table.'

They spoke very little during the meal, though he managed to make them laugh by describing a childish attempt to walk a narrow ledge over a stream and the resulting fall and thrashing.

'How old were you?' Ginny.

'Five or six.'

'Why do they always call it a *good* hiding?' Marguerite's question pleased him.

'I don't think it's fair.' Fay.

'You wouldn't be so stupid as to go mincing about above streams, would you?' her mother asked.

'No.' Fay answered hesitantly.

'But Daddy's not stupid,' Virginia objected. 'Nobody could say that.'

'He's perhaps grown wiser since he was six.' Joanna, sarcastically.

'I might become more stupid.' Fay supported him.

'Not you, chick,' he said.

These small exchanges broke the constraining silence, and not until this snippet was over and they were concentrating on their plates did he connect his fall from a foot or two with Veronica's leap to death. No one else made the connection.

At the end of the meal Richardson said that he would like to deal with the washing-up on his own.

'You won't,' said Joanna, 'when you see how much there is.'

'It'll upset the system,' Ginny, who drew up the rota, objected.

'Let this be one-off,' he said. 'And we'll carry on tomorrow as usual.'

'Not fair.'

'Let's put it back one day, then.'

'The names and days are not,' said Ginny righteously, 'chosen at random. I tailor them to requirement.'

'She doesn't want to alter her list.' Marguerite, shrewdly, for

Virginia's roster, in three colours, was something of a work of art. Her sister pulled a gargoyle face at her.

'Let him make a martyr of himself, if that's what he wants.' Joanna.

'My dad's made a tomato of himself.' Fay tried the sentence.

'That would make him an Indian,' Ginny told her.

'It wouldn't.'

'He'd have a red skin if he was a tomato.'

Fay giggled in despair.

As they were about to clear the table, Richardson asked Marguerite, 'Have you seen Stephen today?'

She shook her head. The rest froze, standing or sitting.

'I wonder if it would do any good to ring Mrs Brooks or Stephen. We could ask them over, if they wanted to come.' Nobody said a word; Margot's chin rested sullen on her chest. 'I don't know how they're off for relatives or friends.'

'They've friends.' Marguerite's voice squeezed out of her throat.

'You wouldn't mind if I invited them?' The rest waited. 'Stephen, I mean.'

'No.' Not quickly, whispered, uncertain.

'We'll need to do our homework, you know,' Virginia said, self-righteously hoity-toity.

Her father gave a bark of a laugh, but put his hand out to her, touching her shoulder.

'Right then. That's settled. I'll phone as soon as I've finished the dishes.'

'That'll be about ten o'clock,' Virginia taunted.

Joanna said not a word, but came into the kitchen to help. She flourished the tea-towel.

'You go and sit down,' he said. 'You've been in here all day.'

'Whenever have you known me sit down at this time in the evening?'

'You don't mind about asking the Brookses?'

'No.'

'I thought I'd better put it to Margot first.' She did not answer. 'I don't really want them here.'

'Don't ask them, then.'

53

'We must, Joanna. Somebody has to . . .'

'If we must, well then, we must. Don't make such a song and dance about it.' He would have liked to put his arms round her, but his hands were wet. 'It must have come as a shock to you.' Her voice had warmed. 'It's only a week or two, isn't it, since you went to see her about this university business?'

'I know. I don't understand it at all.'

'You're surprised, then?'

'Yes. She was an odd girl, no doubt about that. Determined to go her own way. But suicide was the last thing I'd have thought of. She was rather plump, comfortable-looking. I guessed she'd put herself into a rut, liked it and wasn't really prepared to climb out.'

'Depressed people nibble between meals.'

'I suppose so.'

He stood, leaning forward, hands immersed in the grey suds of the washing-up bowl, not moving, in a vice of stagnation, so that it was with a start of surprise that he came to to find his wife staring at him, and guessed she had been so occupied for some time.

'It had nothing to do with this university entrance, had it?' she asked. 'It couldn't.' He recognized the kindness of her cruel question; she'd rescue him if he needed it.

'That's what I've been asking myself ever since Margot told me.'

'I thought as much.' Rough, comforting.

'I can't think it was my fault, the last straw or anything else. One can't ever say. How can one? I hardly know anything about the girl.'

'And her mother didn't make it any clearer?'

'My impression was that Veronica was a little corner of the house that needed tidying. Not very important, but mother's neurosis, if that's not too strong a word, caused her to niggle about it and nag from time to time, when nothing else presented itself.'

'Mrs Brooks isn't a steady character?'

'Um. Hard to say. Drinks too much. Lonely. But I don't know about the breaking point. I tell you what.' He was now confidently handling saucepans, the end in sight. 'If anybody

54

had committed suicide in these last few weeks, I'd have thought it would have been young Moore.'

'The driving instructor's . . .' Typically Joanna. 'And he's all right?'

'He's hanging round one of the young women in the domestic-science department.'

'Is she suitable and available?'

'She wouldn't suit me.' He laughed at himself.

'Oh, Lord. Who would?'

As soon as they had finished Joanna ordered him out to ring the Brookses.

'What does she drink? Gin? We can supply her. Be kind,' she warned. 'Especially to yourself.'

That opened his eyes.

'You're one in a thousand,' he said. 'You are. You are.'

Felicity Brooks answered the phone, and he plied her with sober, suitable words. She answered without overt emotion, almost casually, perfunctorily, allowing him no time for phrase-making.

'We were wondering if you or Stephen or both of you would like to come over for an hour.'

'That's very kind of you.' There followed a long-drawn pause; he could hear nothing of her, no breathing; she might well have disappeared off the face of the earth. Not a patient man, he considered interruption of her silence. 'I'll go and ask him,' she said finally, fretfully. Again he was left to wait, and once he heard her shouting the boy's name as though she had no idea where he was. Suddenly she clattered back to accept his invitation, but put down the phone in the middle of his smooth sincerities. He returned disheartened to his wife.

An hour and a quarter later the mother and son arrived.

Richardson shook their hands in the hall, relieved them of their coats, offered more condolences. Joanna did not show up; she was presumably in the bedroom beautifying herself. The children, television blaring in the dining-room, occupied themselves with homework, reading, conversation, bickering.

'My wife will be back here in a moment,' Richardson said, leading his guests into the drawing-room, where Stephen refused a drink as his mother asked for a very small gin. Mrs

55

Brooks looked remarkable in a long, dark green dress, wide-skirted and pleated, decorated in sparse serifs of gold embroidery. The sleeves were tight at the wrists; the square-cut neck-line low. It seemed theatrical, too heavy to wear for any length of time, and yet sombre, dark as her grief. Her face and neck stretched strained, plaster-white, lined; green eye-shadow had been blindly, generously applied, and her features were equine.

He made remarks about the weather, at the hints of spring. They both took him up; the boy was immediately good as he outlined meteorological lore. Richardson examined him so that the question and answer grew animated and once all three laughed out loud as Stephen stumbled over a word, stuttering it, charming them. The young man had the social graces, and he rose the moment Joanna entered, hinting obeisance.

Richardson had no need to introduce the women, for his wife announced herself clearly, said how shocked and troubled they all were, how glad that Mrs Brooks had managed to come. Joanna's delivery was both bracing and sympathetic; it suggested she understood the depths of the bereaved mother's grief, but that it would not be allowed to exceed certain bounds in this room. She ordered her husband to prepare her a martini and lemonade, almost, it seemed, to clear him out of the way for a minute or two while she established a proper atmosphere. Her dress, he could not remember seeing it before, was in large red and blue checks, smart with no inclination toward mourning, a bright garment for young middle-age, no nonsense, no licence for extravagance.

When he returned with the drinks Felicity Brooks was describing how finally she had got through to her husband.

'He must have been out on a location,' she said, 'miles from anywhere, but they radio'd him and he rang this afternoon.'

'Will he come back?'

'Oh, yes. They have fixed the inquest. I could give him the date. He insisted on coming back. Veronica was his favourite, wasn't she, Stephen?'

The boy murmured agreement, smiling pacifically.

'Before you sit down,' Joanna ordered her husband, 'just take Stephen in to the girls. He'll enjoy their company.'

'Will you be all right, Mum?' he asked, not rising. The plebeian diminutive seemed endearing.

'We shan't eat her,' Joanna said.

The dining-room, redolent of the evening meal, struck brighter and warmer. Fay had bundled herself up on the hearth-rug and leaning back on an armchair shaded a colouring book with a sheaf of crayons. She worked slowly, methodically, pausing often as if a false stroke would bring disaster. Virginia and Marguerite sat at either end of the long table; Virginia was upright, face furious, surrounded by an untidy rampart of books. Marguerite, at ease, lounged before a science notebook, a jotter and one thick tome, *Inorganic Chemistry*. They looked up, but then all three added a word, a formula, a line, before they gave the males their attention. Ginny dropped her pen, said, Joanna-fashion, 'Hello, Steve.' Margot stood, walked across and quite beautifully, without embarrassment, laid her head against her young man's waistcoat, and gently circled him with her arms. Fay, face alight, sat straight and held up, turned her picture for the visitors to enjoy, a sun rising with formal rays over a sea crowded with bathers and yachts and a smoking paddle-streamer and two beflagged piers.

'Can you look after Stephen?' Richardson asked.

'Somebody already is,' Virginia pointed at Margot. He was answered. 'I'll go and make coffee. Do you want any in there?'

'Not yet, thanks.'

'They're boozing,' Fay suggested.

'Quite right,' he said, but she had immersed herself again in her work.

'There, then, Stephen, I'll leave you,' he said. 'Shout if you want help.'

'Is Mummy in with you?' Virginia asked.

'Oh, yes.'

'Good.' She strutted out for the kitchen.

Joanna had moved along to the end of the settee and was now sitting close to Mrs Brooks, bending forward. As far as he could make out she had not touched her drink; Felicity Brooks's glass was almost empty. The hostess spoke quickly, in a low voice if intently, so that he did not latch on straight away to the subject of the harangue. The other sat bonelessly, mouth slightly open. When Joanna had finished with speech, she turned to smile at him, like a flash of March sunshine.

'Husbands aren't too useful,' she said, in clarity.

'Especially this one,' he answered her.

Felicity explained the difficulties Conrad would have in returning just at this time; he appeared from her description to be involved in the construction of some huge complex of laboratories for an academic foundation, but she insisted, though without force, that once he had set his mind on a course of action nothing would deter him.

'The inquest will be over, they say, by the time he arrives, and we'll have the date of the funeral.'

'Still, you'll have company. Support. And that's essential. Comfort.' Joanna.

'Yes.' A wintry smile played briefly. 'He'll stump about the house, because he won't know what to do. His work's his life. And he'll realize he's being a nuisance, and so he'll want to drag me out to lunch or to go sight-seeing.'

'Where?'

'Some seaside hotel. Scarborough.' She laughed. 'Certainly London. He'll take me round the theatres.'

'You don't want that?'

'No. If the plays are serious I shan't be able to stand them. If they're rubbish I shall resent the time I'm wasting. That's ungrateful, isn't it? He's good-hearted, but . . .' Her voice choked; she dropped her head. She recovered in a few seconds; her eyes shone. 'I dread . . .' She stopped; they waited. 'I dread clearing Vernie's room out. You've seen it.' She laughed, brokenly. 'It's piled to the ceiling. She was a magpie, couldn't bear to throw anything away.'

'I'll come round and help you,' Joanna said.

'You've got enough to do.'

'You say when, and I'll be there.'

'I'll hate it. I shan't know what to ditch . . .'

'You're like her?' Richardson asked.

'Yes.' Mrs Brooks was weeping as she sat straight-backed, making no attempt to hide her tears, dabbing them away with a lace-edged handkerchief an inch or two square. 'She was a

58

marvellous girl in her way. We didn't always see eye to eye, I admit that, but she was so lively.'

For the next ten minutes, encouraged, she talked about Veronica as a child, as a young woman, and although she began in tears she ended calmly. She regretted that their mode of life had meant that they had sent their children away to school. 'One doesn't know what one's about. Not that it would have made any difference, in the end.'

She accepted a second gin, curbing his lavish notions with hand signals. As soon as that was over, Joanna offered to start the clear-up next day.

'It will be awful,' she said, 'but the sooner we do it, the better. We'll have a warmed-up dinner; we were having that anyhow, and you and Stephen can come back. Will you?'

Mrs Brooks sat overwhelmed with drill-sergeant organization, rocking slightly in her chair, obviously unaware of her movement. A shout of laughter burst from the other room, and a door banged.

'To be young,' the visitor said, and her hands played in the air. As if in answer, one of the girls began to thump the piano in the dining-room.

'Who's that?' he asked.

'Ginny showing off,' Joanna said.

'What is it?' Felicity.

'Beethoven's Minuet in G,' Richardson answered.

'Oh, yes.'

'Her signature tune.' Joanna.

Felicity Brooks stayed for an hour and a half, ate a home-baked scone, spent a few outwardly cheerful minutes in the dining-room, walked upstairs to say good night to Fay.

'She's usually tucked up well before this,' Joanna said. 'But the hussy'll do anything to stay up.'

'I've ruined your system.'

'She'll be none the worse for it. We approve of good habits, but they mustn't rule our lives, now.'

Mrs Brooks thanked them effusively as she stood at the door with her son holding her arm. Her face had lost animation again; seemed grey, rough-cast. Joanna briskly said she'd be round at ten o'clock next morning.

'You'll be ruthless, won't you?' Felicity spoke plaintively.

'I'm a holy terror.'

When the Brookses had left, Joanna dropped her hands in weariness or mock desperation.

'Well,' she said. 'That was hard work.'

'You were superb.'

She grinned, formidably, but her voice sang small.

'Thank God I've got those two big pies. They were meant to give me a free day on Saturday. Oh, the best-laid plans. I'll tell you something. You've got a really nice way with you, if you put yourself out.'

'But I don't use it often enough.'

'You said it.' She dashed off for the kitchen, where she spent an hour preparing the next evening's meal, whistling, and cursing happily.

6

Joanna banged in home from the Brookses' house at about five o'clock, face smudged.

The family had been warned that dinner would be on table at seven so they had filled in as best they could from the biscuit tin.

'And it's straight to bed then for you, miss,' the mother warned Fay. Excitement buzzed.

Richardson joined his wife in the kitchen, offering his services, hoping to hear how the day's clearance had gone.

'Dirty. Easy,' she said. 'We kept a bonfire going once we'd started. She went mad, and just hurled great boxes of papers on to the fire unopened. As if she was drunk. I hope to God she doesn't regret it. Thank God it was fine.'

Peeling potatoes, he asked, 'Did she talk about Veronica?'

'We took time off for lunch at about half-past one, had a cheese sandwich and coffee, and then she began to talk, and never really stopped. It didn't prevent her from working; she's energetic, physically, but she really spilt it. It was odd, because

60

she gave the impression she was spouting it, spurting it away, and yet she'd stagger out with a pile of stuff for the bonfire and come back ten minutes later and take up again exactly where she'd broken off, as if she had real control. It puzzled me.'

'Had she heard any more from her husband?'

'No. Didn't expect to, she said. He'll ring from Heathrow and that'll be it.' Joanna rattled her scales, drowned communication in the whirr of the mixer. 'There was a man, in the Veronica business,' she said, in a half-moment of silence, 'as you'd suspect. I'll tell you about it, when we're on our own.'

The dinner blazed with success.

They sat down, Brookses and Richardsons, exactly at seven, to marrowbone soup, meat-and-potato pie, and a vast trifle. They laughed, drank red wine, and Stephen scoffed enough for a navvy. Veronica was mentioned, but it threw no blight on the party, rather added an underlying seriousness to the hilarity, a cause for its existence not an excuse, decent pauses not breaks. Richardson began to enjoy the occasion when he saw Joanna's open pleasure, and his own doubts dissipated.

By eight-thirty, when Fay had been put to bed, Virginia to her books, the rest sat in the drawing-room. Stephen and Margot, bloated, slightly tipsy, occupied one end of the settee, hand in hand, pink, smiling out towards the oil painting of Newstead Abbey. The parents, much at ease, played with scalding black coffee.

'This is a restful room,' Felicity Brooks pronounced. 'Harmonious.'

The visitors crept out before ten and Richardson barging into the bathroom found Margot sitting on the clothes basket in tears.

'What's wrong, chick?'

'Everything.' She put a bright face on.

'Such as?' He did not dare touch her; she would have shrugged away.

'What does anything matter, when something like this happens?'

'I know. How's Stephen taking it?'

'It doesn't seem to make much difference. I suppose he's sad; he is, I know he is, but, well, not deeply, not for her, more

61

generally. Oh, God, I don't know what the hell I'm talking about.'

'Yes, I think you do.'

She looked up at him quickly with something of Joanna's sly shrewdness about the glance, disconcerting in the daughter he considered like him.

'You knew her,' she said.

'Yes. Not very well. Or, not very long. But she came over as thoroughly alive, and a bit eccentric for anyone her age, so that it seems wrong for her to have disappeared. I grudge her death.'

'That's right.' Margot bit her lip. 'She was the last . . . Why did she do it, Daddy?'

'No . . .'

'She was funny, didn't have much to do with me, or with anybody at home. But she seemed comfortable up there in her room with her cassettes and coloured walls and kimonos. She'd have to walk up that building, twelve storeys, the lift was out of order, and then climb out.'

'You think it wasn't in character?'

'What is?' Dismissive.

'I think it did them good to come up here for the evening,' he said.

'They'd forget it?'

'Temporarily. They feel cut off from the rest of society, unpleasantly different; not quite lepers . . .'

'Pariahs.' That was his girl.

'And to sit and eat with somebody and hear Fay on about playgrounds and collages . . .'

'Does she understand what's happened, do you think?'

'Fay? I'd say so. She didn't know Veronica, so the impact's less vivid, but she's bright, and takes it all in.'

'She'd know that they'd never come back, crumble away in the ground?'

'I'm not sure. About bodily corruption. Not being seen again, yes.'

'I daren't ask her,' Marguerite said.

'She might ask you.'

'What do I tell her?'

'Something like the truth. If we know it.'

'You don't believe in after-life, do you?' she asked.

'No. It seems not impossible logically, but no. I wouldn't like the idea of living for five hundred years with my present mental equipment, never mind eternity. Not even if I didn't get older and slower and dafter.'

'I wouldn't mind that.'

Joanna poked her head round the door.

'What are you two on with?' she asked. 'Can anybody join in?' Richardson was glad of the interruption; he hadn't talked like this to his daughter since she'd reached her teens, but enough was enough.

' "On man, on nature, and on human life," ' he said.

'Oh, your bloody poets. Are you all right, Margot? Don't listen too long to your dad.'

'Why not?'

'He thinks everything is curable by words.'

'Gross calumny,' he said.

They broke up soon, and he could hear the music centre in Marguerite's bedroom thumping, subdued but reassuring. His wife, tired out, grumbled, said nothing about the dead girl; she'd go to help Felicity again straight after breakfast.

He slept badly, and was interrupted next morning after assembly by Anthony Moore, who was dressed in a garish tweed suitable only for the golf-links. His air itself was cocky, and he kept his hands in his pockets as if guarding fists full of loose change.

'Would you read this?' He dropped a letter on the desk; Richardson noted that the envelope had been jaggedly opened with a finger. That annoyed, unreasonably. Another short note from the errant wife. She had left Wallace. It had all been a terrible mistake. Could he find it in him to forgive her? Sandra.

'Sit down,' Richardson ordered. Moore jigged about as if he might throw a fit, but finally carried a chair across the room to place it exactly opposite the headmaster's. Moore's victory.

'What do you think of that, then?' Moore asked.

'You're glad, aren't you?' Quiet as a lamb.

'Glad. I am not. Who does she think I am?'

'I see.' Thin-lipped.

That checked the man who expected his senior to join him in

indignation. Now he frowned, writhed again, and hammered the side of his chair with a clenched fist.

'Come on,' Richardson said, more friendly, 'just tell me what you intend to do.'

'I don't know.'

'Do you want her back?'

'After she's been screwed by that dirty bastard? What do you think I am?'

Richardson pointed towards the wall and the outer office into which strident voices would carry. Moore jumped up, as if stung.

'When did you receive this?'

'Just as I was coming out this morning. Bloody marvellous start to the day.'

'I could think of worse.' Richardson picked up the note again, reread it, tapped it with his fingernails. 'This address, where is it?'

Moore leaned forward to snatch the paper.

'No idea,' he said. He reread it now, blowing out breath from between clenched teeth.

'There was no address on her last note?'

'No, there wasn't.'

'You don't know where she and this Wallace man were living?' Headshake so vigorous that the chair creaked. 'This isn't likely to be the place?'

'Quite possible. He might have left her stranded. He'd a wife and family.'

'Presumably he's gone back to them?'

'Don't know what he's done, and I can't say I care much.' Moore muttered his gall, but Richardson encouraged him to talk on, to describe his wife, their relationship. The man spoke badly, to himself, as if cantankerous over the circumstances or inhibited by the headmaster's presence. Perhaps five minutes of gutter swearing would have purged him.

'Are you going to answer the letter?' Richardson asked, in the end, watching the clock.

'I don't know what to do.'

'What are your feelings towards your wife just now?'

'Dislike. She's despicable.'

64

'It's very early to ask you this,' Richardson spoke pacifically, almost musically, 'but you're an intelligent man,' he did not think so, 'and it has to be decided sooner or later.' He watched Moore, whose brown eyes protruded hare-like. 'Is there any possibility of your taking your wife back?'

Moore loosed his muted volley; she was a bitch, deserving nothing. What if she was pregnant? He wouldn't put that past the feckless cow. His abuse rambled; he'd done so much for her: this was the way she repaid him.

'You've not answered my question, Tony.' A startled jerk upwards of the young man's sallow face. 'Are you willing to take her back?'

'What would you do in my position?'

That seemed pathetic, justifying himself by prolonging the argument.

'I can't answer that, because I've no idea how you feel towards your wife, what experiences you've shared together. You're the wronged party; I see that and I see it makes a difference. But my inclination would be to take her back.'

'Even when she'd dumped you for this illiterate sod?' Would Joanna leave him, he wondered. And for what sort of man, and in what circumstances? They hardly seemed meaningful questions.

'If marriage is anything to you beyond a legal contract which she's broken.'

'She's done that.'

'Yes. But one thinks back to the time you first met, your wedding day, the things you've done together, the house you're buying . . .'

'That's sentimental.'

'If by that you mean that emotion is involved, you're right. But so it should be. I asked you to think, to use your head, but that's not the be-all and end-all of a human relationship. You're hurt, Tony, and shamed; you think the neighbours are talking . . .'

'They bloody well are.'

'Yes, and it does your self-esteem no good. I understand that only too well. If you want my advice, write to Sandra at that address and arrange a meeting . . .'

'On neutral territory?' Useless man staking some claim.

'As you please. I would invite her, myself, back to your house. It doesn't seem to matter much. Then you actually see her, physically, that is important, and hear what she proposes.'

'When?'

'The sooner the better. If that's what you decide to do.'

'I can't tomorrow, there's a parents' meeting; and on Friday I'm going to the theatre with Miss Allbright.' He looked nastily at Richardson. 'We've been seeing a bit of each other . . . you know . . . since Sandra left.'

The man spilt out these confessions like a schoolboy in trouble.

'And that alters the situation?'

'It's not serious if that's what you're getting at. She's been very good to me these last weeks.' He waited for comment.

'I'm glad. You'll consult her?'

'Um. Possible. Um.' Meanly. 'It wouldn't do Sandra any harm to make her wait. I'm not at her beck and call, and the sooner she gets that into her thick skull the better.'

Richardson nodded, mandarin silent.

'I'll think about it.' Moore jumped up, knocking his chair away. Without a word of thanks, he rushed from the room, leaving the stranded chair. Miss Taylor, on the alert, immediately entered with a sheaf of papers and news of the next arrivals. Smiling, the headmaster tidied his room, watching his secretary, half expecting her to open a conversation about Moore, half disappointed that she did not. He enquired about her mother. No change. The day went on.

That evening Joanna cornered him, made him pour her a drink. She had spent a second long day emptying Veronica's room, expected a further stint. She praised Mrs Brooks, who had worked hard, acted sensibly, had spent time in clearance after she had returned from dinner with them.

'She must have gone on into the small hours. There were six or seven big boxes for burning when I got there.'

'How does she seem?'

'Too excitable. And yet too reasonable with it. The inquest's fixed for Monday. If that goes without a hitch, the funeral will be the following Friday. Will you be able to go?'

'Surely.'

'Nothing more from the husband. You'd think he'd make some attempt. There are telephones where he is, however out of the way. I don't think he bothers. She says as much.'

'She's a good witness on the subject?'

'I wouldn't know that.'

'What does she . . . ? Has she said anything about Veronica? In explanation?'

Joanna settled herself comfortably into a chair, clasped her hands in front of her and raised her heels, feet together, from the floor, as if at a yoga exercise, or making up her mind by these physical means whether this was the correct occasion to reveal confidences.

'She was having an affair with a near neighbour.' Having released the sentence, Joanna sat, pleased as a doll. Richardson knew better than to interrupt thus early. 'It's been going on for something over a year. He's a married man, with three children, a director of an electrical company, to do with telephones, I think.'

'How old is he?'

'Early forties. Not ever so much younger than Felicity.'

'How old is she, then?'

'Forty-six.'

'She told you that?'

'Without prompting. Now, are you going to let me talk, or are you not?'

'I'm sorry,' he said, self-deprecating. 'I'll be quiet.'

'It was all very secret. Until a few months ago, when Vernie, as she calls her, thought she was pregnant. She wasn't, but that's beside the point. She told her mother, quite bluntly; no shame about it, as far as one could tell. Just "I'm having a baby"; take it or leave it.'

'But if she wasn't?'

'All the odder. No talk of abortion, either. Two periods missed. Then it righted itself, and that was announced just as plainly. But she'd told her mother the name of the father. It was all part of the package.'

'Did Mrs Brooks know the man?'

'Yes. Very well. They were quite close friends, neighbours.

Conrad apparently had some business connection with the man's firm. I'm not sure he didn't act as a consultant. They met quite often socially. Meals in the home or out at restaurants.'

'What sort of a man is he?'

Joanna made a small gesture of exasperation.

'His name is apparently Simon Howard. You don't happen to know him, do you?' He shook his head. 'A very nice man, quiet, fond of his family, according to her. He married rather late as the children are young. The eldest's eight, I think. He was a technical man, a scientist, who's changed over on to the administrative side not too long ago. The last man you'd think of in this connection, she says.' Joanna paused, expecting questions.

'And he broke it off?'

'That's the oddity. As far as Felicity knows, not so.'

'Has she seen this Howard man since . . . since it happened?' he asked.

'No. Veronica went out to dinner with Simon the week before the suicide. Vernie told her mother; she did usually. And she came back not very late, quite cheerful. Her mother was still up when she came in, and they sat talking for an hour or more.'

'She hasn't seen Simon, you say. Does she intend to?'

'I don't know.'

'Does his wife, I mean, has his wife any suspicions about . . . ?'

'Apparently. He told her.'

'And she . . . ?'

'Again, I don't know. My impression was that nothing had happened out of the ordinary. If there was some sort of crisis, it was in Veronica's mind. The girl had decided, perhaps, that nothing was going to come of the affair, and that she couldn't go on.'

'Was that like her?'

'I asked. She thought not. At school Veronica had been a nuisance, disobedient and unreliable and bolshy and all the rest. She'd been pregnant, once, had an abortion. Her mother put that down to what she called their nomadic life when the girl was small. But recently she'd put weight on and become more settled. It was almost as if this affair with Simon Howard was what she wanted, that it wasn't unsatisfactory to her.'

'She left no note?' It appeared not. 'She didn't show any signs of disturbance? The day or two before?'

'No, she went off to work that morning. And according to people at work she seemed just the same as ever. Did her work efficiently; didn't look or sound any different. But she went off to this block of flats in Radford.'

'Had she any connection with that?'

'Again that's a mystery. It would take twenty or twenty-five minutes to walk there from her office.'

'She could have caught a bus?'

'I suppose so. Again my impression is she walked. She would sometimes go out in the hour they had at lunchtime for shopping or fresh air.'

'So whatever caused it must have come suddenly?'

'Except that she deliberately made her way to these flats,' Joanna said. 'They're too out of her way.'

'Are they well known? A spot for suicides?'

'Not particularly. The police talked some girl out of jumping from there. It was in the local newspapers. But that was some months ago.'

'Veronica would have read this?'

'They have no idea at all. She'd not mentioned it. The girl was unknown to Veronica; in fact, I think she was a stranger to the city. It's all a complete mystery. As you say, it must have been a sudden impulse, a brainstorm, something right out of character.'

'There's no possibility of foul play?'

'No. She was seen outside the flats on her own. She walked up on her own. Again there were witnesses. A well-dressed young woman. Some old dear thought she was a social worker.'

'What sort of place is this?'

'Working class. Council flats. Names from the Lake District. This one, the first in the estate, is called Windermere. Very decent tenants. Not much vandalized. One of the better places, apparently. Rather quiet at lunchtime.'

'How long was she up there? Before she . . . did it?'

'Not long at all. As far as they can make out, she walked straight up, and out.'

'She must have already decided on it?'

'No. One can't even say that. She might have been distressed, decided to walk it off, made her way towards these flats not caring much where she was going, and then, having got there, takes her decision. It's unlikely, but so are the other explanations. It's all out of character.'

'Could one see from outside, at ground level, that it was possible to . . . to . . . ?'

'Don't know.'

They sat; a wintry gust rattled the sash-windows; the television sounded faintly elsewhere: Fay would be asleep.

'Did her father know about this Simon Howard business?'

'Apparently.'

'And what was his view?'

'Nothing much, or so I gather. Refused to write to her about it. Said she was an adult, and must make up her own mind. Expressed surprise that it was Howard, thought he was a colourless individual, not likely to step out of line. Felicity doesn't speak very highly of her husband. She says his interest ceases once he's made adequate financial provision.'

'Is that why he's abroad so much?'

'No. He's always worked out of England. There's big money in it, she says. And he'd be quite willing for her to live with him, but she dislikes the Middle East. The climate doesn't suit her, women have to keep out of the way, there's absolutely nothing to do except to sip iced lemonade.'

'Is he likely to be there much longer?'

'He's building a university and a power station at present and that will mean a term of another three years, and then the contract's likely to be renewed. There are a whole host of projects. Money's no object.'

'How old is he?'

'Fifty-seven. And he'd been married before. A German girl he met when he was over there after the war.'

'Divorced?'

'I think so. I'm not sure. No children, or at least . . .' She leaned back again, emptied the dregs of her glass, refused

70

another drink. 'I think she's thoroughly baffled by what's happened.'

'And sad?' he asked.

'What? Upset, you mean? I'd say "yes", but I wouldn't know what I'm talking about. I guess she's genuinely undisturbed by what others think, because she doesn't have a great deal to do with them, and doesn't much care for the opinions of people she knows only slightly. She's not overwhelmed by grief, as far as I can tell, and criticizes Veronica as if she were still alive. I don't know. She talks a great deal, very freely, but she doesn't give herself away, if you know what I mean.' Joanna smiled crookedly. 'Unless I'm missing something.'

'They don't seem a normal family.'

'Now,' she contradicted, 'I would have said they were.'

'Husband and wife living apart? Not put out by suicide?'

'Have it your own way.'

They argued, with animation, for the next half-hour, enjoying the exercise, failing to remove the puzzlement before Joanna swept away to her kitchen to race through the morrow's chores and so allow herself further time with Mrs Brooks. She preferred action, at any time.

7

Richardson and Joanna drove to the funeral.

The Anglican service, not well attended, fell expectedly flat in a modern yellow-brick crematorium, a cross between an Italian villa and an eccentric church, where Conrad Brooks stood stiffly, a man shorter than his wife, with oiled hair, dried skin, a neat pointed grey beard. He shook hands with the mourners. Felicity swayed wind-swept, not in the sense that clothes or coiffure were disarranged, but that her movements seemed determined by buffets of air, so uncoordinated, eccentric did they appear. Haggard, she tried to smile. By contrast, her husband acted host, militarily at ease, stiff-necked, correct.

71

He invited the Richardsons back for a glass of wine, and on their refusal, the headmaster pleading duty, he asserted that he would be in touch. He spoke sincerely, a frog in his throat. That evening he rang Joanna and arranged a visit in two days' time.

'It depends,' she warned. 'John doesn't always keep this diary up to date. He may have fixed himself up somewhere else.'

'In which case,' the clipped voice ordered, 'you could come on your own. I understand you've been very kind to my wife. I'm very grateful.'

When Joanna reported this to her husband she said Conrad had sounded impressive. 'He speaks,' she said, 'as one having authority.'

'And not as the scribes and pharisees.'

'Such as you,' she gibed.

'Exactly.' He was glad when his wife worked off her low spirits so easily on him.

The visit proved genial.

The Brookses had no other visitors and Stephen had been despatched to entertain the Richardson girls in their home. The house here blazed with light; the drinks cupboard was crowded with bright bottles; furniture gleamed; warmth pervaded every alcove, lapping like tropical water. Touch the picture frames, the fingers went unchilled. Conrad strutted about, his standing more dignified than his movement, the thin neck covered by a neatly tied polka-dotted silk scarf. A monocle hung on its thin cord; Richardson had not noticed that at the funeral. The host waved his drinking glass, and his slippers were highly polished.

Felicity sat comfortably, in voluminous but handsome dark clothes, more relaxed, as if she had come to terms with herself. She explained that they had finished the clearing-up in Veronica's room; Conrad was like Joanna, a thrower-out, with no sentimental second thoughts. The husband interrupted to compliment Mrs Richardson again on her assistance; he did not use Christian names, spoke with formal assurance as at a board meeting.

'And do you know,' Felicity's voice, itself hoarse, seemed rich in harmonics compared with her husband's croak, 'it wasn't until the room was bare and dusted and I was up there

72

with the vacuum cleaner that it hit me.' They waited; Conrad's lips were clamped thin, but the brown eyes twinkled. 'The place looked so naked, just marked walls and a carpet. We'd taken all the plants out and distributed them round the house as you'd suggested,' she smiled towards Joanna and pointed at a couple of pots of variegated ivy in wicker covers, 'and suddenly I didn't recognize the room. She'd made it so much her own, with all the . . . the bric-à-brac. It even smelt different.' Felicity paused again, inviting them perhaps to admire her sensibility. Conrad trotted across the hearth, examined his face in a baroque mirror, pushed a silver cigarette box along the mantelpiece as if there was significance in the transfer, and nodded a soldierly apology at Richardson. 'It was as if we'd moved Vernie out. She was there before, in a way.'

'Best thing, m'dear. Best thing by far.'

'The room represented her, was her, and I suddenly thought, "You've killed her, you've wiped her out with what you've just done." It was horrible. I keeled over. Thank God there was nobody there to see me. I got up in the end, but I'd cut my head.' She lifted her hair from the forehead, which was bruised, minutely scarred. 'I must have caught it on something when I fell, though God knows what. I felt utterly shaky for the rest of the day. Conrad sent me to bed in the end.'

'What else? Sleep it off, always my advice.'

'It's odd how things affect one. You'd think with the inquest and the cremation that that's where I'd have got hurt. But, no, it was the bare walls and the picture hooks and the dust marks.' Felicity smiled. 'Conrad's started to redecorate it. He doesn't like delay. No sooner the word than the blow with him.'

Later, two large gins later, Mrs Brooks took Joanna up to see the present state of the room.

'I'm glad you could come,' Brooks said, 'because Fiz admires your wife, who's one of the few she finds steadying. She needs somebody who'll set about things, won't hang around complaining. We've lived abroad too much; it makes you unduly dependent on the servants. Your wife sorted Vernie's rubbish, shifted it, burnt it. Felicity would have been reading every letter, putting it to one side, grieving over it. It wouldn't have done.'

'She's recovering?' Richardson asked.

'As far as one can see. But how does one know? She seems to be. I wanted her to fly back with me to Oman, but she won't leave Stephen. Not that that's surprising, though he's a different kettle of fish from Vernie. And she'd be bored out there. She's not very sociable, if you understand me, but she misses the chance of social life, theatres and restaurants and trips to London. As long as I'm at work, I'm happy. The jobs are interesting, there's a lot more scope there than ever there is over here, and well paid so that I shall stick out there till I drop.' Richardson expected his host to talk technically now about his work, even hoped that he would do so. He'd invite him up to the school to speak to prospective engineers, especially the girls. That was one of his lines, women in engineering. But Brooks paused, said 'It's not much of a basis for marriage, is it, now?'

Richardson made propitiatory noises, slightly disappointed because he liked conversations to develop his way.

'You met Veronica, I understand?' Brooks had begun again.

'Yes. Shortly. About university entrance.'

'And did she strike you as suicidal?'

'No. Not at all.'

'She was her own woman. She gave these schoolmistresses one hell of a time when she was young, but then when we bought this house, she settled down. I mean, I could hardly believe it; the change in her. Attended lessons, caused no trouble, passed her exams. Felicity began to believe in Santa Claus. I was sorry that she wouldn't take a place at university, but it's not the end of the world. Has my wife given you any hint why this,' he turned his head away, 'may have happened?'

'She has hardly spoken to me about it. That's not surprising. She has said things to Joanna.'

'About this love affair?'

'Yes.'

'Could you understand it?'

'I was in no position; I knew too little.'

'Felicity would have told your wife the truth.' The sentence sounded huffy, accusatory.

'Yes, I'm sure.'

74

Brooks turned his back, not as if annoyed but as though he had found himself suddenly at a loss, unable to continue. He appeared, by the flapping of his hands, to be searching for something. He did not turn but spoke with his back to Richardson. 'Excuse me, we seem to have run out of ice.' He snatched up a bowl, scuttling for the door. It would not have surprised the visitor if he had heard Brooks break into sobs; he did not.

Richardson, uncomfortable, crossed his legs, picked up and examined his drink, a very weak whisky and water, put it down again. That morning Lesley Allbright, Moore's temporary girl-friend, had asked in writing to see him, and he had interviewed her, at her request, in the lunch-hour in one of the large store-rooms in the domestic-science block. There he had sat by a table crowded with a dozen electric sewing machines. The others in the department were elsewhere; the head, a forceful woman, who would certainly have barged in had she been about, was away on an in-service course.

'I hope you don't mind my arranging to see you like this,' she began, 'but I wanted it to appear like a chance meeting.'

'To whom?'

'Whoever might be about. And Tony. He comes across. You've heard about us. Tony and I.' She spoke with a genteel simper, a pretty little woman in well-fitting slacks and a frilled pink blouse. Her dark hair was bobbed, her rose-bud mouth shaped with lipstick of an orange shade he did not like; the eyebrows above her almond-brown eyes traced thin rising curves. The long, well-kept fingernails glowed with a varnish that matched the blouse. 'His wife wants to go back to him.'

'So I understand.'

'He can't make up his mind. He doesn't know whether he wants her or not. But you've heard all this. I mean, he's talked to you, he says.'

'Not for some days. His wife had just written.'

She drew in breath, and her little pointed breasts prettily filled the blouse, as she glanced up in suspicion towards the door which he had purposely left ajar.

'We've been going around together,' she said. 'Since it happened.'

'Not before?'

'No. We did not. He'd sometimes come down from the chem labs for a cup of tea in the lunch-hour, but the others were there. There was nothing wrong in it.'

'No.' Noncommittal, barely voiced, long drawn out. 'But now you've become fond of him?'

'Yes.'

'And he's in two minds?'

'I don't think he expected her,' Miss Allbright said, 'to come back. Ever. She'd made her choice, and left him for good. It made him ill, you know.' He waited. Nipples stood out in the pink stuff of her blouse. 'They didn't ever get on properly. He would have liked children, but all she thought about was enjoyment.'

'How long have they been married?'

'Two years. Just before he came here.'

'But now he's not certain?'

'He doesn't seem capable of thinking properly. She's deserted him once, she'll desert him again.'

'May she not have learnt her lesson?'

'You don't know her, do you?' She leant forward; from two and a half yards away he could smell her perfume. 'She was a pretty, fluffy little thing. All she bothered about was dressing up and gadding about.' Richardson kept his face straight, for this was exactly how he'd describe Lesley Allbright. 'There was no intellectual companionship or equality. I mean, this man she went off with, he wasn't what you'd call educated, or anything else. I doubt if he'd got "O" levels.'

'And yet Tony thinks he might take her back?'

She looked at him, suspicion stamped suddenly into the small, attractive features. At once he realized she did not need his advice, only his support for her views, his approval of what she wanted to happen. She straightened herself and began to talk, to convince him, to convince herself. As she spoke he lost interest, wishing she'd vanish off the face of the earth, or shut up, sort herself out. She and Tony had had sex, but it did not seem a matter of life and death; they had, she claimed, established a mental rapport, an intercourse of minds. She cited a visit they had made to a theatre club to see Ibsen's *Ghosts*.

He asked her, interrupting, if she understood modern

chemistry. In no way put out, she said she did not, but she was prepared to listen, to learn, because Tony was a fascinating, careful explicator. He could make it clear; he wasn't like Stanley Smith, an intellectual snob interested in one or two high-fliers who'd end up with firsts at Oxbridge and nobody else. Not short of words, she set out to open the headmaster's eyes for him. In one sense she succeeded because he had not realized what a garrulous, determined woman hid under this well-turned-out exterior. Again, not quickly, he intervened.

'Has Tony been a good husband?'

Perfect. Perfect under frustration and provocation. She quoted Sandra's thoughtlessness: the bad wife flounced off for hair appointments, games of badminton, even, voice squeaked, discos, leaving him to prepare his own meals. He'd put up with it all, said nothing. Perhaps it would have been better if he hadn't. Miss Allbright dropped into the vernacular. 'She led him a pretty ta-ta, I can tell you.'

When he asked about other men, her face registered disgust, with him presumably. She did not know; she made no accusations; things were bad enough, weren't they? as they were. But in view of what had happened, well, it was likely . . . no, she'd not . . . she had no evidence, she'd be fair.

Richardson looked at his watch, excused himself; another appointment. He thanked her for confiding in him, said that at any time he could be of assistance to either of them . . . He held out his hand. She took it, in hesitation. Her small palm was cold, damp, limp. Glad to release it, he rushed out, catching his hip in the next room on the corner of a high table. He stifled his curses, limping away.

Now Conrad Brooks had returned with a flat dish of ice-cubes. He provided himself with a drink after Richardson had waved him away from his glass.

'You know about Simon Howard?' Brooks began.

'Well, yes. A little.'

'He's a neighbour. We've been friendly for years. One of nature's bachelors, I'd have said. Pale, plump man. Clever, but very quiet. He's in his forties now, and has a young family. We like his wife. Lively woman, much younger than he is, very attractive.'

'How old is she?'

'Thirty at the outside.'

'Does she know about the affair?'

'Must do.' Brooks's face changed suddenly. 'One doesn't . . . one can't say. People are wilfully blind. We knew that Vernie was on the pill. For some years now. There'd been trouble earlier. While she was still at school. Pretty usual, isn't it, nowadays? The pill? I mean with your older pupils.'

'Some, certainly.'

'Most?'

'I wouldn't think so, but I have no means of telling. You're suggesting this was not her first affair?'

'Shouldn't think so. No, it wasn't. But Felicity found out when Vernie thought she was pregnant. And when she wrote to me about it and named Si Howard, it seemed incredible. They'd absolutely nothing in common. He was an academic sort, Ph.D in engineering, and an admin man, a fixer, a quiet, sharp talker, a sorter-out. He was quick and clever and careful and worked twenty hours a day. His firm's involved in my present jobs, and in a big way. He's been out twice to advise us. And he's useful, because though he can see snags he still gets things done. Now God knows when he found time for Vernie, never mind inclination. She was a lovely girl, but geared somewhere else. She'd no ambition; she dressed herself up, sure, but she'd slop around in her room day and night. I used to pull her leg, I can tell you. "Get out," I'd say, "and see a bit of life before you're too old." And she'd smile at me in that sleepy way, like a cat that's got at the cream, and wedge her bottom into an armchair and stay there. I wondered at one time if she wasn't on drugs, but there was no evidence, absolutely none. Nor drink. Black coffee, and soft pop music, and plants, and dolls, and fancy dresses. Doesn't make sense. And yet all the time there she was with Howard. When and where? Fizzy noticed nothing out of the ordinary.'

'Has Howard said anything to you since this has happened?'

'No. They sent a wreath. At least, his wife did. He's been away in America.'

'Were they at the funeral?'

'She was. Netta. Tallish girl. Striking fair hair. Sat over on the left.'

'But you've heard nothing from him?'

'No.' Brooks tapped his monocle on the top button of his waistcoat. 'And it's not likely, either, is it? that he'll come round to tell us he's involved. He probably thinks we know nothing about it. And he's a self-contained chap, not inclined to stir things.'

'Might she have written to him?'

'Possible. But if Vernie could make a mystery of something she would.' Brooks tried to read the expression on Richardson's face. 'That sounds bad. As if it were a game. But my experience is that as people live, so they die.'

There were sounds from the stairs.

'Thanks for talking to me,' Brooks said. 'I'm never sure where I am with Felicity. Keep in touch with her, will you?' He looked all the time for the opening of the door. 'She's like a valuable machine, never properly put to use. And it's wasted on me. She's wasted.' His voice was held out at a low level, ready for switching off the moment the women appeared.

The door swung open.

Both Joanna and Felicity were smiling, larger than life, expansive as if she had braved an initiation ceremony, could boast a new status with confidence.

'You're not getting drunk are you?' Joanna asked.

'Your husband's very abstemious,' Brooks said. 'I wish I could say the same for myself.'

'You're a quick worker,' Joanna spoke warmly. 'You've transformed the room.'

Conrad stood, suddenly quiet, shaken out of his officers'-mess sociability, his English Club sensibility, a poor soul naked in a blizzard. He did not fill his suit; his knees disfigured the well-cut trousers; his sleeves ruffled shorter; the monocle hung a withered joke. Richardson looked away, unable to believe his eyes, then refocused on the man, on his physical inadequacies. Felicity had advanced on her husband.

'Not a bad sort,' she averred. 'To say.'

'To say what?' Joanna.

'That he's lumbered with me.' She took his arm; anchored

79

thus together, they occupied the centre of the room, a senti-mental tableau, into which Richardson tried to read sense. He could not decide whether the Brookses were deliberately acting out a role for their visitors or for their own ironic amusement, or whether raw emotion flung them into these postures.

Both soon recovered. Felicity disregarded the gin bottle, but made some exotically sweet, treacly, black coffee. The visitors did not stay late, and as they said goodbyes in the hall Conrad muttered, 'Push Stephen out, will you? He's all we have.'

At that moment the heavy front door was unlocked, and the son burst in.

'I've had to desert your daughters,' he told Joanna, 'because I've a wretched history essay to complete.'

'All-night job?' she asked. He considered that seriously.

'Very likely.' His smile sugared them all; he was in no trouble. His parents stood back, reticent in pride.

8

'Felicity Brooks has been in,' Joanna announced to her hus-band, signalling him into a corner with the children out of the way.

Richardson removed his overcoat. He had spent the day chasing heating engineers. The weather, at the onset of spring, had struck cold; overnight frost had whitened the playing fields and the laboratories were without heat. The tussle with caretakers, the science staff, the education office, had resulted in the arrival by midday, a near miracle, of two men in a small van. These had inspected the damage, blown hot and cold about the chances of setting damage right, and had settled down industriously to their thermos flasks and sandwiches; three times during the afternoon he had toured the stricken block, given his permission for actions he did not understand. The two men seemed unsure of the cause of the trouble, or rather waxed fluent on the different possibilities; pupils huddled in anoraks and parkas; bunsen burners flared; overcoated teachers warmed their hands round mugs of tea. The workmen tangled with Stanley Smith, muttering to him that it was not as easy as he made it sound; to the headmaster they blamed the caretakers who had not followed instructions a child of three could understand; the second-in-command of the physics department, a union man, led the headmaster to the thermometer, 51°F, threatening action on the morrow if the required 62° did not show. Richardson, fuming, waiting at the phone, had finally wrung a promise of calor-gas heaters out of the education officer for nine the following morning when the junior of the workmen had summoned him back at three-forty to the science block, where heat had been restored, though it was barely noticeable, and he was instructed to assemble the caretakers for a demonstration how to clean the 'combs' of the fan heaters. The janitors played awkward, claiming they had their own chores which would occupy all the time and letting it be known that their men in the labs were both absent. Peace was patched up, but Richardson, thoroughly pessimistic now, did not cancel the calor-gas reinforcement for the morning. By the black looks on the faces of caretakers and heating engineers, next day would probably find the whole school ice-cold and, for good measure, a corpse or two bloodily hacked by the boilers.

The headmaster hated his helplessness. These problems had nothing to do with education, and yet would annoy and hinder two hundred students, probably because somebody had stupidly forgotten to turn a screw here or switch something off there. He could do nothing except blow his top one minute and spread soft soap the next, and all without expectation of amelioration. It was utterly likely that next morning things would be without improvement, if not worse. He tried not to work his frustrations off on Miss Taylor or the two pupils he had managed to see, and did not succeed. He had kicked his hatstand at five to five, had reached home, barely gratified that his tyres were at the correct pressure, that his engine had fired and that nobody had run into the back of him.

He recognized signs of recovery as he sat in his car, for he was already preparing a humorous pot-pourri from the argument about responsibility between caretaker and plumber.

'You didn't clean that radiator, did you, nor set it properly?'

'I didn't; you're right. I never touched the thing.'

'Isn't it your job, though, to see to it that your mate does it?'

The caretaker, a bony, clean man with a quiff and an ever-open mouth, wrestled hard with that.

'I haven't got an 'undred eyes, have I?'

'You've got a tongue. Use it.'

'To lick your dirty radiators out?'

'Well, it would be a start.'

The two delivered these sallies cheerfully, without much ferocity, as if asserting their status in the headmaster's eyes. When he interrupted, they looked at him in displeasure, mildly hostile, rasping their hands in concert, saying they hadn't the whole afternoon to stand about gassing.

Now Joanna's deliberate sentence meant his anecdotes must be deferred.

'Oh?' he said. 'What's troubling her?'

'Conrad has taken it on himself to face Simon Howard with what he's done.'

'And has upset Felicity?'

'Well.' The word dropped at length, promising more revelations, as she dashed back to her saucepans. He knew that she could have summarized the situation there and then, but typically had left him on tenterhooks, establishing her rights. It would probably have to wait now, she'd arrange it so, until the children were in bed, or bedrooms, but this did not displease him. They might run an interesting duet, Brooks v. Howard, caretaker Jones v. Heating Engineer Meldrum. As he laid the knives and forks on the table he tried, recalling this small snatch of conversation, and remembering that his wife had gone out of her way to corner him, to discover whether Joanna had been affected by the incident, and decided he could not. There were at least two opportunities during the evening for their talk to continue, but she brushed him aside, lashing out at her chores, laughing to herself as she left him in the lurch.

It was past ten when they talked, and even then she had insisted on hearing the radio news. He sat patiently, very tired, wishing to go to bed, or that he was a smoker so that he could settle his fidgets with a cigarette.

'Come on, then,' he said, turning the radio off. Joanna sat with the expression of one agog for twenty minutes of commentators' wisdom. She raised her eyebrows. He thought she'd begin an actressy procrastination, and he reddened in anger, but she settled prosaically straight into her statement. It never seemed possible to understand or keep up with her.

'He went round to see Howard, apparently, saying nothing to her. Just slipped out of the house. She thought he was somewhere reading, she said. There was a programme she wanted to see on the telly, and it's easy to lose one another in that barn of theirs. Anyway, he went. And he didn't come back until past eleven. She thought then he'd gone out to the pub.'

'Is that usual?'

'No. But one's never quite sure with Conrad, she said. It's not quite a rush of blood, but now and again he will do something a bit out of the ordinary. He's not impulsive, she thinks, but he doesn't, well, exactly consider what he's doing. Just occasionally. Anyhow, this evening he came back, and he could see she was worried. He looked at the clock and said, "God, is it as late as that?" He'd disappeared before eight.'

Joanna tidied already tidy hair.

'I've been to see Si Howard,' Brooks had said. His wife sat back, legs trembling.

'About Vernie?' Felicity asked.

'Yes. Do you want a drink?' She had refused; Conrad poured himself a bitter lemon, searched for ice. 'It didn't do,' he had said. 'I couldn't let it drag on.'

Felicity had waited for, almost on, him, frightened by his calm. He toyed with the monocle.

'He was quite open with me. Didn't attempt to deny anything. But basically he was as puzzled as we were.'

'He had not heard from her? No letter?' she asked.

'No. Taken aback. Shocked. Netta told him. He was relieved I'd gone to see him, he was so shaken. He was in love with her. He needn't have said that now that she was dead. But he'd had no intention of leaving Netta and the children.'

'Does she know about it?'

'I couldn't make that out. One minute I thought he was suggesting she did, and then the next, no. She seemed to have some notion something was wrong. He was going to confess everything to her, but I told him not to be a fool.'

They had sat facing each other, lost for words. Brooks roused himself.

'I felt sorry for the man. When I went there it was to throw bang-slap in his teeth what he'd done. But one could see he was . . . ruined, as if he'd been paralysed in the will, or like somebody trying to talk underwater. He just cringed. And then I got him to speak about Vernie. He called her Veronica. For all of ten minutes he'd been biting his lip and rocking about in his chair. It was like a wailing mourner, a woman, but without the sound. He looked at me, as if I'd hit him, and then stood up and tiptoed to the door and listened and then locked it. I thought, "Bloody hell, he's going to have a go at me." But not Si; I couldn't believe it.'

Brooks caught his own breath, rapt, pale, monocle forgotten.

'He spoke so well of her. She'd renewed him, he said. It was such a rum word. Like religious conversion. He and Netta hadn't quarrelled; they got on well, sexually and financially and every other way.'

'That doesn't seem likely,' his wife objected.

'It's what he said. He spoke of Vernie as though she were a kind of goddess, outside ordinary goings-on. When I report that to you, though, it sounds ridiculous. If the boot were on the other foot, and you were telling me, I'd just think you were fanciful. But this was something I've never met before. It wasn't somebody crazy with love, not like that daft Scots lad in Bahrein. Not at all. Vernie had intervened into a normal, extremely satisfactory life, in all respects, his own words, and had transformed him. Deeply. He was not just pleased with himself because at his age he was getting it on the side with somebody young enough very nearly to be his daughter. It was, he said, as if the values of the world had changed.'

'But he wouldn't give up his wife and family?'

'Veronica wouldn't have it.'

'That's what he said.'

'He seemed to believe it. He convinced me. I thought he was talking like this because she was dead, but it wasn't the case. She might have been a saint. I couldn't understand it. I mean,

Vernie had a good deal going for her, and was or could be very attractive if she set out to be so, but she was a bit idle, wasn't she? and very self-centred. And yet . . .'

'You think he'd made it up?'

'He must have done. And yet he's the dry-as-dust type. Scientist. Accountant. Make sure of your facts. Sort it all out. And I tell you another thing. While he was on with this, saying what the effect of Vernie was, and it was the same boring voice he uses in the office, he burst into tears. He was speaking, and suddenly his face cracked, broke, y'know, and he sobbed.'

'If Vernie meant all this to him, why wouldn't he leave Netta?'

'Oh, I asked him that. He said I thought he wanted his bread buttered both sides. About right. I did. But Vernie had made it plain to him, and when he told me this he said it differently, as if he were reading holy writ, that they were getting as much out of it as was possible, that if it altered it would be spoiled, and that that was that for the time being. When I said that sounded more like him than Vernie, he just answered, "Believe me or not as you like. It's the truth." '

Joanna, offering her long résumé of the conversation, said how beautifully clear and detailed, how authentic Felicity had made the dialogue sound. She had not exactly played the part of her husband, but had differentiated between his voice and that of Dr Howard.

'It was marvellous, really. You couldn't say she was acting, but she brought it to life. It was a performance.'

'So you didn't think she was distressed?' Richardson asked. 'While she was . . .'

'Excited, rather.'

'Over what was said? Or her recital of it?'

'I can't tell you.'

'But her daughter has died?'

'I know. I know that as well as you do, but that's how it seemed to me. She was intent on making me believe that her dead daughter had so affected this man. There it is.'

'She must be recovering?'

'Must she?' Joanna mouthed doubt. 'Isn't it possible that all this is a cover-up, that she won't admit to herself how badly

Veronica's suicide hit her?' Joanna's face ironically mirrored a scientific detachment. 'Why did she have to run to me to tell the tale? After all, she could discuss it again with Conrad, and had done so, she said. So why spread the tidings? I don't think she's as steady as she'd like to make out.'

'That's what I asked you.'

'And that,' Joanna replied, 'is what I can't answer. The more I think about it, the more baffled I find myself. It was wonderful. I can well imagine that I was there eavesdropping on Conrad and Si Howard, and yet, remember, she was reporting what her husband had said.'

'So he must be pretty good? At spinning the yarn?'

Joanna shrugged, displeased with her husband, or disappointed.

'Do you think she made it up? Or some of it?'

'I've told you,' Joanna said, 'as best I can. For all I know, Conrad invented it, or Felicity did, or while we're exploring every avenue, possibly I did. Now you tell me.'

'You're worried,' he said.

'I wouldn't say so. I'm puzzled. I don't like it, but I'm not troubled. She's an odd case, as you very well know, so I'm a bit at a loss why she came to me with the tale in the first instance.'

'Did she tell Conrad she was coming?'

'Don't think so. She asked me to treat it confidentially, but said she didn't mind if I mentioned it to you. I was naughty and said, "Don't you want to tell him yourself?" But she didn't seem to notice.'

'What are you, we, going to do about it?'

'Nothing.' Joanna sounded stiff, stern. 'This is not a case of talking in the French lesson or running along the corridors. She wanted to get it off her chest to somebody, perhaps to sort it out in her own mind, and let's hope it's achieved that. She can come again, whenever she likes. As can Stephen. But I've no magic wand to wave and raise the dead. The trouble with schoolmasters is that they think all problems are soluble. They aren't.'

Now he had the opportunity to describe the heating crisis.

Joanna enjoyed the recital, giggling away at the verbal duels between caretakers and plumbers, especially pleased that Dr Smith had been dragged into the contention, saying, 'He's worse than you are. He thinks life's a chemical equation.' When Richardson defended his head of science, she merely laughed again, ignoring the arguments as she claimed, 'I'll say this for myself, I can recognize a human being when I see one.'

They went to bed pleased with one another, and made love, tired as they were.

Richardson, still vaguely content next morning, had just returned from a hot science block when Miss Taylor said there was a man on the phone who refused to give his name.

It turned out to be Tony Moore ringing from a callbox, begging the headmaster to drop round at his home in the dinner-hour.

'I don't want people to know I'm consulting you.'

'What people?'

'Lesley, for one.'

Richardson drove out immediately he had finished his lunch, only to find Moore had not yet arrived. He sat in his car listening to 'The World at One'. Moore dashed up, miserably apologizing, led him into a house that was cold, smelt stale, had been cheaply furnished, rarely dusted.

His story, once he'd made a token show of hospitality, gesturing towards the kitchen, was as before. He could not make his mind up; his wife bothered him; Lesley Allbright was likely to prove awkward.

Richardson sat still, listening without encouragement to the ill-at-ease delivery. Moore writhed in his chair. Both women pressed their claims; he seemed to dislike both equally; people were unsympathetic and curious; Smith had issued disguised warnings; his pupils wrote obscenely about him in the lavatories. Paranoia was not far off.

'Look Tony, I haven't too much time. It's only because a meeting was cancelled that I could come at all. And I don't much like this cloak-and-dagger stuff, not giving your name. Enid Taylor's no fool. She'd recognize your voice. But what do you want me to do?'

'Give me some advice.' Moore, sullen.

'How can I? I don't know enough about it?'

'God. I've been through it enough with you.'

'Let's begin,' Richardson said, 'with what I think. Not that

that is of any value. From what you've said today, I gather you like neither woman.'

Moore leapt up from his chair, stood tottering, subsided.

'Oh, well, if you're going to play bloody fools with me, it's no use continuing.' Richardson nodded, buttoned his coat, rose. Moore's face fell. 'No. Sorry. I didn't mean that, sir. I'm grateful for your time.'

'You do prefer one to the other?'

'In a way.'

'Which?' Moore thrashed about again. 'If you were not married, which would you choose now?'

'If I weren't married, Lesley. But I am.' He scowled. 'Because I know what Sandra's like now.'

'You don't think Lesley . . . would find some difficulties in living with another person?'

'Might. We all do.' Moore grinned; his face suddenly grew attractive.

'Do you feel, I want you to be honest, any obligation towards your wife? She's treated you abominably, but do you still consider that as her husband you are bound somehow to look after her? For better or worse?'

'Richer or poorer. That's just it. I don't know.' He bit his lip.

'Go on. Expand that. Why don't you know?'

'I'm different from minute to minute. Sometimes I'm so raging wild I could beat her face in. And then I'll remember something we did together, and it will seem,' he stumbled, looked up, 'sweet. I was reading how the maquis in France shaved the heads of the women who'd slept with Germans; made them parade naked through the streets. She deserves something like that.'

'You want her punished?'

'No. I don't know what I want.'

Richardson rubbed his chin. His good shirt, tie, suit, his attitude of careless alertness, the high polish on his shoes, the uncreased socks, made the chair seem shabby.

'I don't know whether I'm breaking a confidence, but Miss Allbright has consulted me about this. Did you know?'

'She said something.'

'I gather she thinks you shouldn't take your wife back?'

When Moore made no reply, he said sharply, 'Isn't that so?'

'She would say that, wouldn't she?'

Discouraged, Richardson essayed another tack, without much hope.

'You've seen your wife, haven't you, since we last talked?'

'Yes.'

'How did you get on?'

Moore screwed his mouth in boredom or distaste.

'I invited her back here,' he began. 'Well, that seemed the best thing. She came in reeking of scent, and do you know the first thing she did when she came in the house?' He frowned, moved his mouth as if removing wet crumbs from his teeth, and pointed at a picture, an unattractive print of a ship under sail. 'She straightened that.'

Richardson smiled; Moore sniffed deeply as if to clear the room of heady perfume, and continued.

'We talked to one another. At least, she did most of the talking. She said she was sorry, she didn't know why she'd done it, that she must have been mad. Could I forgive her? She was very unhappy. And all the rest of it. My impression was she'd practised what she was going to say.'

'She would have gone over it time and time again in her mind.'

'Probably.' Moore's bottom lip projected. 'She sat where you're sitting. All dressed up like a dog's dinner.'

'She'd taken all her clothes with her?'

'She'd tried, but she was so bloody slapdash, she'd left things all over the place.'

'And while she was saying this, Tony, what were you thinking? I'll tell you why I ask. It's a very good thing to consider all this very closely, to talk it over with a friend or friends, but sooner rather than later you'll have to make your mind up. You can brood for too long.'

'Well, I don't . . . You see . . .'

'The breach is there, like a bad wound. If the process of healing is to be managed, then it should start quickly.' Simile and metaphor added emotional weight, not out of place.

'You mean,' Moore said, 'I should start thinking myself into the state of mind where I can take her back.'

'Yes, and I'll tell you why I say that. The fact that you're undecided still makes me come down on that side. It has its disadvantages. As you say, you'll have to convince yourself. Against the way you feel, sometimes. She's hurt you.'

'You can say that again.'

'But we can't leave it there. Just now I'm obsessed by a suicide I know about, a useless loss of a promising life, and it must have originated with some failure of some sort.' At the thought of Veronica his throat choked, chill raked his skull, though he knew he was making mere emotional noises, designed to panic Moore into acceptance of his views.

'Whichever way I move now,' Moore said, 'somebody will catch it, either Sandra or Lesley. I don't say they'll commit suicide. I don't know. It's bloody terrible.'

Richardson hummed soothing sounds.

'It's not as though it's my fault,' Moore continued, doggedly ugly in voice and face. 'She upped and left me.'

'You turned to Miss Allbright.'

'I had to go somewhere. I'm human, aren't I? You talk as if Sandra's deserting me was nothing. It was like death, and I felt like death. And that's how Lesley will be now if I drop her.' His chin sank to his chest. 'If I tell Sandra to stay away, at least she'll only have herself to blame.'

'Mightn't that make it worse?'

Moore did not answer, shrugged argument away. Richardson had no idea whether the man genuinely wrestled with a moral or emotional problem, or sloshed about in a mash of self-pity.

'I shall have to go,' he said, headmasterly, not even consulting his watch. 'There are one or two matters I must attend to first-off. I've told you what I think you should do, but the decision's yours, not mine. This is a fearful dilemma, but I can't see any advantages in delay.' He stood, pulled at his cuffs, glanced at his smooth hair in the dusty, oval mirror over the mantelpiece. Moore sat staring downwards. 'I must confess I feel so inadequate, but if I can do anything, talk to Miss Allbright, or your wife, if you think that will do any good, I'll do so with pleasure.' As Moore made no response, Richardson put a hand out on to his colleague's shoulder; the fingers shone cleanly with health. 'Can I give you a lift?'

Moore mumbled thanks, but did not move. Richardson let himself out through the front door. Pink, ruched lace curtains disfigured the bow-window, but paint on the woodwork shone new; Moore had spent his summer holiday to good effect.

Back in his study, the headmaster felt relief to be caught up again in the ordered chaos of the school. He threatened two idlers, discussed careers with a clever, attractive sixth-form girl, promised the sports king that he'd look round for money for a further trampoline, answered three short phone calls, gave his blessing to a sponsored walk for the disabled, explained to the head of maths why he could not at the moment promote a young computer expert who was muttering his discontent, signed his letters, indulged in five minutes of personal self-aggrandizement with Miss Taylor and set off at twenty minutes before the final bell for the laboratories.

Moore stood on his dais, in a white coat, scribbling efficiently on to the scroll of his overhead projector. His sixth form grouped itself negligently round, taking the information in or down. Nobody paid attention to the watching figure. One floor below, Lesley Allbright marched across her room, laying the law down, to a group of sixteen-year-olds. Her approach was brighter, sharper; she turned swiftly to silence two West Indian girls who had ventured a word to each other. She noticed the head outside the door and raised a pretty hand, a smile, much in control.

He acknowledged her salute.

Lessons went on, though everybody looked forward to the holiday. Work proved prayer in these temples of technology, and it gratified him. He wished that somewhere in the place someone was learning Greek, but he knew it not to be so. Cheerfully whistling, he made his way back to his office, Miss Taylor and the end of the academic day.

9

Richardson and his family spent the Easter vacation on Anglesey.

There had been talk that the Brookses might join them, but Conrad had been called back to his work, and he, his wife and son spent the last four days of his leave in London, wasting money like water, piling up earthly treasures by day and losing time and energy in the theatres and clubs by night. Conrad, according to a letter Joanna surprisingly received, had left Heathrow exhausted and cheerful, Stephen had seen nothing like it but was glad to return to his textbooks and quiet, while Felicity had managed, as her husband had expected, to forget herself for a day or two.

The weather near Amlwch had blown stormy, but with long periods of cold brightness as if the rain and hail had cleared the air for an hour or two. At Cemaes Bay they had sheltered amongst the rocks from driving snow, and five minutes later had been clambering in sharp sunshine. The sea slopped dark and frozenly dangerous even in the protected havens, but the family ran and shouted, red-nosed and excited, along the beaches. Back for six o'clock, they ate enormous and delicious meals, walked the lanes for half an hour's twilight or played Scrabble before Fay was packed off to bed with hot water-bottles and the rest gathered round the open fire to read, perhaps talk.

Joanna enjoyed herself, seemed young, sillier and noisier than her daughters, once out of doors, as if this lonely place had freed her. She planned each day's activity, covering the floor with maps, reading passages from the solemn guidebook, ridiculing its pretences with her sing-song, synthetic Welsh accent, consulting their landlady, daughter of a sea captain, about what was worth visiting. Mrs Morris-Jones believed in education and regarded holidays as times for broadening the mind; she had spent her few childhood breaks from home with relatives in Liverpool, where she and her sister had been put to it as unpaid skivvies. The Richardsons neither saw television nor listened to the radio, and only once did the father buy a newspaper, which lay unconsulted, a wrapping for litter.

Three days into their second week, as they returned one blustery evening cold but exhilarated, Mrs Jones handed over a telegram. It was from John Bentine, the senior deputy, asking the headmaster to phone him, 'utmost urgency'. After dinner the whole family trooped up the hill-road to the telephone box outside the post office. It was not yet dark, the winds gusted, buffeting smoky clouds across the dull sky; lights glared from the windows of bungalows and shacks perched on the mountain. From the kiosk armed with his torch, his pile of coins, he could see the family playing some kind of tag, a graceful game hardly involving movement of the feet, but body-swaying, swoops of arms, bursts of laughter, as he waited to be connected.

Bentine spoke badly.

Four boys, fifteen-year-olds, on a holiday party had been drowned in a boating accident. It had been in the national press and on television. Richardson explained he had heard nothing, and searched for an envelope to write down the four names. They had taken a boat out, in Northumberland, against the express orders of McPherson, who was in charge of the party. It was the day before the expedition was due to return and the children had been given a few hours to shop for presents. McPherson was devastated; he'd taken these walking-parties for years, in safety.

Richardson said he'd start back early next day and he'd be in the school at lunch to see people; Bentine agreed to make these arrangements, relieved that support had appeared. The head looked again at the four names: Paul Nunn, Terry Grocock, Michael Lynham, David Weekes; they lay, closely written but not neat, inside the small oval of the flashlight. He asked the deputy if there was anything to be done now; nothing, apparently. Bentine would pass on his sympathy to the families concerned, and if they wished to see the headmaster he would . . . The man was lost for his words. The Director had been informed, the local office; they were helpful. Mr Wesley at County Hall was concerning himself with the matter. No, there was nothing the head could do just now.

Another coin. Richardson waited to know about blame. Bentine was not forthcoming; the boys had disobeyed orders; three bodies had been recovered. No, they were by no means wild or indisciplined; it seemed to be on impulse. In a sheltered bay they'd dragged a rowing boat from behind some bathing huts and had launched it. A prank. Ought to have been safe. Talk about currents. They could all swim, it seemed. Nobody quite knew.

Richardson listened, said he'd be in his study as soon after midday as he could, but that depended on the traffic. He thanked Bentine, put down the phone and shuddered, his eye resting, half seeing, on the lighted list. He knew none of them personally; they'd be fourth-formers in the part of the school where he came across only a few promising scholars, outstanding athletes, recidivist wrong-doers.

'That took long enough,' Joanna said as he emerged from the kiosk. The four of them panted slightly from their game, did not notice his distress. He leaned against a garden wall.

'Come on, Mummy,' Fay shouted, wanting to continue.

'Time we started back,' Joanna said. 'It's getting near your bedtime.'

They walked down the hill in the half-darkness, the father bringing up the rear, not speaking, ignored by his chattering womenfolk. Once Virginia asked him a question, but he did not answer, and she did not press him. The grassy lane from the road to Mrs Jones's house seemed dank, colder. At the front door, he took Joanna's arm, held her back.

'Bad news,' he said.

'Oh, no.'

He explained briefly, said he'd drive back the next day.

'Do you want us all to come?'

'There's no need.'

She now had linked arms in return.

'I'll get Fay into bed, and then see Mrs Jones about sandwiches. We shall be able to manage without the car.'

'We were going to Holyhead.'

94

'We can't now. We'll do that the last day. What was the weather forecast?'

Joanna pressed inside; he followed, sank into a chair. Virginia was nagging Margot to play chess. Fay, waiting for her last drink and biscuit, perched herself on her father's knee, her head on his chest. She did this only rarely, near bedtime, and though she sat still, she seemed heavy. He put an arm about her, noticing her warmth, drawing no comfort from it. The child wriggled free when her mother appeared with the drinking chocolate.

When Joanna had bundled Fay upstairs, a small knock on the door announced Mrs Jones. At Richardson's summons, she advanced a foot beyond the threshold, a tiny, flat-chested woman, with grey hair, glasses askew, rather large feet.

'I'm very sorry to hear of this tragedy,' she said, speaking precisely, each word separately pronounced, and polished, very Welsh. The girls looked up at him in accusation, four strong eyes, chessboard forgotten. 'I'll pack you sandwiches and a thermos flask of tea or coffee so that you can start immediately after breakfast. Would you like cheese or meat? And would it be coffee?'

He answered her, thanking her, making his choice. The girls had not returned to their table, but avoided looking at him.

'It is terrible when such a thing happens on holiday,' Mrs Jones pursued her course. 'They act foolishly, as boys will, and this catastrophe is the result. I cannot help thinking of the parents. Perhaps they made sacrifices, money does not grow on trees these days, to allow them to take the holiday, and then this happens. I do not understand it.'

Richardson muttered appropriately, but still she did not leave the door. In spite of her age, and appearance, she was militantly agnostic if not atheistic; she had made this clear to him on their second day. Her husband went irregularly to the Welsh Baptist Church, and that was up to him, but she had wasted more time in chapels in her youth than she cared to remember. So the visitor knew he need expect no portmanteau sentences on divine providence. This small woman waited to serve, wanted him to make some demand on her so that she could in some way be associated with the affair, offer her mite of practical comfort. He thanked her again, said he hoped to be back in the evening.

'I will keep your meal warm,' she said, without change of expression.

'There's no need for that, Mrs Jones. Thank you all the same.'

'I could do no other.'

She felt in her apron pocket, produced a scrap of paper, one inch by two, which she held out so that he had to rise from his chair to take it.

'That is Mr Bedwyr Jones's phone number. At the new house. In case there is any change of your plans. He will be glad to bring a message over.'

Her writing was untidy, unformed, straggling, unlike the neat little body who still remembered Latin conjugations. He thanked her. This time she backed off, pulling the door behind her.

The girls had dropped their game, asked bluntly what had happened. It brought relief to put the affair into plain words. When his daughters wanted the names of the victims, he had no need to consult his paper. The two shook their heads; they did not know the boys. Virginia walked across, not at once, but as if she had thought it out, made up her mind, to touch him on the arm.

'Do you have to go back tomorrow?' she asked.

'I think so.'

'Fay will be sorry. She really likes having you here.'

He clasped her arm and Marguerite, still at the table, smiled; her face seemed to blossom, he thought, with love. Ginny went back to chess, was soon snorting and rearing her head like a mad pianist, but he noticed that now and then one or the other forgot her rivalry and glanced over at him. When Joanna came downstairs, both girls, out of character, asked if there was anything they could do.

Richardson's book lay on his knee.

Thirty years before, on holiday at the seaside, he and his brother James had been turning somersaults on the iron bar of the fence at the edge of the promenade. At eight o'clock in the morning, though the sun was up, it was chilly on the east coast and both mother and father, who insisted on the pre-breakfast walk, wore their raincoats. The boys dashed on ahead, James the elder by two years, always in the lead. Eric, the eldest, was away on his first trip to Greece.

'Head over heels,' James shouted, when they reached the bar. Down he went and over, neat, toes together, a handsome performance, quick as a flash. John joined him, used now to the feat, after days of practice, but remembering the thrill of blood rushing to the head, the moment of uncertainty and the relief as sandals jolted down on to the concrete. There was no danger; the promenade projected at least a yard beyond the rail.

Mother and father were smiling, talking together; father wore a light-grey, wide-brimmed trilby hat.

'Whoo-hoo,' James shouted, did a double whirl on the bar, straightened and jumped outwards and upwards for the sand, six, seven feet below. John did another cautious turn, enjoying the faint dizziness, glanced for his brother.

James lay face down on the fine sand.

John looked again; one never lost interest in James's theatricals; he could groan and writhe after some tumble enough to frighten you to death, or lie crumpled and still until the dead features creased into mischief, laughed at the terror in your face.

The parents caught up.

'For goodness' sake, James,' Mother called. 'You'll be covered with sand. Get up.'

Nothing below; no movement. John and Father were standing together, outside the bar.

'Stop there,' Father said, and jumped down, neatly as James could, though his hat fell off. He felt James, shook him; John remembered it as Father turned him over. 'Jane,' the man shouted up, 'he's hurt. Run across to the Grand there, and get them to ring for an ambulance. Quick now.' Mother set off. 'You stay up there, John,' Father said. 'It'll be all right.'

Mother came back after a long interval; Father had been standing, then kneeling, then standing again with hands behind his back. A man in uniform accompanied her.

'A doctor's coming over,' she said.

'Have they rung for the ambulance?'

'Yes. It won't be long.'

Other people gathered; while they were walking the promenade had been deserted. Now there was a crowd, standing silently, looking down. The doctor arrived, in a sportscoat and an open-necked shirt; a middle-aged bald man, he walked down the steps, did not jump like his father, knelt and did things, stood up and talked seriously. Mother had gone on to the sand, and John joined them standing a yard or two away, with nobody paying attention to him. When the ambulance arrived, the doctor gave instructions, and James went up the steps, wrapped in a blanket on the stretcher. He seemed to John unmarked, face pale, strong legs brown and stockingless, just still, stiller than when he was asleep because then he'd throw out an arm or snort or turn violently. Father went with James in the ambulance; Mother looked round, at last, for John, found him, took his hand. The doctor accompanied her to the main road, saying things about X-rays and neurological consultants, but suggesting that things would very likely clear themselves up with a strong little chap. He had called James a 'chap', John remembered.

He did not forget the breakfast.

The dining-room clashed with knives and forks, the twinkling legs of the waitresses, the talk, the brisk orders to the kitchen staff. Mother insisted he ate his egg and bacon, and he had no difficulty; fright had not killed hunger. She broke toast on her plate but drank cup after cup of coffee.

She rang the hospital, and drove the car down to fetch father. The town infirmary was a small place in red brick with some huts like those classrooms in Father's schoolyard, and the sandy garden-beds were full of flowers. They allowed Mother in to see James, and John kicked his heels on a bench in a room where the nurses talked loudly to each other and smiled at him.

'Is he better?' John asked when they came out.

'He's still unconscious,' Father said. 'They'll do tests.'

Later that day the authorities transferred James inland to a teaching hospital in Leeds and he died there three days afterwards, never coming round. John heard talk about a clot, a fracture, some inherent, the word stuck, weakness, and occasionally, though his parents spoke guardedly in front of him, of an awkward fall, a chance in a million. It had not seemed to happen to him; how could it? His leader, the boisterous James, did what he had done a dozen, a score of, times every day he'd been there, and had been killed.

Since he'd grown up he'd admired his parents' behaviour. They had not spoilt Eric's holiday by writing to Athens; they had treated John with off-hand care; only once had he caught his mother crying and she'd dried her eyes at once and asked him a riddle. They were a remarkable pair, his conservative father and his ambitious twittering mother; they had loved James as they had loved their other sons, and his loss must have crippled their lives, but they kept it to themselves so much so that at the age of sixteen, for example, John would have said the tragedy had made no difference at all to them. They blamed nobody; they spoke of James in the affectionate, not uncritical tone they might have used if the boy had been away from home on a fortnight's holiday; they did not wrap John in cotton-wool. The achievement was great, and the son never learnt the cost.

Richardson was back in his office before midday.

Bentine fluttered about; he had left a sheet of actions taken on the head's desk, but insisted on talking through them. Richardson got rid of him on a trumped-up errand and rang Wesley at County Hall, who explained the position about insurance. At one o'clock, he had just opened Mrs Jones's sandwiches when he was interrupted by the arrival of McPherson, the teacher in charge of the party.

McPherson, thin, grey, lined with worry at the best of times, said he could neither eat nor sleep. Very gently, for the man would neither sit still nor check the machine-gun bursts of words, the headmaster led his colleague through an account of the black day's happenings. By the end of half an hour the man answered rationally, though now he slumped in his chair.

'I want to thank you, Mr McPherson,' Richardson said, 'for your frank account of what happened, painful as it must be to go over these dreadful events once again. More than that, I want to thank you for all you've done, not only this year, but formerly in this matter of holiday parties. My gratitude in the past, and this is one of the drawbacks of my job, because time's short, has been all too perfunctorily expressed. You are, and this is as

99

high praise as I can give, a good schoolmaster, and that includes your work both in and out of these buildings. What happened last week was in no way your fault. However you feel, you are in no way to blame.'

'If I'd have taken the party out instead of . . .'

'You did a sensible thing, what they asked for. In your position I should have done exactly the same. You need not reproach yourself. And I hope that next year you will find yourself able to lead another similar trip. They are valuable.'

Both he and McPherson knew that this sort of holiday was becoming too expensive; parents thought they got more for their money by packing their families into the thousand-and-one planes and hotel rooms of Spain or the Mediterranean islands.

He made McPherson promise to see a doctor and pronounced on the value of drugs over a short period. Taking the man by the arm, he led him to the door, along the corridor, out to his car. He shuddered as he returned, because it had seemed unreal to stand in spring sunshine, clouds racing, their shadows suddenly darkening the playgrounds and playing fields, in the deserted yard arm-in-arm with a fifty-year-old husk. McPherson had not cleaned his shoes for some days.

Bentine scurried back, hands full of papers, head of ideas.

Richardson unwrapped his sandwiches, and ate, sure that this would embarrass his deputy, who, offended, at once slouched out.

At one-thirty the headmaster telephoned the homes of the bereaved parents. Two only were in; one asked if she could come down, immediately. They agreed on two o'clock. While he waited for her, he hand-wrote notes of sympathy to the other two families.

Mrs Weekes appeared five minutes late, and when he had comfortably settled her, Miss Taylor provided a tray of tea.

A young woman – she might from her appearance have still been in her twenties – she was brightly dressed, attractive, composed. Her nails were blood-red, her tights dark-blue and unwrinkled. Sipping, she listened to his conventional expression of sympathy, nodding, hardly concerned, as if he instructed her about the sale of raffle tickets at a parents' evening. She sat so quietly that he felt bound to wring some talk out of her. She had one other boy, ten now, and she hoped he'd come here next year. David had been a good boy, had saved up for this trip by working on Saturdays delivering orders for a fruiterer. Yes, she went to work, as a typist at Plumb and Midgley's, obviously expecting him to know all about this concern, but she hadn't been able to go since this had happened, she was so shaken.

'And his dad,' she continued, 'he's haunted, a different man. He looks at me as if he wants to say something, and can't think what it is. We neither of us sleep properly. I'm having to have tablets, and I reckon he will before this is done, though he swore he never would.'

Richardson offered decorous condolences, outlined what the official at County Hall had told him about insurance and the inquest. She frowned, very slightly, as she answered him, as if there existed inside her, or him, some spell, some form of words that once pronounced would dissipate the tragic reality. He promised her help, said she must get in touch with him immediately if any difficulty arose. She dropped a sentence, greyly, to the effect that her husband had said something about suing, but she did not develop this, slipped elsewhere into meaningless pieties.

'You can't grasp it's happened,' she said. 'I expect to hear him about the house. It seems so quiet. Henry, his young brother, creeps about as if he's frightened to speak, and that's not him, I can tell you. You don't know why they did it, do you? I mean, taking that boat out, when the weather was so squally. I would have said our Dave had more sense, but if you put two or three lads together, God knows what they'd get up to.'

She did not stay, replaced her bright scarf and with his help her neat raincoat.

He explained that he was returning to Wales that afternoon, but that he'd be back Sunday evening. They shook hands, and he watched her walk for the bus, a neat, attractive woman who had not shed a tear.

For the next quarter of an hour, he played about with the pile of correspondence, signed the letters, instructing Miss Taylor to send those to the bereaved families by first-class post, and left

101

her Mr Bedwyr Jones's phone number in case of emergencies.

'I'm terribly sorry about this, sir,' the secretary said.

He looked at her in denim skirt and cream blouse, one hair in every four grey now, at the alert. Shaking his head, he laid his hand on her forearm; he had rarely touched her before, but she did not move away as he mouthed the expected.

'But four of them,' she said. 'One's bad enough, but four. It's as if the place was cursed.'

She took off her glasses; she was crying. As the telephone shrilled, they jumped apart. She recovered more quickly, snatched up the red receiver on his desk. The local radio station made enquiries; he stood, spoke smooth, statesmanlike inanities for five minutes while she listened.

'Let's call it a day,' he said. 'Get your coat on. You've had three long spells of this.'

'Well, two,' she corrected. She had wiped her eyes. He thanked her again, and they marched out together. The caretaker hovered in the corridor.

'Is it convenient to ask you about them new orders for polish, Mr Richardson?'

'Not now, if you don't mind.'

'Quite all right, sir. I understand.' He made a quasi-military salute, and shuffled back to his buckets, satisfied that he had demonstrated humanity.

Richardson's journey back to Anglesey proved not too difficult, but he found he could barely recall any of it. He had driven fast and carefully as the pain in his mind had efficiently erased each detail. He did not like this.

Fay burst out of the house to hug him, she'd evidently been on the watch; the older girls made a fuss; Joanna kissed him, ruffled his hair, while Mrs Jones insisted that he sat down at once, not at the large table, but a small circular affair covered with a clean, starch-stiff cloth; she had laid the huge cut-glass cruet, the best cutlery, a serviette in a silver napkin-ring. She had put on a brand-new apron, creased still from its packaging, to serve his meal.

'The fatted calf,' he said.

'Fish and chips.' She stayed just long enough to explain that now and then her laconic husband rang Bedwyr to say he was having a bad day and would be late, and then she knew her course. Serve him fish and chips, and his spirit lifted. Men, she concluded, are in some ways still children. Her mouth twisted into a satisfied smirk.

The family strolled out together in the darkness. A car, headlights brilliant, streaked past; it might have killed them had they been elsewhere by a yard or so. The girls chattered on, telling him of the day's adventures, glad to have him back. Later in the evening, he and Joanna, scarfed against the chill, tramped up and down the garden path together, while he gave her an account of his time at the school. She did not speak, was a supportive presence shoulder to shoulder, strong as he was not.

The exercise, thirty yards this way, thirty that after an about-turn, on a grass-grown path, with the noises of the night, rustle of twigs, birds disturbed, animal scurryings in the hedge bottom, the rare sound of tyres on the distant roads, seemed as unreal as the spot. The lights of the dwellings up the mountain hung in the black air; a dog barked, miles away; Mr Bedwyr Jones banged round in the garage of the new house; the wind could not tear away the cloud cover; no stars shone.

He repeated Miss Taylor's sentence: ' "It's as if the place was cursed." '

Joanna took his arm.

'Sometimes,' she said, 'life's not only inexplicable, it's ungovernable.'

He thought of McPherson, shrunken above his uncleaned shoes.

'We're not in control of our lives,' she concluded. 'Or not as we seem to be at these good times, on holiday when the sun's out.'

Mrs Weekes had intercepted a glance from her husband; his own parents had stepped out along the front with their boys to the smell of frying bacon in ozone. Mr Jones came out of the back door to his dustbin and called in muffled Welsh to his wife. Her answer, which sounded like a rebuke, rang clear as crystal. Jones fiddled with the dustbin lid, he never seemed to do any simple action the once, always repeated it, and as clumsily, then laughed mirthlessly.

Returning darkness closed blacker about them as he shut the door.

10

The family spent the next morning happily in Holyhead.

On their return journey the parents sat sheltering from the wind in sunshine while the girls clambered about. The coast stretched deserted; hardly a car disturbed the bluff spring weather. Joanna, pleased as punch, praised the girls, who had been spending money on themselves.

'They know their minds,' she said. 'Even Fay.'

'And is that good?'

'I don't want imitations of you, or me, or each other.'

She stared out, slapping her knees, to where the girls squatted by a rock pool, muffled in their anoraks, out of earshot.

'Are you all right today?' He recognized, as she intended, the change of tone.

'I felt fine this morning when we were chasing about the streets.'

'And you don't now?'

'I ought to. It's a marvellous day,' the sky had cleared to an enamelled blue, 'we're here. I've got you. And them.'

'Go on.' He did not. 'You can't trust it to last?'

'That's about the length of it.'

Now Joanna hugged her knees, her face hidden deep in a quilted hood.

'And how,' she asked almost carelessly, 'are you proposing to get over it?'

'I'm expecting to feel better in the end because it's always happened before. But the day'll come when I don't recover.'

'How do you know that?'

'I don't.'

'That's right. You don't. God knows what we'd do if you lost your confidence.'

'I've not done that yet. But there's been such bad luck.

Veronica Brooks. Now these boys. I'm looking over my shoulder for the next. It's made me think of my parents. When they lost James. It must have snapped their optimism. Then Eric changed over to Sanskrit, and I wouldn't do classics at the university. I see now how these must have knocked my father about.'

'That was years after James.'

'But he never felt he had a job which tested his full potential. He was ambitious. Made great progress for a start. And then, bang, promotion stopped. At Dame Agnes Street Secondary. If only he'd had a degree, he thought. Or knew Greek.'

'Was that the reason?'

'I'm not sure. I guess he spoke his mind to officialdom, or at least didn't go out of his way to endear himself to his superiors or their political masters. And when James was killed, he was, what, forty-seven, and it must have been obvious that he wasn't going any higher, that people he considered to have much less to offer than he had were promoted over his head.'

'And he did nothing about it?'

'Not much he could. Except at home, where he kept Eric and me hard at it.'

'He had his reward. One son a professor, the other the head of the largest school in the county, before he died.'

'I doubt if ambition can ever be satisfied with the achievement of others. He loved us; it pleased him to see us do well, temporarily, at least. But he felt he'd failed himself. He hadn't produced a textbook, even. He'd soldiered along for twenty-eight years as a headmaster of a slum school they pulled down six months after he stepped out of the place.'

'Somebody has to do these unrewarding jobs,' she objected.

'And I think he did it well, until it knocked the heart out of him. He knew for his last three years the place was condemned. And he spent so much of his time with delinquents. He wouldn't delegate that responsibility. But he wanted to spread education, so that his West Indians would all be reading Dickens and Shakespeare.'

She laughed.

'That was his métier, he thought,' Richardson said. 'To teach people to read and speak properly, and understand mathematics and music. He bought prints out of his own money and framed them to hang in the corridors and classrooms.'

'He wasted his time?' She gave him no relief, chafed, snagged.

'Who can say that?'

'But basically he was disappointed?'

'Basically,' he said sarcastically, 'yes.'

'Sorry.' She'd deliberately used the adverb, he guessed, to discover if he was still alive. 'And your mother? How did she put up with it?'

'She was a different kettle of fish. Clever, but not serious. She was very quick. But had never had the discipline of a really academic background. She did two years in a teachers' training college, and taught for two or three years, but of course as soon as she married she had to give up her job. Not that she minded, I think.'

'What did she do?'

'Housework and meals. And children. Not that that occupied her long. She soon got Dad used to plain cooking. But she read a great deal, in both English and French, and gardened, almost scientifically.'

'Was that enough?'

'She'd never been brought up to expect anything else. And her menfolk were demanding.'

'You included?'

'Worst of the bunch. But we were interesting. And she took up with a Mrs Orston, a scandalous figure because she lived with a man who wasn't her husband, and who made us all go to the theatre.'

'They weren't religious? The parents?'

'No. No more than when you knew them. My father had no interest. "Man is the measure of all things," that was his motto. I think she might have shown some interest in the aesthetic side of church services or architecture, given half a chance, but she wasn't.'

'The year or two I knew her,' Joanna said, 'she'd become very quiet. I know she was ill.'

'She kept my father going until he was sixty-five, and that was a full-time occupation towards the end. He hated it, but he

106

wouldn't retire. It was his duty to see it out. He was great on duty. But I don't think, at least when she was younger, she was dissatisfied with her lot. She was lively enough to occupy herself, and not ambitious enough to envy us our chances, but satirically minded enough to poke fun at us. But then she developed this heart trouble, and that altered her as nothing else did. But I'd started university by then.'

The children were still at their search, though they had shifted elsewhere, and were squatting again, talking, arguing.

'Would you say they had a satisfactory life?'

'My mother could have been an academic. She was very like Eric. But I wonder if, at the end of her time, it would have seemed any better to her. She would have affected a larger number of people. She might have left a book or two behind. But, but, but, but. I don't know.'

'And your father?'

'For the blacksmith's son from a little Derbyshire village, I suppose he did well. His father would have said so, and the other people from Selston. But he didn't fulfil his own ambitions, and you know what he was like once my mother died, a miserable old sod who never opened a book, stared glassy-eyed at the telly, could only rouse enthusiasm to complain.'

'Will you end up like that?' she said.

'Very likely.'

'Is it because we, you, overrate ourselves?'

'I tell you what bothers me, now, and that is the tremendous wasting of time.'

'Sitting here, talking to me?' she questioned.

'No, when I'm doing what's supposed to be my work. And I've no idea what I should do instead, what will turn out to be important, and what won't.'

'Don't you apply your mind to it?'

'I don't get any answers.'

'Is that your fault?'

'I suppose it is. But I'm in charge of a bunch of kids, in all senses. Like a mother. I clear up one mess only to find it there again next day.'

'Except you're well paid and highly regarded by society.'

'By the standards of businessmen, even in recession, my

107

salary's nothing. Not that that worries me. We don't go without. But I'm my own worst enemy.'

'That's so,' she said. 'But if they made you Master of Balliol or Chairman of ICI or the BBC, you'd still be picking the scabs off your wounds. Come on, let's go and join the rebels and dabble our hands in cold water and get our shoes wet.'

'And not be able to answer any of their questions?'

'You speak for yourself,' Joanna answered.

Later, on their way back to the car, he found himself alone again with his wife.

'D'you know,' he started, 'I've had much more yardage out of you than ever you've had from me.'

'Have you only just found out?'

Her question killed the conversation, but encouraged him; his wife blew brisk as the sea air, as healthy.

When the new term began, he attended the four funeral services, was summoned and interviewed inconclusively by the Director who, as usual, did not know what he wanted, and was then invited at short notice to appear on television with the photogenic headmaster of a well-known public school and the Minister himself, no less, in a discussion about excellence in education, and its relationship with financial stringency. He was not allowed time to breathe, never mind think, and yet round him, while he dashed here and pronounced there and impressed the world, his school worked on, in the examination term, nerves tautened, tempers fraying, ordinary as the dinners provided in the steaming, song-echoing kitchens.

They heard nothing from Felicity Brooks.

When Richardson enquired from Joanna, she suggested Mrs Brooks must be away.

'And Stephen? We're seeing nothing of him?'

'No. You must ask Margot about that.'

'Meaning you're not going to tell me.'

'Meaning I don't know.'

'That's unlike you.' He chaffed her, glad of the opportunity.

'You can't provoke me into guesswork.'

'That's a good sentence.'

They parted, both pleased with themselves and the exchange. He made his enquiry of Marguerite.

'We haven't seen much of Stephen Brooks recently?' he said.

'I've got exams this year. Perhaps you hadn't noticed.'

'So you've given him up.'

'To some extent.' She resembled him, with the burnished cliché.

'He seemed a decent boy. Is he clever?'

'I'd think so. He's ten "O" levels, most of 'em As. And they expect him to get three As and two distinctions at "A" level.'

'He's a medieval historian, isn't he?'

'Yes. With Latin and economics.'

'That's a new course, isn't it? For that school?'

'He wants to do law at the university. But he told them he wanted to do one modern subject. The authorities were awkward, but he insisted, and Mr Greene gave in.'

'They were lucky they were able to arrange it.'

'He's a fanatic in his quiet way.'

'He tells you all this?'

'He did. The senior history master wanted him, and backed him up. He works very hard; sometimes he'll stay up all night, not go to bed at all.'

'That shouldn't be necessary.'

'You think,' Marguerite answered slowly, instructing the backward, 'that he's not very well organized. But he is. It's just that he's so interested.'

'But you're not seeing anything of him?'

'Just now and then.'

'And I thought it was serious.' He laughed, but she looked at him with incomprehension or dislike. 'How about his mother?'

'How about her?'

'She's disappeared from the face of the earth.'

'She's staying with her brother in London. He's an MP. And a QC. Charles Stanhope Walker.'

His conversations with Marguerite seemed, he thought, between equals. She never hurried herself, nor appeared too embarrassed, but answered his questions sensibly without emphasis, willingly. He regretted the clever, darting, shrieking infant he remembered, wondering from whom she inherited this compact, unruffled persona, uncertain when and how the

109

next change would come. He could think of no girl in his own school who bore the remotest resemblance in temperament to her, but that merely demonstrated that his knowledge of his students was limited, or his position as headmaster prevented their presenting themselves as human beings. Certainly he could not bring himself to believe that, and determined to question Miss Brandreth, Margot's head, when next he came across her. That would not be popular with the daughters, for he recalled Virginia, who'd not been in the school three months, scornfully dismissing a comment on sixth-formers the headmistress had made and which had reached the national dailies.

'Old Dandruff. She's no idea what's going on in her own head, never mind anywhere else.'

He wondered from whom she picked that gem up.

That evening, as the family sat over the evening meal, Mrs Brooks telephoned. Joanna and the girls had been describing to him, at his request for his sixth-form had raised the matter in a general studies period, a television programme in which young social workers had dealt with problem families.

The viewers had been disturbed by a reunion between a child of eight who had been in care and her mother, an hour's harrowing howling, embracing, swearing in what looked like a waiting-room. The mother, ill-kempt, badly dressed, worse-spoken, had beaten and neglected her daughter over a period of years, as had the man with whom she was now living. All her children had been removed from her for their own safety, and this day after three months she was being allowed to spend part of an afternoon with the girl.

One eavesdropped on the anxious discussion between social workers, the decision taken with reluctance, the explanations by the very young woman in charge to both mother and daughter.

'What will happen?' a smooth broadcaster, a voice of reason, had interrupted to ask.

The social worker's glasses flashed.

'I've no idea, really,' she said, Midlands, flat-heeled.

'You're not optimistic, then?'

'No.'

'Why do you do it in that case?'

'We have to keep trying. They say blood's thicker than water. We have to hope. Besides there isn't the money available to take full responsibility for everyone. If we put into care every child we think might be in danger from his or her parents, the number of hostels we'd have to build would have to be doubled or trebled, and you know what ratepayers and taxpayers would say about that.'

'So you can't do your job properly?'

'That's right.'

The meeting of the mother and the child had buffeted, terrified them all, on screen and off. The daughter had been, according to the programme, put out to very decent foster parents, by whom she'd been welcomed, had played happily with the other children there, had blossomed on square meals, steady attendance at school, baths, toys, regular bedtime, rough but wholesome company. She looked wide-eyed with fright as, hand-in-hand with the social worker, she had walked sunny corridors for the meeting.

At first the mother had created a moderately favourable impression. She had made the attempt to spruce herself up, had brought a bag of sweets and a present, a golliwog, not new, not very attractive, purchased for a copper or two at a jumble sale, for Tracey. Both were quiet, wary of the other; the child refused at first to sit on her mother's knee, but hunched awkwardly in one of the three armchairs. The young woman in charge of the case occupied herself at a desk, distancing herself but encouraging the girl to speak to her mother. Her man, in shabby suit, with a holey pullover and sandals, looked elderly, sixty with his grey stubble, awkward, obstinate, dirty, aggressively saying nothing.

Before long Tracey was persuaded to try it on her mother's lap, and she lay there, eyes closed.

'A' yuh a good girl, then? A' yuh bin schule? A' they lookin' after yuh?'

The mother, aged thirty-seven, the programme said, but appearing ten years older at least, grunted out these questions. The daughter barely snuffled intelligible replies. It seemed a useless exercise, a woman hugging an unresponsive child, an

111

unsavoury man lighting a cigarette and seeing no tray available dropping his match, his ash to the carpet.

'Yo' love your mam, don't yuh, Trace?' the woman crooned, crouped. The child moved on her lap. 'Yuh mam loves yo', my little precious. She does, ne' mind what they tell yuh 'ere.'

Nothing, nothing but decent, institutional furniture, in a room with big windows and trees in sunlight outside.

'D'yuh get plenty t'eat? Is it nice?'

Soon the child was sitting up, offering information, so that the pair smiled together, if uneasily. For all the notice he took, the man might have been sitting in a bus shelter. After a series of such questions, irregular awkward silences, an ill-tempered request by the woman to ' 'utch up a bit. Your bum-bones in't 'alf sharp.' The mother, brushing her child's hair with thick, unclean-nailed fingers, said, 'D'yuh want t' come 'ome wi' us, then?'

'Yes, Mam.'

Triumph stiffened aggressively in the woman's shoulders.

'There,' she shouted across to the social worker, 'you 'eard, did yuh? You 'eard what Trace said. She wants to come 'ome.'

'Yes, Mrs Ridley.'

'What yuh goin' to do abaht it, then?'

'I'm afraid it's not possible just yet, Mrs Ridley.'

The woman's face wrecked itself into anger, a wild searing of wrath.

'That's just like yo' boggers, in't it? She's my daughter, een't she?'

'We have to do what we think is best for all of you, Mrs Ridley.'

The woman now held the child tight, and rocked her fiercely from side to side, so that Tracey's head lolled and jerked like a stuffed puppet's.

'Best?' the Ridley shouted. 'How d' yo' know what's best? You know nowt. I wouldn't gi' yo' a job swabbing a sailor's shithouse out. Yo've got na children; yo' don't know what it's like to 'ev your own flesh and blood took off yer, t'ev young gels barely out o' their nappies tellin' me what's best for me and mine just because they've been to some bleddy soft-sods' college.'

112

Marguerite and Virginia reconstructed the dialogue, shocking mother and father, astounding Fay.

By the end of the hour Tracey was screaming hysterically, the man was boasting that he, an old Notts and Jocks man, would fix the social worker up with 'what she wanted, me fuckin' fist straight in yuh bleddy ugly goggles,' and Mrs Ridley stamped about the floor in red rage, uncontrollably. The child had been bundled out, ripped from her mother, to whom she had clung in an agony; Mrs Ridley abused and threatened the social worker and her male superior at the top of her voice; she, young woman, stood petrified, explosion-shocked, her mouth frozen into her pretty face.

'Presumably the camera crew were in the room?' Richardson asked.

'Must have been.' Margot.

'And it made no difference?'

'Might have made her worse,' Joanna said. 'You could see that she was convinced that she loved her child, and that the heartless authorities were robbing her of her own.'

'Didn't the social worker remind her of how she neglected the child?'

'Not once.'

'Why not, do you think?'

'Poor girl, she might have been frightened half out of her wits,' Joanna said. 'I know I should have been. Or she thought the woman was incapable of reasoned argument at that moment.'

'Was she, though?'

'I don't know how much the programme was edited. But I guess so. The woman was in the grip of a single, violent emotion, which dominated her to the exclusion of everything else.'

'I don't think,' Marguerite, very serious now, 'that they should allow that social worker to be treated like that. It wasn't her fault, and it was an absolute ordeal.'

'Was she in danger, physical danger, d'you think? I mean with all the TV people there?'

'That wouldn't have affected anybody in the woman's state.' Joanna nodded agreement with her daughter. 'She was mad.'

'Possessed.' Joanna.

'Was the young girl, the social worker, allowed to make any comment afterwards?'

'Oh, yes. We saw her later. She seemed quite calm, then.'

'And did she say anything interesting?'

'No. She smiled a bit. Apologetically.' Margot smiled at her own word. 'And she just said, "We did our best. You see how difficult it is." '

'Do you think,' Richardson asked, 'that they'd chosen this Mrs Ridley because they knew she'd play up, on camera or not?'

'Very likely.' Joanna.

'It makes no difference. The young woman ought to have been protected,' Margot said. 'They ought to make people like Mrs Ridley realize what they've done to the child.'

'But somebody had probably done something equally evil to her when she was young.' The father.

'It has to stop somewhere.'

'How? Execution? Flogging?'

Margot did not lose her temper.

'Don't exaggerate,' she answered. 'By the look of that woman, I'd say it was medical treatment.'

'Drug her into quietness?'

'Yes. If it's necessary.'

'Yes,' said Joanna. 'I don't see too much wrong in that.'

'I guess,' Richardson, chin-rubbing, 'that a good percentage of our lower social categories regard all DHSS offices, job centres, hospitals, even post offices, as places where you're pushed about, insulted, made to wait, to explain all your private business in public with very little advantage at the end of it all.'

'That's right,' Joanna agreed. 'Bureaucracy appears unfeeling by its nature, its unintelligible jargon, its slowness, its adherence to system and precedent. But . . .'

'But what?' Virginia, surprisingly, with a fierce, small frown.

'I don't see how it can be altered. People won't obey instructions. And some can't understand anything you tell them. And a few try to cheat. Still, hospitals could reorganize themselves with advantage, I agree.'

The phone rang. Virginia skipped out to answer it while the others remained, in anticipation, silent, stupefied by the discussion; even Fay stared down at the tablecloth, unmoving.

'For Mummy. Felicity Brooks.'

Ginny sat down, justified. Joanna, notably curt on the telephone, was out all of five minutes.

'She wants you and me to go up and see her. I've fixed it up for Friday. I knew you were free.'

'Aren't you going to tell us why?' Margot, smiling, diplomatic, but speaking for the curious.

'The pleasure of our company. Some people love us. Is that all right?' Richardson nodded, because his wife looked placid, was plotting something. 'Another thing she said was that Stephen was complaining about seeing too little of you.'

'More lies?' Virginia, upright and cocky.

'Somebody loves Margot,' Fay said. Her sister reddened.

'I'm not surprised,' Richardson intervened. 'I do myself.'

'Mr Black,' said Virginia, 'who teaches us biology, said that parents tend to love their firstborn best. Is that right?'

'The man in the Bible,' Marguerite, 'Jacob, loved the youngest, Benjamin.'

Fay clapped her hands, excited.

'And the Good Book is always right?' Richardson.

'No, just evidence to the contrary.'

'I imagine that he is generalizing from his own experience,' Joanna said. 'Is that what they call "extrapolating"?'

'Not in this house it isn't. I just don't know. There must be some research. It seems slightly likely.'

They laughed at his caution, but by now had had enough post-prandial conversation, and turned to their evening chores.

'How was the Brooks then?' Richardson asked, passing his wife in the hallway.

'As usual. Been on holiday. Conrad had rung her up once or twice.'

'She's all on her own?'

'Stephen's there.'

Joanna left him. She was humming, but he could not tell what.

11

John Richardson did not accompany his wife on the visit to Mrs Brooks, because the BBC rang to ask him to take part in the recording of a chat programme on Friday evening.

Though the producer was quite honest, admitting that two people had dropped out, Richardson was glad, as always. That the programme was not about education but about travel pleased him even more; his name was becoming known. He felt no qualms about letting Mrs Brooks down, for he trusted Joanna to get out of her what it was the woman wanted.

Thus he walked smilingly about the distant corners of his school, in token of his euphoria.

Joanna's shrewd eye would be on him; he could expect her cynicisms on the cult of personality, but she encouraged him. She had now convinced herself that it was to her advantage to have a husband who looked handsome and laid down the law on television, whose views were canvassed on radio and in the Sunday posh papers; she pushed him into accepting engagements which would bring him kudos, though she did not dare call them 'prestigious' in his hearing, and to turn down flat those which did not. Afterwards she would let him know if he had not shaped well, or allowed somebody to upstage him, or had fidgeted unacceptably with tie or legs. In her view, he either did it properly or wrote himself off.

So as he walked his corridors, preoccupied, alert, smartly dressed, even dignified, he prepared sentences for use in the broadcast, quotations from the portentous 'Not one returns to tell us of the Road/Which to discover we must travel too' to the facetious 'Travel broadens the behind', anecdotes of stops in the Dordogne, fruity wines, languages, architecture, high mountain snows, the poetry of railways, serendipity, God around the corner. He'd look out the diaries Joanna kept, scrapbooks with menus, tickets, photographs, dates, addresses. He'd not be at a loss, if he could help it.

'What's he doing over here?' the junior asked the senior lab technician, who did not answer but slipped snake-fast through a prep room to meet the head by chance three doors down. No one trespassed on his empire.

'Good morning, sir,' he greeted Richardson. 'This is unusual, if I may say so. Can I help you?'

'Good morning, Mr Spendlove.'

'Is there anything you wanted, sir?'

'No, thank you. Just travelling on life's common way.' Wasted.

'Yes, sir.' The eyes narrowed as the head moved on. 'The sly sod's up to something,' Spendlove told his underling, and then wondered if Dr Smith knew of the visitation, hoping not.

One storey up, Richardson ran into Lesley Allbright, who blushed, manoeuvred her hair into place.

'Ah, Miss Allbright. I'm glad I've seen you.' When he enquired about her health, she gushed and simpered, standing with her head on one side. Neither mentioned Moore, who, it was rumoured, had taken his wife back. The woman, he had to admit, dressed with a crisp cleanliness. 'I wanted to ask you about your form.' The broadcaster acknowledged the verbal play, but to himself, for now he was serious. Terry Grocock and Michael Lynham, two of the drowned boys, had been members of her 4D.

Immediately Miss Allbright understood his purport, and it took her a little time, she launched into an account of how she had read of the accident in the local paper. Again he had to admit she held his interest. She had noticed the black double headline, 'Four Drowned in School's Holiday Tragedy', with the most casual eye, and it was not until she caught the name of the school and the victims that she was stricken.

'I couldn't believe it. You can't, can you?' She described how, after the jolt of surprise, she had made herself reread the damning words. Her eyes brimmed as she talked.

He listened, judging her performance as he would a lesson, marking her high, but short of the highest class. Excellent on the surface, lacking depth, B plus. Allowing her to finish, he asked,

117

'Has it affected the other pupils in any way?'

It was clear she had never considered the question. She pulled faces, side-stepped, placed her hands breast-high, wide of her body, finger-tips upward. Yes, they had been shocked at first. But now. Back to normal. As far as one could tell. But one was never sure. 'They're a mystery sometimes.'

'Let me know if you notice anything, won't you? It is worrying for us all. Thank you, Miss Allbright, thank you very much.'

He set off down the corridor, and she accompanied him, a pace to the rear. She turned into a doorway, where she fiddled in her handbag, presumably for keys, but he neither stopped nor looked back.

On the Friday, Richardson left school an hour early to pick up from home the good suit necessary for radio before he set out for Manchester. Joanna inspected him, said she would apologize again to Felicity Brooks, to whom he'd already spoken on the phone.

'You'll go and come back by taxi,' he ordered. They considered they could not afford a second car.

'Probably.'

'Now you're trying to make me feel guilty.'

'Impossible.' She smiled, preoccupied. 'Do well.'

'I'd be interested to know how she's shaping,' he said, hanging about.

'Get along. You'll be late. And I'm busy.'

Felicity Brooks appeared quite normal, said she was glad that John had given her notice, two days, of his absence, otherwise she would have drummed up one or two other couples to make a dinner party. Now she and Joanna could eat sparingly, and that suited her book. Stephen was neither seen nor heard.

Over the delicious light meal, marvellous omelettes, gooseberry fool, she talked at length of Conrad's work, explaining that he had to be a diplomat, careful of religious sensibilities, knowing when to coax or threaten, even bribe.

'Is he good at it?'

'He knows the Middle East well. He's worked there so long. He's also had tremendous successes.' She named two palaces Joanna had never heard of, a hospital, harbours and a mosque, an enormous marvel of restrained magnificence which had demanded not only the most up-to-date technology but a finesse in playing off not one party against another, but one sub-sect against a second minor faction. Felicity spoke with animation, expressing open admiration for her husband, contempt for what she called 'the London corner'. The names she reeled off meant nothing to Joanna, a careful reader of the *Guardian*; with regret she re-learnt that dozens of sane, complicated, fascinating worlds existed outside her own.

'I shall never get him back,' Felicity said briskly, without rancour, with approbation. 'He's fifty-seven, and he'll work out there until he drops. He's hardly lived in England. "The engineers are all accountants," he says. "Penny-savers." ' Joanna was invited to look where that had landed us. The anecdotes piled as they stacked the washing-up machine, not yet half full. 'I'm not his first wife, you know.'

The remainder of that confession was delayed until they sat over brandy.

'He married in Germany straight after the war. He wasn't fit to go into the army, eyesight and a heart murmur. It's odd because I can't think of anybody fitter than he is now. But he qualified as an engineer and was sent out to Germany as a civilian, and there he got married. To tell you the truth, I know very little about it. I think her name was Inge, I'm not sure. Neither family approved and it lasted just a few years, four or five at most. He had two daughters.'

'Does he ever see them?'

'No. Nor hears from them. They'll be in their thirties now, and presumably married. In Germany. Probably with children. We don't know. Correction, I don't know. Her family took over after the divorce; they were manufacturers of some sort, well-to-do. Like mine. But he never talks about it.'

'That's sad.'

'I'm not sure. It's a part of his life he's never shared with me. He was young, and perhaps he acted rashly. Germany in 1946 wasn't a stable place. But he's quiet. Or quiet on essentials. I would guess,' her voice assumed strength, 'that doesn't mean he won't feel it. Do you know, Joanna, I sometimes feel I don't know my own husband.'

119

'Don't we all?'

Mrs Brooks went on to say how she and Conrad had met. He had been sent up to one of her father's factories, by chance, because the usual man was ill. He knew nothing about that line, but he had three days to spare and hated to waste time and considered no job connected with machinery either uninteresting or beneath him, and so had appeared. Fortuitously, the local hunt had held its annual ball; Conrad joined her father's party; visitor and daughter had danced, got along well, but she had been shattered three days after his departure to receive a letter from him proposing marriage. It had been flatly written. 'I had "impressed" him. He didn't say why.' Felicity laughed now. ' "You and I could make a go of it." ' He was, he told her, off to Canada, and would return in a month, and that would give her time to 'consult her feelings and the family'. She laughed again. 'He was insistent about the family. Perhaps it was his German experience. If I took him seriously, I was to talk it over with my father and mother. My father would be able without much difficulty to find out what his prospects were.'

'Extraordinary.'

'He wouldn't think so. It wasn't my first proposal. I was twenty-one.'

'And Conrad?'

'Thirty-two. I don't think he saw anything out of the ordinary in it. He'd made his mind up, and this was the sensible way from there on.'

'He'd made his mind up,' Joanna said. 'That was the extraordinary thing.'

'Oh, I don't know. That's typical of him. He's like all these mathematically inclined people; I did "A" level maths and one man who taught us always seemed to miss a couple of lines out in the middle of a proof. "That's obvious," he'd say when we chivvied him. Not to me it wasn't. Conrad's like that; his conclusions surprise you because you don't see the reckoning in between. He's socially a bit eccentric, but I put that down to his odd life.'

'Sheep's eyeballs with the Bedouin?'

'That sort of thing.' Felicity almost sprawled in her chair, much at ease. 'In some ways, I know I shouldn't say this, I'm almost glad your husband, John, couldn't come. I'm a bit frightened of him.'

'Why's that?'

'He's very assured, isn't he? He's nothing like my age . . .'

'Thirty-nine.'

'He doesn't look it. But when he talks to you he seems to have it all worked out. Conrad's good at his job, but compared with John he's dishevelled, and not only with his clothes.'

'It was hair originally.'

'Hair?' Felicity frowned, at a loss. Joanna made no attempt to explain. 'John is neat, and handsome, and knows what he thinks, and why he thinks it, and can put it in plain language. He gives the impression of being utterly conventional, and I don't think he is. Is this all fantasy?'

'No,' Joanna said, 'not at all. I see so much of him that I begin not to see him. It does me good to hear you. Go on.'

'He's clever? And ambitious?' Now Felicity Brooks spoke tentatively, in questions, as if afraid of annoying her listener.

'He's that all right.' Joanna spoke strongly. 'The parents were keen; they lost one boy, and wanted the other two to succeed. They're both competitive. The elder brother's a full professor of Indian languages at Yale, and every five or six years he brings out some learned book on the language of the Mahábhárata or epic conventions in the Rámáyana and this frightens John.'

'Why?'

'He thinks Eric will leave these memorials behind him. Eric, who's very like John except darker and much much quieter, poohpoohs the idea. "My views will be out of date in twenty years' time, so that if some future scholar actually blows the dust off my books, it will only be to conclude what an unintelligent, unenlightened obstructionist I was." ' She mimicked well. 'But neither of them believes that. All I can hope is that John finds some opening that matches his ambitions.'

'Such as?'

'That's the snag. He might become a professor of education, but he doesn't think too highly of mere theory. And universities are sniffy about schoolmasters. He might have to move out of education.'

'Politics?' Light bursting on Felicity.

'Not John. Too chancy. His present life's bad enough, but he doesn't depend on the voters for the continuance of his job. He'll combine caution with ambition.'

'They don't seem to fit, do they?'

'Probably not.' Joanna had had enough of the subject. 'I must say that it's most pleasant sitting here. This really is a beautiful house.'

Mrs Brooks explained how her grandfather had built this cul-de-sac for his own family, he thought. She herself had lived here for a time as a child, not long really, but all four houses had been sold off. Conrad had re-purchased the place when they had decided that Felicity should settle permanently in England to oversee the children's, especially Veronica's, education.

'It's a pity my parents didn't hang on, and then I'd have had their furniture.'

'Who did you buy the house from?'

'A consultant surgeon. His family were growing up, and his wife wanted a smaller home out in the villages. So. I've spent years in the sales, I still go, to get the right sort of large furniture.'

'And what did you use in the meantime?'

'Makeshift stuff. The bedrooms still are full of it. I'll show you. We've an enormous amount of foreign rubbish which I hate.' She tapped a table. 'Oh, and Conrad's sister suddenly presented us with quite a lot, his family pieces, because she moved to America.'

'But it all matches so beautifully.'

'It doesn't in fact.' Felicity spoke masterfully, pointing round. 'These come from different periods. But furnishing a house is a bit like living your life. You put there what you can lay your hands on, and hope the result's not too disastrous.'

Joanna laughed out loud and Felicity stopped short as if the homespun philosophy embarrassed both. They walked the rooms together, leisurely, taking nearly an hour, but even then they neglected some doors, did not approach the top storey.

'I expect you wonder why we keep such a huge place on. The cost of heating it is enormous.'

'Why do you?' Joanna, now on the first-floor landing outside a bedroom, looked down at the solid, chunky woodwork of the balustrade, the florid chandelier, the red darkness of carpets, the whiteness of doors and skirting-board, the floral decoration on the hall table, the gold-framed glum pictures on the high, light walls, and was satisfied.

'I often ask myself. Money's no trouble. Conrad is very well paid, and isn't taxed out of it at all either. But it takes up a great deal of my time. I have help, of course, inside and in the garden. I've just found an Irishman who's ever so good. Says I'll never have to buy another vegetable. It's my hobby, I suppose. Do you find that unreasonable?'

'No.'

'Not that an educated woman should spend her time on what's really high-class housework?'

'Most of us spend it on low-class.'

'I always looked forward to a home in England. We've lived in very beautiful houses where Conrad's worked. But this seems permanent, not fool's gold. We've flitted about too often. I try sometimes to remember the names and faces of our servants, but I can't.' She lifted a many-armed goddess in bronze. 'We bought this in Agra, years ago. We were on a holiday. Conrad was working in Bombay at the time. It's followed us about the world.'

She rushed into a room, snatched a lace cloth up, revealing a table of dark wood, fretted, deeply in-carved with snakes, convoluted limbs, flower stems, roots, wildly intertwined; even the centre of the table-top itself seemed sculptured, a dark and shallow pond of bubbling figures; Felicity had not turned on the light, so that it was barely possible to make out the nature of the horizontal surfaces in the glow from the door.

'Ugh,' Felicity said. 'I hate that. Beastly. It's ugly.' She dashed back the cloth, raced to the switch, dazzled them both. 'Not like that. That's beautiful.' Above the draped table on the wall hung an Afghan mat, dirty-white with a decoration of floating lines, suggestions of flowers, randomly, sketchily put together, but elegant and immediately convincing. 'Look at all this junk.' The room, large enough, was stacked with furniture, boxes, cases, as if for a sale. 'These are all our oriental stuff. I'll never get round to sorting it out. I don't like it enough.'

123

'Isn't it valuable?'

'Some of it. Oh, yes. There's another room upstairs just as crammed.'

Felicity turned, rudely switched off the light, and when Joanna emerged was sitting on a black, carved chest on the landing, her hands gripping the front edges, humming to herself with concentration. She beat time with her heels, and appeared both tense and excited, like a girl at a fair, just before the waltzer, the roller-coaster lurches off.

Suddenly the subdued sound changed, altered itself strongly, clarified itself into words. Felicity was singing now, though sitting exactly as before.

> 'I leaned my back up against an oak,
> I thought it was a trusty tree,
> But first it bent, and then it broke,
> And so did my true love to me.'

The voice rose youthfully in the wide space of the stairwell.

Joanna, back to an upright of the still-open door, watched, listened in the rich but subdued lights of the hall. Felicity Brooks sang easily, in a white voice, clear of harmonics, like that of a choirboy, but judged exactly in volume to suit the amplification of enclosing walls; she projected the sound with a naive skill, both careful and uncaring of effect, forward, out, as though exactly to some invisible but critical listener.

Felicity broke off at the end of a verse.

She was crying now, but so silently that it surprised Joanna when she first noticed the quantity of tears. The still face of the singer glistened wet, theatrically, with glycerine drops.

Joanna, uncertain, embarrassed by her own reaction, tiptoed the three steps to sit down by the other, and prised her left hand from the edge of the chest. Felicity, again histrionically, laid her head on Joanna's shoulder, uncomfortably, unfitly so that the pair leaned awkwardly, unmatching.

They moved soon, Felicity first.

She straightened up, removing her hand from Joanna's, then dabbing at her face, then smiling.

'Oh, dear,' she said. 'Oh, dear.'

'What was it?' Joanna asked, caught out.

Felicity shook her head, then kissed her companion full on the mouth. Joanna, taken aback, did not flinch. The kiss was sexless, the way her two younger daughters kissed her, not snatched, but not lengthily held or pressed, healthy, undemanding, perfumed.

'Thank you,' Felicity said, withdrawing. 'It was too much. I see these pieces of furniture, and there they are, not changed one iota, and Vernie's gone, doesn't exist any more, a shovelful of ashes. And Conrad and I are apart.'

'I'm sorry.'

'Oh, no. It's fair enough about Conrad and me. We'd get on each other's nerves because he's interested in manipulating men and machines. The sexual part doesn't mean much now. It did once. It's nearly impossible to remember it was so. But Vernie. Why wasn't she allowed to live on? Are you religious?'

'No.'

'I'm surprised. I thought you would be. Don't you ever go to church?'

'No.'

Felicity shrugged at Joanna's monosyllables, nonplussed.

'The girl had barely made a start. And what she had done consisted of mistakes. It doesn't seem fair. We did our best. You don't agree with that either, do you? You think we shouldn't have packed her off to boarding school. But it's what all our friends did. And their daughters seem ordinary and happy enough.'

'Seem,' Joanna emphasized.

'I want permanence,' Felicity continued, ignoring Joanna's word. 'I wish I believed in God. I could, easily. No, that's wrong. But everything wastes except bits of Benares brassware and ugly tables.'

'They don't last for ever.'

'Why can't you convince me that something exists in perpetuity? Mountains. They do. But we are capable of moving them now. With bombs not faith.' She laughed, crowing, tinnily. 'I know I'm asking the impossible, but every so often it all overwhelms me.' She stumbled on the verb.

'Even before Veronica . . . died?'

'Yes.' Felicity's voice hardened to sanity. 'But she annoyed me with her fooling about and I suppose that kept me from thinking. She made me so cross, because she wouldn't be helped. She lived on the edge of a volcano I knew nothing about, and now I think I blame myself for not trying hard enough. She had an abortion before we came home. At fifteen. And she tried suicide. Thank God there was a woman doctor who fixed things up for her. Lived near, had some connection with the school. We thought that had calmed her down. It had, somehow. She did well enough at the day school here. We don't know, we just don't know.'

Joanna stared, stunned, at the luxury about her.

'I find it impossible,' Felicity Brooks spoke drily now, as if reciting some theory she had committed to memory, 'to imagine what she must have gone through. Up here. On her own. And here we were, and your husband, talking about university entrance. It doesn't bear thinking about. It does not.'

She snatched herself up from the chest so violently that Joanna feared she'd throw herself at, over the balustrade, but she rushed to another door.

'Look,' she shouted. The voice, strangled, held no echo of the singing. 'Look at this.'

The door now stood open, the light already switched on. Joanna followed her companion inside. The room newly decorated, smelt slightly of the fresh white paint, but not one stick of furniture was to be seen. Floorboards were bare; even the dustless lamp-bulb lacked a shade. Clean, and hateful.

'This was Vernie's hidey-hole. It was full of shelves and plants and knick-knacks, and piles of books and clothes, and posters all over the wall. You couldn't move, but she wouldn't straighten it. Conrad redecorated it while he was home. And I wouldn't let him put any furniture in. He thought I was mad, and I suppose I was. So there it is. No curtains, no chairs.'

'I understand,' Joanna said, evenly. 'I saw it.'

'I didn't go in much while she was alive. But I chuntered at her. It wasn't the amount she had. It was the cleaning. Mrs Molloy used to complain that there was dust everywhere. We don't know when we're well off.'

126

She flicked off the light, ushered Joanna out, closing the door, slow-paced, melancholy.

'This is a beautiful house,' the visitor said, on the landing, to break extended silence.

'Do you think so? What shall I do about Vernie's room?'

'Furnish it.'

'It's white, and clean, and dead now. She liked purples and reds and deep greens and bead curtains.'

'Make it ordinary. And come up and sit here.'

Felicity pulled a wry face, but deliberately, in control of herself.

'Perhaps I will.' She looked at her wristwatch. 'What time is your husband on the radio?'

'It's not tonight. They're recording. It will be on Sunday evening, in a week or a fortnight.'

'I misunderstood. Again. I don't think I ever get anything right first time. Shall I tell you a good thing? Since Vernie died and Con went back, I haven't drunk nearly so much. Why's that, do you think? I thought I'd be . . .' She shrugged unpleasantly.

'You've Stephen here.'

'He's no help. Give him a desk full of books, and he's satisfied. There he sits, the schoolmaster's pride. He's no more feeling than . . . than a clothes-peg.' Felicity, now beginning to walk downstairs, said over her shoulder, 'I know what you're thinking. "There's another she's got round her neck." That's right, isn't it?' Insistent. 'Isn't it?'

'No.'

'Oh?' A rising tone, a query. 'You're lucky. Some people are. What shall I do?'

Joanna, on impulse, sat down on the stairs, wrapping her arms round her legs, lifting her feet slightly. As she took up the position, she realized how unlike her everyday self she acted. Felicity stopped, two from the bottom.

'Sing again,' Joanna ordered.

'What did you say?'

'Sing again.'

'Why do you say that? That's no help at all. It won't solve anything.'

127

'I enjoyed it.'

'Oh.'

But Felicity did not comply, walked straight-backed on, left hand out queenly to the stair-rail, and when Joanna gave her husband an account of this, she said she was surprised at the banal nature of their continued conversation. Mrs Brooks spoke with real liveliness about clothes, about the theatre, about a cruise Conrad had taken her on, about her new Mercedes.

'She was everything a hostess should be. Pleasant, full of information, interested in what I had to tell her. She didn't drink much. We discussed slimming. She's started to skip. But she seemed a different woman from the one on the stairs.'

'I see.'

'Which is the real one?' Joanna asked. It was a Virginia-type question, innocent and gravelling.

'No use asking me,' he answered. 'There are obviously areas of her life where she's very sensitive, and the emotion's near the surface. But again she's capable of separating them from the ordinary run of things.'

'Are we all like that, do you think?' Richardson shifted uncomfortably at his wife's catechism. Under the questions skulked the implication that he should, but did not, know the answers.

'Oh, yes. But it's a case, isn't it, of how different the two, or two hundred, states are? If there's not much difference . . . Oh, I don't know. That might be as bad. When I went to see Veronica Brooks about university entrance, she asked me what my Christian name was. Everybody uses first names these days.'

'Your pupils to you?'

'No. Not yet.' His lips set grim. 'When I told her John Bernard Neil, she said she would call me Bernard. Now I've wondered about that often enough since. Why should she, on the verge of suicide, want to do that?'

'There's no telling that she was on the verge of suicide,' Joanna snapped. 'I know she had tried before, but on that day at that time she was just a rather embarrassed young woman, trying to please Mum, and impress an authoritative, handsome old gent who'd been foisted on her. Every girl would act, would react. Many would be shy. But those with spirit would look for, oh, a chink in the armour. So she calls you Bernard, a big, cuddly, life-saving stupid dog with a flask of brandy.'

'Thanks.'

'Are you worried about Felicity Brooks?' Joanna asked.

'You are, obviously, or you wouldn't ask the question. Yes, I suppose I am, but,' he held up his hand to forestall interruption, 'my job makes me worse at this sort of thing. I have to stand back so often, to come in at third hand. I'm insensitive, case-hardened. What does Margot feel about Stephen? I don't know. I don't know how to find out. And yet she may be breaking her heart.'

'Go on.'

'It's just that when Veronica commits suicide, I begin to wonder who's next.'

'I don't think Margot will kill herself. She's too much like you.'

'And Felicity Brooks?'

'Ummh.' Joanna hummed ignorance, but half jovially to set his mind at rest.

'What happened to that friend of hers who had to put her mother in a hospice?'

'I asked her,' Joanna said. 'The old lady died, oh, quite suddenly. Pneumonia and heart. They let her go. The daughter's quite settled about it.'

'Does Felicity do much of that sort of thing? Has she any friends?'

'I doubt it. Acquaintances, yes.'

'Where do we stand?' he wanted to know.

'I guess she's let out more of herself to us than she's used to. And now she's afraid of what she's done. Well, apprehensive. But you ask her.'

12

The Richardsons invited Mrs Brooks to accompany them to the theatre, took her out with formality to a restaurant one evening and on another for an hour and a half's conviviality in a country pub. She seemed cheerful and even claimed to be busy, saying that with the better weather the garden occupied her. Stephen, in spite of imminent exams, was seen again at the Richardsons', and this delighted, the parents noted, the younger daughters as well as the noncommittal Marguerite. Joanna expressed doubts to her husband.

'He's like you,' she said. 'Hard-working and ambitious. Concentrated on the advancement of Number One.' She could manage such accusations without giving offence, in that she chose a time when Richardson felt comfortable or satisfied to speak the truth.

'So you wouldn't recommend him as a husband?'

'It depends what she wants.' Joanna grinned. 'I'm not complaining.'

John Richardson felt his life to be broadening. The outline of his book on the aims of comprehensive secondary education, its first three chapters completed, which he had submitted to a publisher, had been enthusiastically received, and a contract signed. The editor allotted to him, a young woman, was bright, singular, full of ideas, had stimulated him, but wanted the first draft finished quickly. He was amazed to find such direction and help, and writing letters all over the country, as well as consulting local colleagues, was inundated with advice, so that he often stayed up to the early hours now, alive with creativity he told himself, to meet her deadline.

'Write it quickly but to the correct length,' his editor ordered. She, in her early thirties, had a brilliant career in classics and philosophy at Oxford, been don and civil servant, and was now married with a young child, working part-time.

Incisive, out to make a name, she made him feel snail-slow. 'This draft will have to be done again so get it out of the way. It will give you a good idea of what you think.'

'I know that.'

'I doubt it. No, you're clever and restless. You'll change your mind.'

'In detail perhaps.'

'Get the bloody thing written, friend,' she said, putting a hand on his own, 'and then we'll see who's right. There could be plenty in this book for you, if you don't hang about.' She handed him a further series of answers to his questionnaires she had elicited from distinguished acquaintances. Though tired out often enough, he felt on the top of his form, alive, alert, sharp with words, brimming with ideas.

At the same time some television pundit invited him to take part in preliminary discussions for a series on modern civilization for BBC2 in the autumn; he met an eminent and likeable philosopher, an admired Catholic historian, a brilliant scientist, Marxist in leaning, an eminent literary lady who aimed to score off men, and an ennobled architect. They excited him with their talk, flinging witticisms lavishly about, while he tended to shelter his thoughts, or produced them straight-faced like a poker player only when necessary. The local university recruited him for a public lecture; his Oxford college called him in for consultation about entry; the director of education invited him over for a chat about the forthcoming book, and thereafter sent subordinates out scurrying for figures on English as a Foreign Language, Community Relations, Ethnic Minority Publications. 'This book is absolutely necessary at this time, John,' first names, oh, yes, 'but we must get it right.' Richardson saw that his superior was alarmed, but could not find out why and wondered what was being brushed under the educational carpet.

Finally, and winning his family's approval, he was called up to stand by for appearance on one of the BBC's half-intellectual panel games, a programme about which he had spoken slightingly often enough, but now he boasted.

'I'll do anything for money,' he told Stanley Smith.

'Aren't you afraid of making a fool of yourself?'

131

'Of course.'

Smith was now on a direct route to the inspectorate, strongly supported by his headmaster, would in fact take up his appointment in the new year, and therefore often dropped in for an hour while they discussed the place of science in the comprehensive school. Both knew the other's game; Smith's ideas were politely but ferociously pummelled by Richardson as they would be by interviewing panels; the same ideas, source acknowledged in a note, of course, polished by questioning, refined by wide considerations, would eventually form a cogent chapter in the head's publication. It suited the books of both.

Richardson felt, to use a word he palmed regularly out on the platforms of local school speech-days, 'fulfilled', that is, busy with what he thought valuable and could master. His puritan upbringing made him question his activities; he had been trained at home to distrust what came easy, and this left him happy. He put his doubts to Joanna, suitably disguised.

'I'm neglecting you all,' he said.

'Oh?'

'I'm flying here, there and everywhere, and when I'm at home I sit up there at my desk, right out of the way.'

'Is it any different,' she asked, 'now from other times?'

'Oh, yes.'

'I hadn't noticed,' she said.

That set him back.

'You don't object, do you?' he enquired, and sharply.

'It wouldn't make much difference if I did. You'd do what you wanted. When I get thoroughly screwed up with it, I'll scream at you.'

'Is that likely to be soon?'

'It depends on the other elements, doesn't it?'

'Elements.' He mused, in affectation, and she left him to it. Though she spoke equably, he discerned tension, and tried to make it up to her. He organized a family outing on his one free Saturday, when they made for Derbyshire, visited a small zoo for Fay's sake, where all five enjoyed themselves, sat down to a lunch in a large spa hotel to disappointing food and expensive wine, ran to the river and were caught up in a sudden thick drizzle which showed no signs of lifting.

'Never mind,' said the founder of the feast, 'it will do your mother's garden good.'

Typically they discovered when they arrived back home that not a drop of rain had fallen, good, bad or indifferent.

'What did you like best?' he asked Fay.

'The waiters,' she said.

'They were mostly girls,' Virginia objected, accurate as usual.

'Ours wasn't.'

'They seemed Italian,' Richardson said, 'the waitresses. At least they spoke Italian to one another.'

'I'd like to do that,' Fay said.

'Speak Italian?' Joanna, in correction.

'No. Be a waitress.'

'In a foreign country?' Margot.

'Anywhere.'

'It would be boring,' Virginia said. 'At everybody's beck and call.'

'I'd give the nice things to the nice people,' Fay told them. 'Like us. That wouldn't be boring.'

One evening, as John Richardson scrambled at his desk through a sheaf of papers from a university education department, he was called to the telephone. A Mrs Moore wished to see him. Yes, she would be round in an hour.

Publicly sighing, he returned to his work with relief. An hour would serve to distil what he needed from these submissions; they confirmed, with some evidence from experiment, what he already knew. He prepared to make a quick note; one card into his index would suffice. He was ready for Mrs Moore when she arrived, ten minutes late.

Sandra Moore was as he expected, a slightly less assertive version of Lesley Allbright; her perfume stung his nostrils, swamped his study.

'I told Tony I should come and see you,' she said, 'but he didn't think I dare.' Richardson waited. 'He's beginning to hit me.' She paused, head hanging.

'Go on.'

'Since I came back to him. He's no time for me, or patience. If I do something he doesn't like he swears at me, and now he's started to beat me.'

133

'More than once?'

'Yes.'

'Seriously?'

She unbuttoned the front of her blouse and slid the material off her shoulder. Across the shoulder blade, the pale skin was blotched red, and in one place perhaps broken. She moved the strap of her bra, slightly, for no reason except to make the rise of her breast more apparent under the lace margin.

'That was last night,' she said. 'He hit me with a dish.'

'He threw it, you mean?'

'No. It was in his hand all the time.'

He motioned her to fasten her blouse, but she seemed in no hurry.

'This never happened before you went away?' he asked.

'No. Tony could be very moody, and nasty sometimes, but he never hit me.'

'Mrs Moore, I'm sorry to have to ask you this, but do you think you've done the right thing going back to your husband?'

She drew her blouse together in rebuke.

'I don't know. I couldn't do any other, could I, really? And I put my savings into the house as well.'

'Could you support yourself?'

'There is the chance of a full-time job coming up at the library. Mr Grainger says I can have it if I want it.'

'And you will take it?'

'Yes. It'll be sensible now. I've as good as said so. At first when I went back to Tony, I thought that, well, we might, could have a baby, y'know. To make it up.'

'Would you like that?'

'I thought I would. Until he got as he is. I'm not so sure now.'

'I see that. Why do you think your husband is acting in this way?'

'Well, I did leave him for another man.' At least she understood so much, though her expression was quizzical, doubting whether he grasped the force of her statement. 'I don't think he's forgiven me.'

'But,' Richardson felt he must press her now, 'the marriage must have been fairly unstable for you to make off like that.'

'I don't know. When I look back, I can hardly realize that I actually did what I did. My life was dull. The two and a half days in the library, that was fine, but the rest. Clean the house, prepare and cook the meals, nothing else to do. And we never went out. Tony wasn't happy. He thought Dr Smith had a down on him, and hadn't given him a fair timetable. He had some rough forms; children who didn't want to learn, he said. He'd sit glowering over exercise books at night, and complain, complain, complain, all the time.'

'Did you try to help him?'

'How could I? You don't know Tony, obviously. That's why I started driving lessons. To take my mind off things. And then Wallace Gordon was nice, smooth-tongued. And he started to bring me back home. He was a fast worker, hand on your thigh first lesson.'

'Mrs Moore, I can understand the temptation. I can understand a casual affair. I don't say I condone it, but . . . What I really can't understand is why you left home, with a married man who had children, something of a rake, by your own confession . . .'

'It seemed perfect. A little flat. Wallace promised to live with me.'

'How could he afford it?'

'Others can. Others have done it.'

'He had a family, hadn't he?'

'Three.'

'Is he well paid, as a driving instructor?'

'Not badly, if he worked hard. With a few private, cash only, arrangements out of hours. And he lived in a council house. His wife worked. Her mother looked after the children when they came out of school. She lived nearby.'

'And you,' he pursued, 'saw this as a permanent arrangement?'

'I suppose I hoped so. The attraction was sexual. The sex was out of this world, just marvellous. I'd never known anything like it, I can tell you. You don't follow that, do you? You don't know what I mean.'

' "Sexual intercourse began
In nineteen sixty-three," ' he intoned, rather loudly.

'Nineteen sixty-three? I was only six then.'

'I'm sorry,' he said. 'It's a quotation from a poem.'

'Is it?' She looked doubtful. 'I like poetry. I did at school.'

He shut his mouth, as she buttoned her blouse, quickly, efficiently. Her hands seemed quite beautiful, with long, blood-red fingernails. They had the blandness of the face, but lacked its banality; they possessed shape, distinction, whereas the features were pretty, forgettable, useless, vulgar, to be despised. Now she smiled, a sad, poverty-stricken re-setting of the lips.

'I'd hardly moved in,' she began, 'before I realized I'd made a mistake.' The voice had changed, for the better. It admitted his reality. 'Wallace didn't come often, and never intended to leave his wife. And the place was uncomfortable, and money was short.'

'Did Wallace help you, financially?'

'No. He couldn't really, could he?'

'Had he encouraged you to leave home?'

'That's the oddest thing,' Sandra Moore answered. 'I thought he had. I could have sworn he had. But he said he hadn't. When once I'd done it. Said it was stupid.' She sniffed.

'Had you, do you think, anything in common with Wallace besides the sexual rapport?'

She thought about that, wiping at her left eye with a squarely ironed handkerchief.

'No,' she said, at last. 'No. It didn't seem to matter. And to be frank, there doesn't seem much between Tony and me since I came back.'

'I take it the sexual relationship was resumed?'

'Yes.'

The face offered no clues to success or otherwise there. She directed her prettiness to devalue itself in stubbornness.

They talked for another half-hour, retracing the same subject matter, in boredom, in self-assurance. Richardson gave her the address and telephone number of a friend, a woman solicitor, who had close connections with a hostel for battered wives. Mrs Moore had bridled.

'It hasn't come to that yet,' she protested. 'A hostel.'

'No, but Mrs Barker-Smith will tell you what to do, if the

136

worst comes to the worst. I hope, of course, that you'll both settle to a new life. But, better to be safe.'

The whole of the evening's conversation seemed packed with 'of course', a phrase, a sop, to contradict the bleak remainder of the sentences.

Sandra Moore congratulated him on the comfort, the tidiness of his study, comparing Tony's littered 'den' with his, saying she daren't touch anything for fear of her husband's anger, but admitting she made slight alterations to see if he noticed. She expected his congratulations, obviously. They shook hands; the beautiful fingers were limp.

As soon as she had gone, he made his way back to his room where he slumped down to recover. The place stung with her scent, but that was better than her presence. He had hated the hour in her company. He ought to ring Janet Barker-Smith to warn her, but he would not be fair; he'd prejudice her against the odious Sandra. No, she was not odious, but feeble, slimy, crippled in moral sense. If he'd had any gumption, he'd have set about her, forced her to imagine how she had mangled her husband's confidence. He had asked why she had married Tony, and she had described how he had been a prefect when she was a fourth-former, how he had gained an honours B.Sc., how he had tried to seduce her after a disco. Oh, she had been impressed. Richardson immediately guessed how this important young sprig, this personage of consequence, this intellect, this man of the world, had deteriorated into the shabby dyspeptic nonentity whom nobody could, or wanted to, please. He stroked the arms of his chair to calm himself.

Marguerite and Virginia sat over hot drinks in the kitchen. The television was off. Joanna perched on the edge of her easy chair, legs straight out, hands clasped in the fashion of a knight on an alabaster tomb.

'She'd patronized Woolworth's scent counter,' Virginia announced, in aggression.

'She, as I keep telling Fay, is the cat's grandmother,' Joanna said.

'Daddy's lady-friend. I don't know her name.'

'Mrs Moore,' he informed her, digging into the instant coffee.

137

'More more than less.'

'What does that dark saying mean?' Joanna.

'She seems not to do things by halves. Spraying perfume, for example.'

'Is that good or bad?' Her father.

'Is she pretty?' Margot interrupted. 'We didn't see her, only smelt her.'

'Your children,' he expostulated to Joanna.

'You see what I have to put up with while you are interviewing the pretty ladies. Is she in trouble?'

'Yes. Of her own making.'

'Your father,' Joanna instructed her daughters, 'is prepared to assist only the deserving poor.'

'That's better than the undeserving rich,' Margot defended him.

'We don't know any of them.'

'Mrs Brooks,' Virginia corrected her mother. 'Apologies, Margot.'

'Don't mind me,' Marguerite shook with laughter, as if some deadly satirical missile had struck mid-target. Richardson felt proud of his daughters, and suspicious.

'There are beds upstairs,' Joanna said.

The girls made an unhurried departure, after which he gave his wife an account of Sandra Moore's visit.

'So you never did find out what she wanted?'

'Not really.'

'Well, you can't win 'em all.' Joanna sometimes turned to the demotic, to shoot her husband down from the upper air of education to reality. 'I keep on telling you that you can't solve the problems of this street, never mind the world.'

'I'm learning.'

'I doubt that,' Joanna said. 'I shall have to start protecting you. You're on a high now; there's nothing you can't do; it all comes easy. So in between your book and your telly and your lectures, you think you can raise the dead. You can't. And there'll be a reaction.'

'You're probably right. But this is preferable to stagnation. I'd sooner . . .'

'You've a long way to go,' she announced. 'You've more than

138

twenty-five years of working life left. Do you ever think about that?'

'Yes. And it terrifies me. The long decline. That's why I feel I have to get it all done now, while I'm capable.'

'You don't consider that you'll grow wiser or saner or more mellow? Go on, does that cross your mind?'

'Well, I hope so. I sometimes doubt it, but that's what I'd like to think might happen.'

'But?' she asked, heavily emphatic.

'Energy will disappear. That's what bothers me.'

'Will you never rate being above doing?'

'Not at present. But what are you on to, now? The mystic East? Into the ashram?'

'All my life consists of doing. Sorting the girls out, making meals, ironing your shirts, shopping.'

'In my opinion,' he said, speaking slowly, headmaster in assembly, 'those are just as important as anything I do.'

'In my opinion,' Joanna's face was pleasant, comfortably thoughtful, pitched nowhere outside this room and his advantage, 'when you say that you either deceive yourself or have taken to lies.'

'That's not very complimentary.'

'You think, and probably rightly, that your work and your writing are important because they affect a large number of people. I don't disagree. Though sometimes I think, or suspect, that your, I nearly said "antics", methods spoil your skills at one-to-one, if you understand me. I may be wrong.'

'You may well be right. I need to be an actor, and I don't know sometimes when to stop playing the part.'

'Well, don't start Uriah Heep now.'

'I think you're good for me, Joanna. You don't let me pull any wool over my own eyes.'

'I should be even better for you if I were a nuisance, or a neurotic or a burden. Then you'd be goaded. Stanley Smith's wife's a mouse, but she scours the educational advertisements for jobs, and has been known to send off for application forms without consulting him.'

'You can't believe Edith's made him the man he is.'

'No. He's clever and energetic and dominating. But she's his

139

coach. She constantly psychs him up. Technical term in sport,' she said in answer to his sour face. 'Why, I don't know.'

'But you think you do.'

'To get her own back. Easy. He shouts and orders the kids about and decides on the holidays and schools, but all the time it's to make sure that the colourless, pretty lady he married won't be able to deduct a sharp mark for carelessness or lack of effort.'

'He'd get on if he were a bachelor.'

'Yes, I agree. But not so far or so fast.'

'Tell me,' Richardson said, headmaster in the study, finger-tips together, 'is that a good basis for marriage?'

'At present. When he's some great panjandrum of the educational empire, it may be different. Or if he fails to be that. He's very conventional. And sexually satisfied, I guess. Edith's a cut above him socially, and that counts for something in Scunthorpe or Wigan or wherever it was he started life. So he's not likely to lose his head, or his job, over other women. Or not yet.'

'And she won't leave him?' he asked.

'Like our Mrs Moore? Not while there's something there for her. She has a young family, and a bit of money of her own, and a real stake in his progress. She'll live adequately through him.'

' "He for God only; she for God in him"?'

'Right, though it's not all one way, by any means. It doesn't suit the feminists' case; it doesn't suit me, but there are women of that sort. You might have done better for yourself marrying one of them.'

'I'm satisfied,' he said, warmly, putting out a thankful hand.

'Because things are going well for you now. Wait for the bad times.'

'That's when I'll depend on you.'

'We'll see.' Both were acting, glorying in it. Curtains, Act One.

13

Sandra Moore left her husband again early in June.

Richardson learnt this from Miss Allbright as he walked one morning round the hall and the gymnasium where public examinations took place. Miss Allbright, invigilating, trapped the headmaster in a corner, whispering, 'Tony's wife's gone again. Keep your eyes on him, please.'

With that, she flitted back to her solemn patrolling of rows of desks, a sheaf of paper at the ready for insatiable candidates, pretty and conscientious and a credit to them all.

He met her the next day, this time crossing the senior playground.

'I haven't seen anything of Tony,' he began. 'Is he coping?'

'I think so.' Fresh as a toothpaste girl.

'It wouldn't be wise to say anything unless he raised the matter with me, do you think?'

She smiled even more, broadly. A gust of wind chilled the sunshine.

'It's shaken him up. You'd have said it was just what he wanted, but he seems shattered. I don't know.'

'Why has she gone?'

'Must have liked her independence.'

'Are you looking after him?'

'Well, I feel sorry for him, but I'm keeping my distance. I'm not at his nod twenty-four hours a day, whatever he may think.' She sounded aggrieved.

'I see.'

'That's why I asked you to keep an eye on him.' She straightened the pile of folders she was carrying. 'Look, he made his choice, and he must abide by it.'

'Will he do . . . anything . . . foolish?'

'I shouldn't . . . No. I'm sure. No.'

'It must have been very worrying for you, Miss Allbright.'

She half closed her eyes, spoiling the even smoothness of her face.

'I was fond of him,' she said. 'That I admit. But I'm not a puppet on a string.' Bridling, she again re-ordered her folders. 'Tony has a lot going for him, if only he'd see it.' He looked questioningly at her. 'He can teach. Clever and dull alike. And it's not everybody who can. And the stupids have a right to be taught as well as the intelligent. But he's always complaining, questioning. He's never sure of himself. He blames everybody else but himself.' She fluttered incredible eyelashes at him, film heroine of a golden oldie. 'I ought not to talk like this to you.'

'Whyever not?'

'You might hold it against him when it comes to promotion. And then there's another chip on his shoulder.'

She was out, he could see, to damn her former lover.

'I don't think so,' he said. 'This is confidential.'

She made no comment on his lack of logic, so that he wondered if the cream of his voice had drowned her wits.

' "Sam" Smith won't support him.' He smiled at her use of the students' nickname. 'Tony's too independent for him. He wants yes-men and nothing else.' Once more she hoisted her folders. 'There I go, talking out of turn again.' Her smile broadened; pearly teeth eliminated all other features.

'I'm always interested in what you say. You don't speak much in the staff meetings. These private words keep me on my toes.'

She looked at him now, in distaste. She could not disguise it.

'Yes,' she said, vinegary. 'If you want my opinion, staff meetings are a waste of time. Especially at this part of the term. Three or four shooting their mouths off.'

'Isn't it democratic, though, to give the staff the chance to voice their opinions in public?'

'It may be democratic, but it's boring.'

'You must liven it up, then.'

'Who'd be interested in what I thought about education? I think I know how to run a good dressmaking class, and I'd be interested to know what Mrs King,' the head of the department, 'or Thelma thought about it. But amongst ourselves.'

'Are you advising me to dispense with staff meetings?'

'Oh, no. I suppose you have to have them.'

Lesley Allbright made her final adjustment to the armful of folders, murmured an apology, bobbed her head and walked across the yard. Urged by end-of-term frustrations, marking of papers, totting up, listing, she had for a short couple of minutes spoken her mind, and was now regretting it. She wouldn't boast of her candour, but would fear that next time he wrote her a testimonial he'd hold this morning's conversation against her.

He pushed into one of the boys' lavatories, always a signal of his displeasure. It stood empty, with no smell of cigarette smoke. The walls were thick with graffiti, mostly small, neat and moderately well spelt. The largest letters, high up and in capitals, were reserved for a crayon message: 'Richo is a wanker.' He wondered what he had done to cause some large boy to scrawl that. Was it a cry against authority? As he left, he noticed Mr Moore's alleged lust for Miss Allbright commemorated in an ancient but improperly scanned verse. A coat of paint would be more effective than a moral lecture. It was worth, perhaps, a paragraph in his book.

Morality rose rampant the next day.

At a quarter to ten when he and Miss Taylor were dealing with the mail, Bentine, the senior deputy, hammered the door, Gestapo-heavy, and burst in. A red spot burnt on his sallow cheekbones.

'We've caught a boy cheating,' he said. 'In the "A" level Physical Geography paper. He had made a crib on a sheet of the Board's paper, and had it there in front of him.'

'Who is it?'

'James Walters.'

'Does he deny it?'

'No. He couldn't, could he?' Excitement, triumph, lit up the shame.

'Where is he, now?'

'Waiting outside.'

'Could you get me his file, Miss Taylor, please?'

Nothing was said while the secretary was out. Bentine stood, though his posture suggested he was about to break into a run, bolt-eyed, breathing harshly, unaware of the sound. Miss Taylor laid the packet on the table. Walters, James Brian, in black felt-tip, with two photographs, one of the eleven-year-old entry, one of the sixth-former. Fair-haired, the small boy wore glasses, the senior had either dispensed with optical aids or wore contact lenses. Richardson remembered the face from general studies, that of an earnest, steady boy, prepared to write a note but not to indulge in controversy. Salt of the earth. Father, he read from the topmost document, manager, department store; mother, school secretary; brothers and sisters, none.

'What does he say?' Richardson asked.

'Nothing. Seems shocked.'

'Do you know the parents?'

'Not really.'

'I'm wondering about talking to them on the telephone. You'll have to inform the Board.'

'I've looked up the procedure.'

'Get hold of Higgins or whoever it was who taught him geography, and his tutor. I'll see them. And we'd better have a series of strict warnings in the next few days to candidates and invigilators. This is bad.'

'I'll see to it.'

'Good. Send him in.'

Bentine bustled out, efficient under orders, and Walters entered, stood in front of the headmaster's desk. He was taller than Richardson remembered, but pallid, boneless; he wore a clean check-shirt, jeans, and carried a shabby briefcase under one arm.

'Sit down, James.' The boy looked about for a chair, at a loss, before he found it one yard behind him. 'Mr Bentine tells me you were cheating in the geography exam. Is that correct?'

'Yes.' Hardly a word, a sound.

'Why did you do it?'

The boy opened his mouth, froze, closed it, then shifted minutely but violently so that the chair legs creaked.

'I didn't think I could remember enough.'

'Is this the first time?'

'We've only had maths so far. Cribs are no use there.'

'Did you intend to continue cheating?'

'I don't know.'

144

Richardson tapped the papers Bentine had left with him.

'This must have taken you a considerable time to prepare.'

'I did it for revision purposes.'

'But it's on examination stationery. You had been warned under no circumstances to take that out of the room. You had, hadn't you?'

'Yes.'

'Then why did you do so?'

'I don't know.' Walters shook his head, dazed, beaten.

'It was almost certain you would be caught. The staff are most careful.'

Walters grinned weakly, about to be sick.

'I shouldn't think I'm.the only one.'

'You mean there are others acting dishonestly?'

The boy waved his hands in a vague wristy motion, denying sanity to anyone who would ask such a question.

'You realize this is a serious matter. We shall have to inform the Board, and it is very unlikely that they will allow you to complete your examinations. I shall also have to tell your parents. Will there be anyone at home now?'

'No, sir.'

'They're both out at work?'

Walters nodded and kept his neck twisted to one side.

'What is the best way? Would you prefer to let them know yourself or would it be kinder for me, say, to ring your father?'

The word 'kinder' stuck choking in his throat. As far as he knew, this was a decent lad, with decent parents, already worried sick about their son's performance. Why should he be set up in judgement? The boy was speaking; his own distress had caused him to miss the muttered sentences.

'I beg your pardon. I couldn't hear you.'

'I said you'd better tell my mother.'

'Would you prefer to tell her?'

The boy sat clenched in his chair; as if one had asked the question in an impenetrable foreign language. He roused himself sluggishly.

'All right.'

'Will your parents be upset?'

'What do you think?' A proper flash of temper.

'I see from the reports here from Mr Higgins and Mr O'Hare that they thought you'd at least get a B.'

'There's too much to learn. I couldn't get it to stick.'

Walters answered reasonably now, if sullenly. Richardson, hitching up the burden of his duty, advanced one or two more solemn sentences about the seriousness of the affair, and received no reply. The boy's face was flushed, his attention elsewhere. The headmaster carefully avoided certain words, 'disgrace', 'shame', 'punishment', but could not help feeling throbs of an abstract anger which dissipated itself as soon as he looked back at the awkward figure in front of him.

'This is bad, James,' he said, finally, convinced he'd get nothing further from the victim, 'but it's not the end of the world.' He explained that, though he would not be allowed to complete the examination, there was no reason why he should not repeat it in November or the following summer, and though that meant he would have to put back his entry into university, that was perhaps not altogether a disadvantage since this episode had demonstrated, if nothing else, that he was not yet ready for the change.

Efficiently, the headmaster instructed the boy to go home, collect his books and return with them that afternoon at three, when he'd be unlikely to meet other examination candidates or juniors who'd be in lessons. Richardson would consult Mr Higgins and perhaps some arrangement could be made about borrowing texts for revision.

'I shan't be allowed back here, then?'

'No, I think not.'

'Why?'

'I have to consider the effect. On the others.'

'You think I should spread cheating like a disease.' Again, the hot flush of the boy's resentment. 'There's plenty going on.'

'So you've said.' Richardson could now feel dislike. 'Do you wish to say anything more about that?'

'No.' The word rumbled, bestially.

'I'll prepare a letter for your parents which I trust you to take home this afternoon. It will give you the chance to tell them first.'

Walters sat, left hand across his mouth as if he'd forgotten something, but seemed unwilling to go. Richardson left him there. He studied the now pallid cheeks, a dirty thumbnail, the decent clothes, the cheap briefcase, the outward and visible signs of what could not be said.

'Is there anything you wish to say to me, James, before you leave?'

'No, sir.' Return to formality.

'I'm sorry this has happened. I'll see you this afternoon, then, at three.'

Walters stood up, nodded, looked round as if for all the world he'd no idea where the door was.

'Thank you,' he said, crystal-clear, and walked out.

Richardson listened to the footsteps along the corridor, ordinary sounds, before Bentine trundled in again. He had been lurking somewhere, ready with his news. He had been in touch with the Board, and they would give their decision later that morning. Geography was out, but they might just allow Walters to sit the rest of his maths and economics papers, if that was what the school wanted.

'What do you think?' Richardson asked the deputy.

'We shouldn't allow it. Look at the example.'

'He might not want it himself.'

'I never thought of that.'

'He's coming back here at three. Chase the Board for a decision before then, will you?'

Bentine, delighted with himself, wanted to stay, to talk, and his headmaster, bored, but not impatient, allowed him ten minutes of fervour. The deputy, not yet fifty, talked like some Victorian evangelical, sure of his principles, ready with his precepts, hating the sin, going through the motions of loving the sinner.

Richardson heard him out, flicking ostentatiously through a pile of letters he'd already dealt with. In a pause, before the thunder of morality sounded out again, he said, drily, 'Thank you very much, Mr Bentine. There is just one other thing, and then I must get this desk top cleared. Walters claims he was not the only one cheating. I don't know the truth, but I want a quick investigation. I want the staff and candidates warned. I saw an invigilator marking. Oh, he hid his papers.'

Bentine's face fell. He did not like his senior, privately disagreed with his views, might even be driven at this time of term to express his disapproval to his cronies if the head allowed Walters back to complete his examinations, but he would say nothing here, in the study, or rather would huff and puff his way through paragraphs of empty rhetoric. Mildly, because Bentine was both conscientious and efficient, Richardson wondered what the man's breaking-point would be. That a man of principle should risk his neck so very infrequently for what he believed did not surprise him; Bentine knew his mind and that was about all he did know.

'Do you think we might need more staff on?' the deputy faltered.

'That's a possibility you could investigate.'

'That would mean that I had to rewrite the whole invigilation schedule. And it wouldn't be popular with the school exams starting.'

'Are we serious about this, Mr Bentine, or are we not?'

Richardson concentrated on the letter in front of him, took up a pen and marked the third paragraph of a useless missive advertising photocopying machines. He nodded, in sagacity, to himself, not allowing himself to look up. Bentine withdrew, tiptoeing, cowed. Richardson screwed up the letter, dashed it into the wastepaper basket, and condemned himself as both cruel and mischievous. He had no intention of having an efficient system of supervision altered, as Bentine should know. Perhaps he did. He tapped his button to recall Miss Taylor. Bring on a human being.

He saw Walters that afternoon.

The boy had not contacted his parents, but pocketed the letter Richardson had prepared. It was explained that the Board would not allow him to complete the examinations, but that he should contact Mr Higgins, who would permit him to retain books in preparation for the November sitting.

'Shall I have to fill in another UCCA form?'

'I'm afraid so. That is, if you still want to apply for university entrance. Talk it over at home.'

'Will you act as academic referee for me?' The plain sentence tumbled dully, broken, like coal from the back of a distant lorry.

'Certainly.'

'Will you have to say I cheated?'

'I don't think so. After all, I'm hoping you'll make good.'

'But it's not fair to them,' Walters glumly objected. Richardson could barely believe his ears.

'What to you mean by that, James?'

'They won't want a cheat will they? I could start again. Once I realized I couldn't take it in, remember it, I made up my mind how I was . . .'

'James. I am not underestimating the gravity of your offence, and I am glad you see it in the same light. But what you have to do is to try to put this behind you. If each time we went wrong it meant we would never again attempt to act honestly, we'd be badly off. I see what you mean, and your reservations do you credit. You've gone against the ethos of this place, against your upbringing, but you're not depraved. Surely, surely, you don't believe that.'

Walters's eyes filled with tears; he swayed in his chair. The two talked on for twenty minutes and in the end shook hands. Richardson sat at his desk, after the boy's departure, both dazed and yet pleased with himself. He had shown what humanity he could, and yet he could hardly grasp the difficulty Walters would have coming out with his confession to his parents, and their problems with grandparents, aunts and uncles, the neighbours, perhaps between themselves. He wished to God the whole day could start again, and he could take James Walters by the arm as he stepped into the examination room.

As he walked out of his office, with nothing in mind except not to have to sit, he passed the boy outside the door of the staff common-room, with Higgins, head of geography, the master's face like that of a blinded Oedipus, and hovering, hands full of papers, Bentine, neither in on the colloquy nor out of it.

All three looked up as he approached, guiltily, it seemed.

He nodded to them, passed by on the other side.

14

That evening, immediately the Richardsons had finished their meal, Conrad Brooks telephoned.

He was in Saudi Arabia, it appeared, for a three-day conference and he'd found the Richardsons' number written in the back of his diary.

'I don't know why I'm doing this. I saw your name, and it was straight up to the hotel room to ring. I want you to go to see my wife. And write me a letter, airmail form's best, telling me how you found her.'

'Haven't you heard from her?'

'Yes. But she puts on a show for me. I'm not sure.'

'Won't she do the same for me?' Richardson asked.

'Very likely.'

'Am I to tell her you phoned?'

'Of course.'

'Is it easy to get through? On the phone, I mean?'

'Oh, yes.'

'Will you try her now, then?'

'If you say so.'

'You tell her I will call this evening. I'll check later to see that she's in. Anything you particularly want me to cast my eye over?'

'Look, Richardson, I've no right to ask you to do this. And there's no good reason, either. It's mere impulse on my part. But I want you to go.' He dictated his address.

Richardson promised to make the visit and said he would post on his findings the next day. He made a few remarks about their meetings with Felicity, the last a fortnight before. Brooks admitted comfort, but stressed again his confidence that he was doing the right thing by ringing.

'Wouldn't it be better if Joanna went?'

'Take her with you by all means. But I want you to write the report.' The clipped tones might well have been addressed to some subordinate dispatched to assess costs of materials or availability of skilled labour. 'It's not that I don't trust women.'

'But what?' Richardson laughed, hoping the line was as clear the other end as at his.

'Probably it's me; I just don't always understand what they're getting at. They don't exactly say one thing and mean another, but they seem to talk a good way over my head.'

'And you think I shan't?'

'We can try. I mean, here am I, women's intuition stuff, calling you like this. It's not drink. I'm teetotal out here. Nor overwork, nor the sun addling me. But I saw your name and number, and it seemed a good thing to do.'

They talked very little longer. Brooks would ring his wife immediately, and then Richardson was to try in thirty minutes. Brooks became gruffer; one could hear him clearing the sand or the hotel's treated air from his dry throat.

When half an hour later he contacted Mrs Brooks, she was on her way out to a dinner party. She was excited, she said, that Conrad had rung him, and she would be glad to receive Richardson the next evening if that were possible. She spoke graciously, but as if the taxi were waiting outside.

He asked Joanna about the two matters puzzling him. On the first, Conrad's sudden whim to send him spying on Felicity, she shook her head.

'Perhaps he's learning to have a conscience. Or perhaps something particularly horrible had happened to him. She says he doesn't suffer from loneliness, that he prefers it, but then we don't know. He may be changing.'

Conrad's views on women's writing she dismissed.

'I guess women put down what they think and feel more clearly and more strongly than men. ". . . the awful way their poems lay them open/Just doesn't strike them." '

'Who's that?'

'Kingsley Amis.'

'Is he such an expert, then?'

'Well, not really. But anything that's said has to be interpreted, and old Brooks has convinced himself he doesn't understand the language.'

'Why should he do that?'

'No idea. Perhaps this first German marriage. Probably no one reason. Veronica. Anyhow you go and ask Mrs Brooks.'

'You're coming with me.'

'No. Go on your own. She likes men. Besides, I've a WEA committee.'

Felicity Brooks began uncertainly, he thought. Her skin stretched dry, elderly, though she had taken considerable trouble with her hair, which was piled, and with light-blue eye-shadow. She wore an extraordinary robe, or wrap, belted, of ankle length, in orange and gold silk with an azure lining. She carried the dress well, its wide hems whipped across the floor, but the garment seemed melodramatic, as though any minute she'd fling it wide to reveal stark nakedness underneath. In fact, a glance at her ankles above gold shoes showed she was wearing stockings or tights. Her conversation in contrast was low-keyed as she spoke about Stephen's 'A' level papers and her care to see that he went off each morning after a substantial breakfast. His anxieties, if any, did not blunt his appetite, but she would be glad when it was all over. No, he had not complained about the papers; he had done less well on one economics paper than he had hoped, but that was his own fault, he claimed. As soon as he had finished, that is, next week, he'd be off to Italy. They had discussed inviting Marguerite to go with him, but had decided against it.

'We thought perhaps she was a shade young, though nowadays they gad about the world with the opposite sex. I didn't think you'd approve, though I don't know, really. I suppose you have a fair number of pregnancies in your school, don't you?'

Her sentences dodged without connecting links, like the writings of Joanna's mathematicians and Conrad's women. Pleasantly he put over an anecdote or two of the sort she wanted to hear. Felicity seemed uncertain about the room in which they were sitting, constantly asking if he were comfortable. In the end, at her proposal, they moved into a small square place, overlooking the large and floriferous back garden, which was bordered at the far end by three huge lime trees. She had no idea of the original purpose of this closet, guessing perhaps it was an office for her grandfather if not the housekeeper's room. Nor had she thought to ask her neighbours if they had an equivalent.

They sat in brocaded chairs, almost side by side, facing a blank television screen.

'That's better,' she said. 'Or don't you think so?'

'I'm fine.' Between them, on a small, inlaid table were the soft drinks they had carried in from the drawing-room.

'Were you surprised to hear from Conrad?'

'Yes. I hardly know him.'

'I suppose I mention your family rather a bit in the letters. I write regularly, once a week, I have a set day, always have, it keeps us in touch, and I like him to be able to visualize what's going on. And you and yours are amongst the more interesting exhibits about here. That's why. He'd feel he'd know you well.'

There seemed no answer to that, but Richardson, never at a loss, strung words together about letter-writing, its value and its decline in the day of the telephone. She was prepared to wait.

'What did he want you to do?' she asked, easily, when he'd concluded his paragraph.

'To ring you, to come round here, and then write telling him how you were.'

'Why should he ask you to do that?'

'That's for you to answer rather than me. Is it like him? In character, I mean.'

There was silence in the room; she sat still as a stone, but as far as he could see out of the corner of his eye, quite relaxed now.

'You'd say,' she began, 'that it wasn't, but there. He gives the impression of the imperturbable, but sometimes . . . He's holding a curious job down. He's more of a diplomat than an engineer.' Again, as to Joanna, she listed his achievements, his difficulties. Her voice was light and the account accomplished, even polished, as if she had rehearsed it. Richardson, interested, questioned her, and she answered with detail. An hour passed in no time.

She broke off to make coffee.

'What are you going to tell him?' she asked, pouring.

'That his wife greatly admires him. And that's unusual.'

'Do you think so?'

'No man's a hero to his valet, they say . . .'

'Doesn't Joanna . . . ?'

'I shouldn't think so. She sees too much of the hesitation and vacillation and procrastination.' Felicity opened her eyes wide at the list, suspecting irony. 'And perhaps she's too close. She sees the papered-over cracks.'

'But she admires the actual work?'

'After a fashion. It's difficult to evaluate. At the end of one of your husband's stints, there's a solid hospital standing, not dropping to pieces. That's tangible. I turn out a pupil with an Oxbridge scholarship, and next thing we hear he's in prison.'

'Conrad's . . . One of his most beautiful, useful buildings, a block of flats, really elegant, beautifully delicate in spite of its size, was shelled to pieces this week.'

'The plan is there. They can build it again.'

'If they have the will.' She jerked her head. 'What's your school like?'

'Too large.' He laughed. 'Seventeen hundred pupils. But it's in a good catchment area, so that makes it just about bearable. Plenty of parental support and money. And we've a big sixth form. We even steal; no, that's not quite right; pupils come across to us from other schools.'

'Is that good?'

'Not really. But I can't prevent it. And probably they get a better deal with us. More teaching time, more competition, more outside activity.'

'Have you any sort of control? I mean it seems large. You'd be surprised how few men Conrad will employ these days, even on a tremendous contract. They use machines.'

'I've some say, in some areas. Like curriculum. Like general studies. I can encourage, and kick behinds, and give the impression my beady eye is there and open. My job is to build up the confidence of the place, I suppose, and to make sure that the good things get praised, and the bad stopped, checked, reprimanded.'

'You're the figurehead?'

'Yes. That's what it seems like often enough. And I suppose there's some value in that, if not much. And I do some of the things headmasters did with smaller schools in the old days. I congratulate pupils; I discuss their problems; I see their parents. But I must confess I've no idea whether the most important cases come to me. We've heads of upper and lower schools, and heads of houses, and heads of departments, and deputy heads in charge of welfare and examinations and university entrance, and God knows what they all sit on, or clear up, without my knowledge.'

'It sounds chaotic.'

'It is, but I think I've developed an ear. I've an inkling when the whole machine's working properly.'

'And if it isn't?' she asked.

'I'm in, with both feet.'

'Not tactfully?'

'My middle name. But my staff know I'll interfere if I think it's necessary. But they're on the whole well intentioned, and pressures from society are running our way, especially in this area. We've made a name for ourselves, with good examination results mainly, but plays and operas and football teams.'

'So it's not too difficult?'

'Impossible, sometimes. I feel as if I'm driving a bus from the back seat, bound and gagged. But the road's straight just now and well made up and lighted. And those at the wheel will now and again obey an instruction or act sensibly on their own.'

'But if things go wrong . . .'

'God knows. I thought they were off target just when I started teaching, and remember, I've only worked in favoured schools. The economic depression has steadied some of the hot-heads, but I guess it's meant anarchy in some inner-city places. The middle classes hog all the privileges.'

'Some,' Felicity Brooks said, 'some. Not my Veronica.' He waited for her; she studied the reflection of the window on the television screen. 'Simon Howard has been to see me.'

'Did your husband know that? When he rang up?'

'No. It was only this week.'

'But he spoke to you on the telephone?'

'I didn't mention it.'

She bridled, as if he criticized her, and so sat silently, feeling at the arm of her chair with her left hand.

'Had he anything interesting to say?' Richardson had to

repair the break, made his attempt with this rough and ready question.

'No, he hadn't, really. He's very quiet, of course. I don't think one should expect anything.'

'But he came round?'

'He did.'

'Did he mention Veronica?'

'Yes.' Felicity cocked her head. 'He said he loved her. And nothing would change that. Not what had happened or anything else. It was a miracle.'

'Had he told his wife?' Richardson would not let her ride easily.

'No. Why should he? That would only mean trouble.'

'Do you think she didn't know?'

'I'm sure. There was sex between him and Vernie, and some outings. But not many. He never came here privately to my knowledge, for instance. The majority of it went on in his head. Perhaps that's why Vernie found it so unsatisfactory.'

'Did she?'

'She didn't kill herself for nothing.' Felicity Brooks breathed fast, through her nose. 'We shall never know. He's making a romantic thing out of it, and perhaps that's best.'

'He didn't express any guilt?'

'Of course he did. He's not a block of stone. It was his usual cough and splutter, but . . . I didn't encourage him to blame himself. It wouldn't bring her back.'

Mrs Brooks's calm, subdued voice judged Richardson. He found himself wanting in that he slapped out these crude questions which prised information from the woman who remained, in spite of hurt, civilized. It was possible, he concluded, that she knew little, and so refused to exaggerate her feelings. He admired her, and said so. She raised her hand at the compliment, a small gesture, as a golfer holing a not too difficult putt acknowledges a scatter of applause.

'I have to go on. And I suppose I'd deceive myself if I could find any advantage in it,' she said. 'But Vernie was sly about this. There was some sense in that, because she wouldn't have got much encouragement from me, I can tell you. It's not the way I wanted it.' She stared him straight in the eye. 'I can remember her as a baby, and what we thought of her then. That's sentimental, isn't it?'

'By no means.'

'I'm hanging on here, putting a lot into the house. I'm trying to learn Arabic. I have Stephen about, but he doesn't make many demands. I feed him, but I sometimes wonder whether he'd notice if I served up bread and jam for every meal.'

'I wouldn't wager money on that,' he said. She smiled.

'You might be right. I've friends and acquaintances. I write regularly to Conrad, as I've told you. I go on holidays. In all, I don't have much time to sit and brood. But it's nothing but bits; there's no overall pattern. It was exactly the same, I'll admit, when Vernie was alive; she was another of the bits. It makes me think that everybody should be sent out on regular jobs. That's why unemployment is so dangerous.'

'They might not like the work allocated to them.'

'That's so, and they'd be just as disgruntled as I am now. Men are more likely to find fulfilling work. You and Conrad, for example. Staying at home with babies, even grown-up babies, isn't healthy. You ask Joanna.'

'Shall I report this to your husband?'

'Yes, it will do no harm to worry him. Or to offer him an alternative kind of worry.'

'He did ring me up,' Richardson said.

'He did. So he did. He's a good man, given his faults. And like everybody else he has his moments of depression, and then he telephones you.'

Mrs Brooks spoke cheerfully, as if she'd solved a mathematical puzzle, twisted a Rubik's cube the way she wanted. How near the truth she had arrived he did not know.

'We went to a wedding, not very long ago, when he was over once, to the daughter of a cousin of Conrad's. There'd been a lot of trouble, because the family didn't want the girl to have this man, who was very much older than she was and had married before. They gave in, in the end, after a great deal of hassle. They were married in a nonconformist place, they couldn't have it in the parish church, and that was another cause of trouble, but there they were dressed up, and then on to a hotel for the reception, and people made some very good speeches,

157

and then the bride's father, Con's cousin, who'd been very witty and had quoted poetry, just made a sort of cawing noise and dropped dead.'

Richardson obliged with the subdued, expected noises.

'That broke it up. They put a screen round him. I felt awful, but I remember I was pleased that Vernie and Stephen weren't there. Conrad didn't say much, but when he was driving back he suddenly blurted out, "Well, that put things into perspective, didn't it?" And he was right. Tom, the cousin, had worried himself to death over the wedding, but he didn't know he'd die there. Oh, he was overweight, had blood pressure, smoked. You could guess. But he didn't know. This is a complicated story.'

'I think I see what you're getting at.'

'That's more than I do. There ought to be a moral, but I don't know what it is. Go on, make a suggestion.'

'There are more serious matters elsewhere,' he said, 'than those which are driving us mad.'

'Good. But that's no comfort, is it?' She stirred in her chair. 'Do you know, John, that when your Joanna comes to see me, it makes me sad. That's good for me, but I'm made melancholy.'

'Why ever?' He could be jovial.

'I compare myself with her. She seems so smart, fresh. I don't mean clothes, though she dresses well, but in herself. She's running your family, your daughters and you, making it easy for the four of you to carry off all the prizes and awards and yet . . . and yet she's herself, her own woman, young and, oh, breezy and sharp. I envy her, but I think she'll not stay like that. Something'll finish her, spoil her. Old age. Mrs Allegro, you don't know her, I helped her daughter put her in a hospice where she died, I guess she'd be a Joanna when she was young. You could just recognize it. If your imagination was good. Life is bloody, isn't it? It ruins everything.'

'I hope not.'

'I boast about this house to Joanna, and to tell you the truth she envies it. I don't say she'd change the convenience of your place for this museum, but she can't help but see there's something about it. It's solid and beautiful. It is, isn't it?'

'Well, yes.'

158

'When I've got you here, I just want to explain things, to make everything clear, but with her I want to sit down and cry, for the disappointments and aching joints and Veronicas who can't see their way clear to go on living. Joanna's a real work of art. No, she can't be. A work of God, if I weren't an atheist.'

'A wonder of nature.'

'I see you don't understand,' she said, with acerbity. 'Still, it's not to be expected. You don't appreciate what your wife is. I've only just come upon it.'

'Her uniqueness? My blindness?'

'You can make fun.' She broke off, as if she had just grasped the enormity of her statement. 'I shouldn't talk to you like this. I've no right. But I . . .'

'Go on,' he smiled, encouragingly.

'I'm just letting my tongue wag,' she said, dourly, a twitch reducing the breadth of her shoulder, dulling the proud lines of the gold robe. 'Have you ever committed adultery?'

'That's the sort of question I don't answer,' he replied, primly.

'That would lead me to think you had, if I didn't know you were such a diplomat. You seem to have so much going for you maritally that I wondered if you'd want more. I think Conrad does occasionally. He doesn't tell me, but I can guess. But it's not serious. Or at least that's how it seems. But I'm afraid that one of these days he'll come along and say that his latest fancy is love, that he wants to part from me. It's happened to so many people.'

'Has it happened to people of your background and experience?'

'Yes, it has.' Richardson, still shaken by her question, in that he felt himself demeaned by whatever alternative he admitted, or by truth or a lie. She had hit him low, painfully.

Felicity was speaking again.

'I'm always on the watch for change,' she said. 'Change for the worse.'

He put out his hand, and she took it.

'I think sometimes you're a human being,' she admitted, and dropped his hand.

'What am I going to report to Conrad?'

159

'Just give an interesting account, I'm sure you can do that, easily enough, and let him draw his own conclusions. For all we can tell, he won't want to know by the time he gets the letter. Make it lively. Amuse him.'

'That's me docketed, then. The thinking man's clown.'

'I've told Joanna this.' Felicity now addressed the still-lighted window, but had switched on the table lamp by her chair. 'What worries me most is change. Nothing lasts. Everything's transitory.'

'That could be good. You could always prepare for the next, better, event.'

'It's not like that. I've no control. We enjoy this or that for a short time, and then something else blows up, something bad and black.'

'Is this the result of experience or temperament?' The headmaster.

'What does that mean?'

'Some people, who are averagely successful or more than that, see their lives as disaster areas because they are temperamentally anxious. It's probably physiological, chemical to an extent. But they aren't able to enjoy success, and even translate it as failure.'

'You're not like that?'

'Not basically, no. I'm quick, too quick perhaps, to dwell on my failures, but I recover in the end. When I think,' he paused to watch Felicity, who had now settled comfortably, mannishly almost in the way she had stretched her legs out, 'how I sat upstairs talking to Veronica about university entrance when she was eating her heart out, I wonder what sort of bloody fool I am.'

'You couldn't help that. You were following your brief. I don't think anything could have saved her. She was damned for long enough.'

'I don't believe it. Drugs might have . . .'

'Might, might.' Felicity Brooks was bolt upright again, hands on chair arms, voice hot. 'She went through hell, and looked plump and at ease. Oh, God. Such things happen. But it's no use blaming yourself. Or if you do, what about us, the parents?'

'It seems typical. I investigate something parallel and dis-

160

tanced and unimportant, because that's all they let on to me.'

'No,' she said, woman-sweet.

'No. It's not right, and I'm exaggerating to say so. But it's how it appears on my bad days.'

'You've Joanna, and those daughters. They're beautiful.'

'Do you know what worries me? My work occupies more of my time than they do. And that's not right. It can't be.'

'You've schoolteachers and doctors and travel agents and insurance companies to help you out. You're not totally responsible. And when you have anyone as beautiful and efficient and energetic as Joanna to chase them up or cool them down, there's not much need for a heavy father.'

'It doesn't make sense, because what I do isn't important enough,' he argued. 'Now if I were Mozart or Shakespeare . . . .'

'If you were, that wouldn't of necessity mean you were the genius of a father. Our children are part-time occupations, even for mothers these days. And we can't make of them what we will, nor should we try. Even if it leads in the end to a sadness like Vernie's. Nothing goes exactly our way, and when it does we don't know how to treat it.'

They talked until it was dark.

As he drove home, he began to compose a cheerful letter to Conrad.

15

During the last week of term Fay went down with chicken-pox.

The child was not very ill, and Joanna, busy as ever, congratulated her daughter on catching the disease before they set out for three weeks in France. Richardson made time to read to Fay, recited verses to her, and noticed how Margot and Virginia often showed up for the performances. As he had almost completed the first draft of his book, had given his editor a date on which he would submit it, he was ready to be pleased by their interest. Joanna ragged him, to his satisfaction.

'Sometimes,' she said, after a chapter from an abridged *Oliver Twist*, 'I think you'd make quite a good teacher.'

'Thanks.'

'It's a pity you decided to leave the classroom.'

'There's no cachet or money in teaching.'

She smiled, daughter of two generations of consultants, the granddaughter of a fourth baron, at his small-beer ambition.

'Will this book make your name?' she asked.

'No. Not unless it gets into the newspapers, and that will be by chance. If I mention something that happens to be in the public eye at the time it comes out.'

'Still,' she pressed, 'even if it's a damp squib, you'll have the satisfaction that it's well made.'

'I'm not sure that what I'm saying is exactly true.'

'Don't water it down on that account,' she advised, stalking away. He wondered at her metaphor.

He had received no reply from Conrad Brooks, though the report of his visit to Felicity had taken up five airmail forms in the most minuscule writing and had occupied him two nights in composition, time he could ill afford from his book. But the blue sheets had disappeared into Arabia Deserta, and Richardson felt disappointed. Joanna, sensing this, had made careful enquiries of Mrs Brooks on an outing the pair took to the Theatre Royal to the Cambridge Footlights, but as far as she could make out Conrad had not mentioned the letters.

'The post's odd out there,' Felicity said. 'And he dodges about like a dog in a fair.'

Joanna, saying nothing, grew angry for her husband.

'He'll hear, in time,' Felicity went on. 'Con usually answers letters when he finds he has a spare minute. I wonder, perhaps, if he didn't quite grasp what your husband was getting at. He'd just want to hear that I was healthy.' Mrs Brooks understood Joanna's exasperation. 'You think,' she said, 'that a telephone call from the Middle East is something. To Con it's the equivalent of using a second-class stamp.'

Two days before the family left for France, Felicity Brooks made another appeal. Richardson had been sent shopping; he

162

believed he could think better on his feet, or at least he was glad to take a rest from the last two chapters of his book, unwisely composed together and fraying his nerves. Joanna took the message.

'Felicity's on the warpath again,' she said. 'Would you talk to Netta Howard?'

'About what?'

'She's kicked her husband out. That's Veronica's man.'

'What can I do in any one day? Did you tell her we were off to France?'

'I did. She's every confidence in you. "He's a catalyst," she said. "He forces you to think hard and straight." The very words.'

'Is it true?' he asked.

'May well be in her case.'

'But not in yours?'

'You said that, not me. I'm passing no judgements this morning. She's shown her husband the door, and Fizzy thinks she'll live to regret it. You've just to tell her to take him back.'

'Is that what she said?' he asked, incredulously.

'Not in so many words. I've translated it. But that's about the length of it. But you're to ring her first, Felicity that is, so you're quite sure what she wants.'

'You're enjoying yourself,' he reproached her, not altogether in jest.

'It must be nice to be popular. And Fay wants some more wicked Fagin before coffee while you're delighting the weaker sex.'

He telephoned Mrs Brooks, who was restrained, said she would make an appointment for him to see Netta that evening. She did offer a suggestion that it would be better for everybody if the girl took her husband back, but the whole of her conversation was lack-lustre, expectant of nothing, a counsel of unrealized despair, he thought. She would take him round and leave.

'You realize we're going away for three weeks.'

'Well, yes.'

'There can't be any follow-up. Or not from me.'

'What I want you to do is to talk to her, or to get her to talk to

163

you about what she's done. To a man. Then she might open up to Simon.'

'Are there any suggestions?' Jovially now.

'I want you in there with a clean shirt and a straight face. If Conrad were at home, I'd ask him to go, but he isn't. And I don't think he'd be laying down the law, though I don't know about that.'

He was surprised at his disappointment, that he had expected flattery from her, unearned praise. When he said as much to Joanna, she said he was learning and asked what he wanted for holiday wear.

Felicity Brooks was waiting for him, a light coat across her shoulders.

'We'll walk round,' she said. 'I'll introduce you, and then come away. The children will be in bed. She's a good girl is Netta. I think highly of her. We've had one tragedy; we don't want another.' There was nothing portentous there; she might have been explaining to a plumber why she wished to change a pair of taps. 'Come on. We mustn't be late. She'll be on edge.'

'She knows I'm coming?'

'Yes. And who you are.'

They walked out into the summer brightness of the evening. The warm air was heavy with the scent of late lime flowers; water trickled somewhere; trees were luxuriant with foliage, giants of dark, clustering weight against the polished surface of the sky.

'It's a pleasure just to walk along your cul-de-sac,' he said.

'I didn't notice.'

Netta Howard let them in, shook hands with Richardson, invited the callers into the drawing-room.

'No, thanks,' Felicity announced, 'I'm going. I shall just be in the way.' She marched off, letting herself out. Netta shrugged, politely.

The hall, architecturally a mirror image of that of the Brooks, rose strangely dissimilar. The walls, like the Brookses' were pale, but the sparse furniture crouched modern, streamlined, steely; the spindles of the staircase were staring white, the lightshades thin, colourless star-spearheads like modernist ear-rings; three contemporary abstract prints had their place, stood

164

at attention would be the metaphor, with two tall, narrow stretches of mirror. The effect on him, oddly, was neither bleak nor clinical, but utilitarian. The lengths of white radiator looked efficient, though they were now switched off. It would be easy to leave dirty fingermarks in this place, but equally easy to wipe them clean. The drawing-room into which Mrs Howard led him again presented space, great barenesses of wall and floor, huge and elegant emptiness, emphasized by plainness of carpet, smart gloss, few pictures, not big, not square, brand-new squat furniture under the high complications of the old embossed ceiling.

He was ushered to a chair, plain, slightly uncouth in design but very comfortable. Mrs Howard asked if he would care for a drink; he refused. She stood in hesitation at that, as if his refusal cast a slur on the form of her hospitality.

'Are the children in bed?' he asked.

'Oh, yes,' she said. 'Anna and I did that.'

'How many are there?'

'Three. Tom's eight, Simon six and Victoria three.'

She was a tall girl, younger than he imagined, but different. For some reason he had expected another small, pretty pert woman, another Sandra Moore, Lesley Allbright, a smart, hapless female, limited, feminine. Netta was tall, hadn't he been told so?, exquisitely dressed in dove-grey, without jewellery except for a broad wedding-ring, with large, blue, beautiful, watchful eyes, which seemed to judge him or prepare to do so. She sat, with marvellous speed; at one moment she had been standing, and at the next she was composed in her chair, and the time between infinitesimal or unnoticed.

'I'm glad you could come,' she said. She had recovered. 'I'm very unsure of what I should do. Mrs Brooks, Felicity, said I should see you.'

'You asked her?'

'Oh, yes. Why?'

'I thought it might be likely that her advice would be more useful than that of a stranger.'

'I don't quite look on you as a stranger. You met Veronica.'

'My effort there did no good.' He'd be honest.

Mrs Howard made sounds and signs of incomprehension so

that he gave a brief, unemotional account of his visit. When he had finished she asked, 'Did you talk to her sensibly about university entrance?'

'As far as I could, in the circumstances. I didn't know her well.'

'I'm sure you did your best.' Patronizing?

The young mother spoke diffidently, but from certainty. Here, as far as he could judge, was a person of consequence who, if she did not know her mind, could behave as if she did. No pointers suggested themselves. He waited for her.

'My husband, Simon,' she had begun again, 'had, was having an affair with Veronica Brooks. I knew nothing about this until a fortnight ago.'

Netta paused.

'You knew Veronica, though?' He'd establish his presence.

'Yes. Not very well. We met quite a few times, because Simon had business dealings with Conrad Brooks. We went to dinner there, to the theatre occasionally. Conrad is abroad a great deal, and Simon has to go away quite often.'

'And what was your impression of Veronica?'

'A fat, pretty girl, with a plummy voice. We'd heard something of her history, of course. Felicity made a cautionary tale of it when we talked about bringing up a family.'

'So his confession came as a surprise to you?'

'Yes, exactly. He said he had thought and thought about it after she died, and had decided to tell me. There was no need. I don't think I should have found out. I just don't know why he confessed. Perhaps he felt it was in some way connected with her death, that it might clear his guilt. I was surprised.'

'It was, I take it, uncharacteristic of him?'

'You've not met my husband. He's a scientist, a careful, let's-look-at-this-in-all-of-sixteen-ways man. So, I was amazed to hear that Veronica had attracted him. I could just about imagine his losing his head to some witty, highly intelligent quick-talking woman or to one who was beautiful, in a certain way, unusual, strikingly dressed. But he wouldn't be rushed off his feet. He's cool.' She laughed at her word, or at his facial reception of it. 'He is also very fond of his family. The feeling is distant but deep, if you understand me. He likes the idea of being a father, or a provider. But Veronica was, well, messy. You could see that. Untidy. If she dropped something she wouldn't bother to clear it up. She'd leave it to somebody else.' She flashed a glance at him, eyes momentarily wide, light-blue. He thought of a line of verse he'd learnt as an impressionable youth. *'Toute une mer immense où fuyaient des galères.'* 'I don't want you to think I am saying this out of pique.' She sighed. 'Perhaps I am. You'll have to make your mind up. But in my book Veronica Brooks was the last person he'd have fallen for.'

'But he did?'

'Apparently.'

They left it there for the minute. Netta looked about the room as if she searched for a conversational opening. She was still staring high into a far corner when she spoke again, making no attempt at intimacy, feigned or otherwise.

'I was also surprised that he confessed. That he thought fit to. There was no need.'

'You mean,' Richardson asked, 'that he knew it would cause trouble?'

'No. I mean, I should not have found out.' She slightly adjusted her position into one just as decorous. 'He sat me down, here, in this room one evening. When we were getting the children ready for bed he said he'd something he wished to say.'

'And that was out of the ordinary?'

'Yes and no. He'll ask my advice, and if he wants to do it without interruption he'll do it when the children aren't about. I didn't notice, either, that he seemed troubled. I didn't notice. Or I didn't feel apprehensive.'

'And?'

'We sat down. He said, "I've something I want to say to you. It may come as an unpleasant surprise. Shall I get you a drink?" I didn't want one. To tell you the truth, I thought it was something to do with his work. Perhaps he'd been made redundant. You hear such odd tales these days.'

'That would have surprised you?' Richardson.

'Utterly.' She nodded as if she had checked judgement with memory. 'He then went on to tell me that it was about Veronica. "We had an affair," he said. "Recently? Was it going on when

167

she died?" It was. He sketched what had happened, and I suppose I asked one or two questions which he answered. He said he was sorry, and I asked why he'd told me. He said that it seemed honest. He went on talking, making things clear, and, I'll say this for him, he looked very ashamed. Head hanging.'

'And how did you take it?'

'It's difficult to describe just now. I was taken aback, but there was an element of excitement that . . . that kept me from realizing exactly what it was he was saying. So I just sat there. After a time he talked again about the, the, er, relationship, but I noticed he never offered me any explanation why it had happened. That was presumably because it would have implied that I was in some way to blame, that I had shortcomings. Again, he was very sorry and he hoped I could forgive him, but he couldn't have lived with himself if he hadn't confessed.' Netta lifted her head. 'I wondered straight away if he would have told me if she had still been alive, but I didn't say anything. It was up to him to finish off his piece or damn himself. I think it annoyed him that I didn't make any comment.' She stopped again, as if making sure of her recollection or teaching him the value of silence. Richardson responded in kind. Neither looked at the other. Outside the day was brilliant still. Netta rose, walked to the window, stared out.

'He jumped up in the end,' she said, back to her guest, 'and grabbed hold of the top of his chair. His hands looked agitated. And he spurted out, "What do you say, Netta? Don't just sit there silent. I know what I've done is reprehensible, but at least I've told you, when there was no need." ' She smiled. 'I know he used the word "reprehensible"; it struck me at the time. It wasn't the sort of word I'd use. It seemed typical of him as I knew him, not of this other man who committed adultery with a neurotic girl. I'd no idea what to say. "This is a shock. I shall need time to get used to it." Something of that sort. I mumbled over that a time or two, and even while I was doing it, it didn't seem real. Or pertinent.'

As soon as she had finished speaking, Netta Howard suddenly loosed a small shriek of laughter, quite out of keeping with her appearance. Her face soon restored itself to calm.

168

'I've just remembered,' she said, 'that at this point the phone went and Simon answered it. It was the decorator, and Si knew nothing about it, and had to call me out. And then we had to fix up between us when it was convenient for the man to come in to make a start. It was like a comic turn, and when it had finished we just went back and he started all over again, and I said, "Go away, get from under my feet and give me a few moments to think." '

'And he did?'

'I wish now he hadn't. I didn't know what to do, or think, how to blow my top or calm myself. It was mad. In the end I locked all the doors, the au pair had gone out, took a couple of sleeping pills and went to bed. Simon wasn't about; he'd made for one of the spare beds; we've plenty. I wished he hadn't. We should have had another blazing row, and perhaps got it over. He turned up at breakfast as usual and nothing untoward was said. He telephoned me mid-morning and it was then I told him to clear out. I said the house would be empty between two and three-thirty and he could take out what he wanted and that would be that.'

'You said this suddenly?'

'I half expected him to ring. I'd become angrier, and had made my mind up by that time.'

'Did he not attempt to argue?' Richardson asked.

'Oh, yes. You don't know him. Was it wise? What should I say to the children? I ought to see Peter Hughes, our solicitor. Oh, a whole lot of stuff. We mustn't do anything precipitate. It made me madder and I just told him to collect his belongings that afternoon before I changed the locks. By the time I'd finished, I was convinced I'd done the right thing.'

'But you haven't?'

She glanced up, in arrogance.

'Why do you say that?'

'What does Mrs Brooks think?' He'd trade question for question.

'That I should have him back.'

'Is she a sensible woman, would you say?'

'Yes. But her sense, or wisdom, or whatever else it is she has, didn't save Veronica, did it?' His own argument returned.

'Why does she think you should allow him back?'

'The children, mostly. They need a father.'

'Would you agree?'

'Yes. I suppose so. Yes. I'm not sure, though, if the parents are fighting like cats all the time.'

'And that's what will happen?'

Her face registered a spasm of boredom.

'Possible,' she said.

'You wouldn't try to . . .'

'Try,' she interrupted. 'I might not be able.'

He paused, having no idea whether he was making progress. T. S. Eliot's epigraph drifted into his mind.

> 'Thou hast committed
> Fornication: but that was in another country
> And besides, the wench is dead.'

Marlowe, was it? *The Jew of Malta*? He'd never read it. Epigraph to what? He could not remember and this angered him, slightly. Joanna would know.

'Now,' his voice purred, 'you must tell me what you think you should do.'

'I change my mind. Sometimes I'm bloody angry. And then half an hour later I think we might make a go of it. I miss him sometimes. I'm used to his being here.'

'That's better than nothing as a start.'

'Is it?' A dry, clipped question, out of keeping with the young beauty.

'It's not the be-all and end-all, but at least you are not physically repelled by him.'

'Was that likely?'

'It could happen,' he said, and she cocked her head to give the appearance of consideration of this factor.

'What sticks in my craw,' Netta Howard said, speaking quickly, surprising him with the image, 'is that he could do such a thing, and I'd no idea either what he was about, or that he was capable. It's so uncharacteristic.'

'The secrecy?'

'No. He'd manage that, though I doubt if she could. Even if she cared. No, the affair. She must have led him on.'

'Some men,' he answered, 'do it just to prove to themselves that they're still alive, out of incapacity, really.'

'We had a good sexual relationship,' Netta said. 'Very good. You don't believe that, do you?'

'I've no means of checking.'

'You don't believe it, do you?' He sat back; the repeated question was not strident, quietly insistent on truth, perhaps. 'I wouldn't mind so much, I say I wouldn't, if that weren't the truth, if he was trying to prove himself to himself.'

'She might have tempted him, and he was flattered, and yielded.'

'And gone on yielding?'

'Yes. Isn't there plenty of talk, if nothing worse, in the business circles he occupies about sexual success?'

'No more than anywhere else.'

'You mean the whole of society is obsessed with it?' No answer. 'Was Veronica promiscuous?'

'How do I know? An abortion at fifteen hardly suggests otherwise.'

She faced him now, an enemy, as if his questions had goaded her beyond reason. He waited, weighing her up.

'I think,' he said, 'that if I may, I'd like the drink you offered me earlier.'

Netta seemed not to hear, then leapt up.

'Yes.' Voice unflurried. 'What would you like?'

'A very small Scotch and water, please.'

She had to leave the room for the water. On her return he refused ice. She served him before pouring herself a bitter lemon into a long glass, at which she stared as though it held poison. He touched his lips with his drink.

'I don't think,' he began carefully, 'that anything you've said has much altered the view I held when I came in. I knew that Felicity Brooks thought you should take your husband back. She was also emotionally concerned in the whole business. It was her daughter who died. But you've said nothing to suggest she advises this out of malice. She seems to like you, and your husband. She doesn't hold Veronica's death against him, as she might easily. So, if you press me for advice, you can guess what my answer will be.'

'You hardly know the first thing about it.'

'I admit that.'

'And yet you still tell me what to do. Is it because of the children?'

'In the main, yes. But I feel you'll still be able to cope, to make something of a life with your husband. I'm not telling you that what he's done is nothing. It isn't, and you won't forget it. But you'll come to terms with it.'

She lifted her drink, wagging it so that the ice clipped the glass.

'That's it, then, is it?' she asked.

He nodded.

'How does it strike you?' he asked her. Silence. Her face seemed flushed; a small undeep frown puckered flesh. Her glass, returned to the table, ice-cubes large, floating lemon slice, still dominated her attention. She coughed drily, scourging her throat, before she began to talk, avoiding him with her eyes.

'I've not made my mind up.'

'That's sensible,' he said, 'but you shouldn't delay your decision too long.'

'It makes me angry to hear you laying down the law.' Netta did not sound so. 'You've no idea how I feel.' The tone was off-hand.

'I'm sorry.'

'Oh, I know what you think. I've seen these pictures on television of young soldiers' widows with their children, and I know I'm better off than they are. But they have no choice. They know how they have to move.'

'You're not suggesting,' Richardson spoke with a head-master's asperity, 'that it would have been better if Simon had died?'

'No, I'm not. And you know I'm not. It's just I don't like it when you say I should do this or that, especially as you know nothing about it.'

'That's hardly fair to me. I was invited here, and I thought I'd been particularly careful not to be dogmatic. If it seems otherwise to you, then I can only apologize.'

'It's your whole attitude,' she said. 'You know, and I don't, and that's that.'

172

Her distress, her hot voice demonstrated this, touched him. It did not seem reasonable, certainly, and his vanity was hurt, he had assumed he could help this good-looking young woman.

'You don't know, and you can't know what I feel.'

'Will you tell me, then?'

'No, I shan't. Why should I?'

It was as if she had switched to another personality; the hostess with her controlled voice in the subdued lighting of a modern drawing-room had changed into an adolescent, squaring up to a hostile, unjust world of unsympathetic adults. At any moment, he felt, she might lash out with her feet, physically kick him.

'Perhaps it would be better if I went,' he said, softly, not moving.

She did not answer, but dashed a furious look out beyond, behind her. Action would relieve her, steady her nerves.

'You'd like to punch me on the jaw, wouldn't you?' he asked, without emphasis.

'No.' Gnashed off.

'It might do us both good.'

Netta, locked to her chair, seemed unable to come to terms with spoken language. Her lips moved, were licked, but enunciated nothing. The silence in the room grew; headache plagued Richardson; breathing became difficult. He would have to make the effort, but he lacked the energy. He groped for something to do, noticed his drink, raised it to his mouth, but the movement was without effect. She paid no attention to him, had turned half away, a posture sometimes adopted by children who considered themselves wronged. He finished his drink, weak as water, returned the glass to the table.

Nothing happened.

The house seemed unalive; outside, the dazzle of daylight faded into warm pink. Tomorrow would be bright.

'I'm sorry, Mrs Howard,' he made himself speak, 'but I seem to have done no good. I'd better go.' No sign; the rudeness of non-recognition. 'I'm sure you will be able to . . .' In his lowness he could not decide on a proper form of words. He blew breath out; she did not speak; he abandoned his sentence.

After a moment he rose.

He swayed a moment, shifted his feet and directed his attention down on her.

'Goodbye, then,' he said. 'Thank you for listening to me.'

She shrugged up from her chair, preceded him to the door.

In the hall he held out his hand. The enormous front door was more than half of stained-glass, swirls and ogees of green, blue, dulling yellow, red, lead-lined between the solidity of the woodwork.

'That's a beautiful door,' he said, 'beautiful.'

She took his hand briefly, without hostility, firmly, but did not speak.

'Goodbye,' he said. 'I hope it all goes well with you. I'm sure it will.'

Netta slightly bowed her head, then opened the door for him. He stood on the steps and the heavy door clicked to.

In the open air it was brighter than he expected, warm still. He took to the winding path between shrub roses, large but flowerless now. The few yards along the pavement did him no good; four grand houses well back from the lime trees, behind green depths of front gardens, only upper storeys showing, put him in his place, the stranger in the street, the hawker repulsed by the same notice which directed tradesmen to the back door.

As he unlocked his car, he could make out the electric lights in the Brookses' drawing-room, and he stood for a minute. He could hear a thumping, the insistent bass of a pop record, then vaguely the upper parts, a wailing, a reeling over the drum-heavy beat below. It seemed to come from the Brookses'. Stephen? Felicity?

There were no clues, only the unimportant noise that he might well have missed.

He made for home, and Joanna.

16

The weather in France scorched, though twice the Richardsons were lashed by thunderstorms. They took the car but largely lounged about. 'Daddy amongst the topless ladies' was the subject of the girls' photographs, though they themselves rarely removed bikini tops on the beaches, Joanna never. Richardson was determined that he would go easy for the first fortnight, do not a stroke of work, but found that inaction or the reading of books because they were to hand and for no other reason unprofitable. His daughters were content to dash in and out of the sea, making riotous friends on whom they practised gobbets of French. In the overwhelming power of the sun, the girls, like the hundreds of other young people round about, acted out some ritual of running, leaping, shouting, splashing, followed by shortish periods of roasting stillness. They seemed both younger, so that Fay could join in, with overturned lilo or beach-ball, and particularly in Margot's case older, attracting not only adolescents but at least long appraisal from poncho-moustached, nut-brown young fathers of families. Her parents could not be sure whether their daughter was aware of her attractions, discussed the matter often.

'She's womanly,' Joanna pronounced. Marguerite held a statuesque pose as she waited on her sisters with the thermos; male admiration spread over wide metres of strand around her. The next moment, the flask returned, her limbs flashed across the beach as she outran and outshouted the excitable Virginia and staider people smiled their satisfaction.

'Are you enjoying yourselves?' he asked Fay.

'Oh, yes.'

'But we're only just sitting about.'

'You are,' Virginia said. 'We aren't.'

'Don't you think we ought to see something of the country while we're in it?'

'We're speaking French,' Virginia said.

'You are,' Fay objected.

'Of sorts,' Joanna, in truth.

The girls laughed, sun-drenched, dizzy with the table wine, worn to frazzles by the hot end of the day, ready for anything by the next. In one of the evening thunderstorms the three of them ran circling out in the grounds of the hotel, were soaked within seconds, and joined within a minute by a half-dozen French admirers to play tag as the lightning split or filled the sky and the leaves gushed, spouting like broken conduits.

'Just look at those idiots,' Joanna said, not without pride.

A crowd of guests gathered at the windows to enjoy the antics.

'I'm surprised Fay's out there,' Richardson told his wife. 'She's usually scared of thunder.'

'Behaviour inside the peer group. Isn't that what your book would call it?'

He did not argue.

The garden flashed full of screaming figures, hair in rats' tails, shirts and dresses plastered to young bodies.

'You know who started this?' Joanna asked.

'Margot?'

'No. Virginia. She was out like a shot.'

'You didn't stop her?'

'Too late. No chance.'

'It's not very sensible. They'll be saturated.'

'We've plenty of towels.'

'It's dangerous.' He remembered that holiday, and her lip curling in scorn made him certain she agreed.

The shrieking outside whirled noisier. Virginia had fiercely repeated a phrase she had learnt from childhood stories, which was still quoted, though loftily, by Fay. 'Run, run, as fast as you can; you can't catch me, I'm the gingerbread man.' The sentences were taken up, sounding ridiculous and obscure, shouted by men in French accents, the beaux who took care in spite of the haphazard appearance of the sport to be within touching distance of Margot, a school-girlish but magnificent figure, a goddess round whom the dance gyrated. 'Zheenzhaire brrhed,' boys called, teeth bared with laughter.

Margot led the retreat.

She trotted to the door of the bar–lounge.

'Go round the back, darling,' Joanna warned. 'You'll ruin the carpets.'

'It does not matter, madame,' the host, who had stood among the applauding guests. 'Let them come.'

'Shoes off, then.'

Margot shook the hair from her forehead; its wet straggle in no way diminished the beauty of the fine oval face. She dabbed for a minute with the large handkerchief her father produced, and ran smiling, dripping for the stairs. Joanna called in Fay and Virginia; others followed. Puddles shone on the floorboards. Another job for the servants. A violent flash of lightning was immediately marked by a volley of thunder that trembled profoundly through foundations and walls.

'Close,' Richardson said, to nobody. Joanna had slipped off upstairs to supervise the drying operation.

Outside, in a thick, straight-rod downpour, two show-off boys were left, chasing, wrestling, finally falling into a sheet of water. The guests paid no attention, returning to conversation, newspapers, indigestion. Reason had re-established itself, and as a young lad from the kitchen sloppily mopped up the water into a bowl, the lounge door was shut on the revellers, who had to find their own ridiculous way in through the back.

The storm played itself out, with a further twenty minutes of frightening, sky-shattering tricks, but middle-aged decorum prevailed inside with small glasses discreetly raised. When the trio of English girls returned to civilization, in crisp frocks, small approbationary smiles touched even the lips of firm French mothers. Youth had had its fling, without harm done, and here were the misses as good as new, fresh as paint, hair dry and with books in their hands.

Both parents, proud that their daughters made so favourable an impression, wondered, pondered. The children were obviously beautiful, better mannered than at home, and took no advantage of the admiration they excited.

'Do you miss Stephen?' Richardson asked Marguerite.

'Not really.'

'It's Pierre she likes now,' Virginia interrupted.

177

'You mean, you do.' Fay.

Pierre, a student of oriental languages at the Sorbonne, practised English on Margot's parents, explaining to them with a diffidence denied by his intonation the complexities and beauties of Arabic. He had spoken it, or some unacceptable patois, from childhood in North Africa, where he had been born. He was perhaps twenty and spent his holiday here at this hotel, on his own, like a middle-aged bachelor. Even Joanna spoke approvingly of his tan and his short curls. Margot enjoyed his company, but unlike Virginia made no attempt to seek him out, or monopolize him. He walked handsomely; the fuzz of light hair on his chest glistened to perfection; he could do anything, hand- or head-stands, improvised surfing, rowing, racing, clambering, but Marguerite Richardson could take it all in without losing composure.

'She's not aware of the impression she's made,' Joanna reported. 'I'm sure she thinks he's marvellous, but has no inkling he's attracted in return.'

'Is that usual? Was it so with you?'

'Perhaps. In some ways she's young for her years. But somebody will wake her up to it.'

'That happened to you?'

'It did. And not a thousand miles away from here.'

'Is that why you chose Carnac?'

'Could be.'

Joanna marched off to collect the next set of necessities, grinning to herself.

One or twice Richardson had raised the matter of the interview with Netta Howard, but his wife had been dismissive.

'Forget it,' she had said.

He knew that she deliberately used these snippets of popular wisdom or phraseology because he would dislike them, and this suggested uncertainty on her part. He could not leave it alone, questioned her.

'Look,' she answered, 'I don't like to see you worrying yourself. In your job you're going to have some setbacks. Sometimes because you're only nominally responsible, and sometimes because at your distance there's nothing you can do. You've been lucky so far. And that's partly because you're good at your job, and that's landed you in a middle-class school where the crises aren't quite so unmanageable. But you can't do everything.'

'I utterly misjudged this Howard business.'

'So you tell me.'

'Mrs Howard listened and talked as rationally as I could hope, and then suddenly I found she had set her face against me, wouldn't be helped, disliked me and all I stood for . . .'

'You can't say, John,' Joanna must have been serious for she rarely called him by his first name, 'why that was. It may have nothing to do with you on a personal level. Of course, she may have found you,' pause, ironic teeth-tapping, 'unacceptable, and that could have been something more to do with her, her past, her personality than with anything you are. On the other hand she may have been taking it all in, and profiting from it, when, click, suddenly, crack-bang, she can stand no more, the thin skin's burst . . .'

'I ought to have seen that coming.'

'Don't be daft. How could you? People are unpredictable. If you haven't learnt that in your job . . .' Joanna spoke irascibly, but he judged she was putting it on. 'I don't know this woman, don't particularly want to if truth be told, but if she was sufficiently bruised to show the breadwinner the door, then . . . Well she's either stinking rich, or badly hurt. Too much to be cured with an hour's soft soap, however skilfully applied.'

'I see.'

'I hope you do. Part of your job is to have distraught young women, or disgruntled members of your staff, or undeserving or unbalanced pupils, throwing your kindness back into your face. If you haven't cottoned on to that, it's time you had.'

'What must I do?' he asked, comically, biblically.

'If it was me, when they spat in my eye, I'd spit straight back. But that's why I'd be no good at all. Put up with it. Look pleasant. Grin and abide. Come to tell Mummy all about it.'

'I will.'

'The only work you can be sure is exactly right is when you turn out nuts and bolts on a factory bench. And that's boring.' She stood nearer. 'You're always going to be the rowing coach bawling through your megaphone. Or more likely, the infant teacher trying to control her fractious charges from the far side of the road. It has its advantages.'

'And Netta Howard?'

'I don't know her. By your account she can be unpleasant. And, in any case, people who are going to survive do so because they can sort themselves out. That doesn't do much for your ego, but it's near the truth.'

He and Joanna seemed particularly close that holiday, discussing his book and what his editor would make of it. She approved of his line: a watchful advancing conservatism and prophesied that Laura Wykes, the editor, would try to press him into conclusions more radical than those he held.

'She's in a hurry,' Joanna said, 'and so she'll want ferocity from you.'

'Such as?'

'I don't know. I've only met her once. But I guess she'd like you peddling some fancy line, oh, that the television picture and the computer print-out have replaced the printed page as the high points of our civilization.'

'Oh, I don't think . . .'

'Well, the other way about, then. Value of examinations – strict academic tests for all. Latin verbs for eighty per cent of the population. Firm-handed discipline, respect for elders and betters, corporal punishment.'

'Oh, no.'

'This is an age of extremes. At present in Britain they're held in check, disguised, but they're there. At both ends of the political spectrum. Moreover, she'll regard your book as ephemeral, a bit of pulp journalism, forgotten as soon as the first edition's sold out. Oh, I know, even if you won't say so outright, that you see it as a classic, a document to be consulted by the next generation, a contribution to the history of ideas. But not our Ms Wykes.'

'You've taken against her.'

'Not her, particularly. They're all like that. And that's why she'll tempt you, or push you, or inveigle you, or whatever the word is, into some strong statement that'll catch the eye of the press, and get your name in the papers, because that'll lead to second and third editions and paperbacks . . .'

'And film rights?' he mocked.

'I can see I shan't convince you. You're as good as lost already.'

'But Laura's an academic, with a distinguished career.'

'The second's right. She knows which side her bread's buttered. If she can produce an educational best-seller at a time of recession and retrenchment, she'll go down a bomb with her employers. "Fridges to Eskimos" isn't in it. She's clever. She did well at university, as you did, because she set her stall out, and a well-decked stall it probably was, to please her teachers, and she spent all her time doing that. You and I might well approve of the ideals of the dons she sucked up to. Or, on the whole we do. But she's out in the wicked world now.'

'And what am I to do against this big, bad she-wolf?'

'Know exactly what it is you want to say.'

'That's not altogether me, now, is it?'

'It's not altogether anybody but a few selected lunatics, but most people are more certain in print than in actuality, at least in your line of business.'

He remembered this conversation when he returned. Joanna was proved right; Laura Wykes had her eye-catching line at the ready. Though it did not concern itself with principles so much, it still asserted at greater length than he had intended an idea that he held, but she wanted it stated without disclaimers. It concerned money. She offered him statistics, said he'd know where to find more, to prove that one received back in the educational and social worlds what one invested. Put money in; success. Cheese-pare as at present and the result was a falling of standards and its concomitants in life outside schools. He could not hold this view crudely expressed, and his resulting compromise ensured that when the book appeared it was savaged by national and local politicians on the one hand, and by teachers and their unions on the other, in their case because he suggested that one did not make the most economical use of highly trained people. But it achieved what Ms Wykes wanted: a controversy in the media. He appeared on television, wrote three articles for the *Guardian*, and consequently felt not only unpopular but uncertain of his rôle. Now he stood no longer in the firm Arnoldian tradition, seeing life steadily and whole, but was marked down as a wild boy, a biter of the feeding hand, a traitor to his own subordinates, untrustworthy, a maverick, unsound. Joanna's view that there could be no bad publicity brought no comfort; he had wished to be popular, and had found many enemies.

But while they were in Brittany he prepared to speak expertly.

'You mustn't be disappointed,' Joanna said. 'Or you must be prepared to be so.'

'Why?'

'Who's interested in education these days?'

'I hope this will stir people.'

'It'll be read by lecturers in education departments and colleges and by people who want some ideas to bandy about in interviews for promotion. And that's probably as it should be.'

'You cut me down to size,' he told her, affectionately enough, because he could still hope strongly that she was wrong.

He managed to convince his family that they should visit some of the prehistoric sites. They stood and grimaced, and walked round the monuments, puzzling themselves so that father was pleased.

'At least they lasted,' Joanna said.

'I think,' Margot, 'that they ought to have shaped the stones, chiselled them into pillars, or idols or something.'

'It's the placing of the pieces perhaps that matters,' Joanna suggested. 'Relative to the sun or moon or planets.'

'And maybe they didn't want to interfere with the natural forms.' Richardson. 'They felt the numinous in what existed and so brought it into places where it could be used.'

'I wouldn't like to have to move them.'

'Daddy and I built a rockery once,' Joanna said. 'We had to place what Daddy's groundsman called "horses' heads", only about three feet long, and it nearly killed us.'

'You don't work out of doors all the time,' Virginia told them. 'You're not cave-dwellers.'

They consulted the guidebooks, argued about wooden rollers and wheels and quarrying, without much conviction. Joanna thought that Chaucer's *Franklin's Tale* was set hereabouts, and was compelled by her daughters to tell them what she remembered of black rocks and sorcery. The girls were not impressed.

'There is something magical about this coast,' Richardson said, defending his wife. 'It's old, detached from our civilization.'

'But all of geology's like that,' Marguerite said. 'Rocks existed hundreds of millions of years before men.'

Richardson, delighted with his daughters, who seemed to grasp something of the hidden attractions of landscape and yet kept their heads, asked Virginia what she made of the cromlechs and menhirs.

'Very good,' she answered briskly, 'but a bit boring.'

That was a present for him, a bonus. The girl wanted to please him, but not at the expense of honesty. He could well imagine in another twenty-odd years that Ginny, a second Joanna, would insist on bringing her family out here to lecture them. She'd march them round the museum on wet days: he wondered if Joanna had ever danced in the thunderstorms.

Fay was much affected at the first weekend when some of the guests left. Joanna reported tears, not only for one or two beach companions of her own age, but for some grown-ups, especially one middle-aged couple, who had presented her each day after breakfast with a delicious wrapped sweet.

'What did they say?' her mother had asked, discovering the child chewing one morning.

'Here's something to suck before you clean your teeth.'

'You could understand them saying that?'

'They spoke English. They are English.'

'Do they hand Ginny a sweet?'

'If she's there. I'm always there.'

'You aren't making a nuisance of yourself?'

'No, but they are lovely. French sweets. Bigger than ours, and tasting of real fruit.'

'There's something about these children of ours,' Richardson said. 'This holiday's brought it out.'

'It's given you the leisure to observe it.'

'What will they be like, I wonder, in ten years?'

'There's no telling.' Joanna spoke firmly. 'We don't know what society will be like. It may be the recession will be over, and there'll be jobs for all. It can be that forty-hour weeks will never exist again, and then what?'

'But scientists will want to be working in their research labs at all hours even if, let's say, people in factories or general practitioners only do two days a week.'

'I'm not sure. You're perhaps right. It could be there are some people who'd sooner do boring work than laze in the garden or take up a hobby. Society, our society's all compromise in spite of anomalies. We all toe the line to some extent.'

'And our girls?' he asked.

'They're different from one another. And they change so quickly. Margot now. I'd never seen her so definite as she is at this moment.'

'She's the belle of the ball,' he said.

'I could have told you that was going to happen, but she makes her mind up so quickly.'

'Just like you,' he said. 'And Ginny.'

Joanna drifted away but only by a yard or two.

'I saw some photographs of Veronica Brooks as a child. Felicity insisted on showing me. She seemed like any other little girl. I mean, there was no hint of tragedy. There she stood or sat, lively and sturdy. And I wonder. And I look at Fay.'

'That's one with her wits about her,' he said.

'As far as we can tell.'

The conversation dashed his spirits for half an hour, and he troubled himself imagining what Netta Howard, Sandra Moore, Lesley Allbright were like as children, and then giving them suitably unsuitable parents. His uncomfortable reverie was broken by the arrival of Virginia, who said that as the wind blew this morning they'd visit the museum of prehistoric remains again, and Pierre Thibaud would like to accompany them.

'Hasn't he been before?' he demanded mischievously.

'I expect so. One always sees more the second time round.'

That put him in his place.

'I feel really safe in museums,' Richardson said. She turned back, willing to spare her father a minute or two before she broke the good news to Pierre or Margot or both. She had raised her eyebrows in question, stood waiting exactly like mother for instruction. 'Time has stopped. You have artefacts that have lasted for thousands or hundreds of years, and there they are classified. You don't think about death in circumstances such as that. Correction, I don't.'

'But the people are all dead. Not only the original makers, but probably as well the men who found them, and wrote out the labels.'

'That's true, but the typewritten titles and glass cases don't make me dwell on my own death. Even when I'm thinking about theirs. I get the same sort of feeling in a book-lined study or a library. I'm secure, for the present. Protected from unpleasant thoughts.'

The girl looked at him, with a faint misery, expressed by drooping of shoulders, a carelessness of stance, but she recovered sharply enough.

'It takes all sorts,' she said, matter-of-fact.

There spoke the mother's girl; the body firmed, confirmed itself as she wheeled, and darted away, not looking back, but Joanna reported that Ginny had told her that Dad was morbid sometimes.

'And what did you say?'

'Nothing. "Morbid" often means "what I dislike". I wondered what you'd been telling her.'

He repeated the conversation as best he could. Her eyebrows rose, comically, and then she laughed.

'One couldn't say you hadn't tried to educate your children.'

That cheered them both.

The last week of the holiday passed quickly. Richardson remembered how this happened in his boyhood. Monday, Tuesday, Wednesday stretched luxuriously long; Thursday and Friday flashed by; when cases were packed, his father walked the family down to the beach, half deserted even in sunshine, for a final breath of sea air. John did not want last glimpses; he loved the sand, deck-chairs, ice-creams, pierrots, only so long as they were his all day.

The final chapter of his book was planned in his head; he could write it in less than a week once he arrived home. Virginia arranged to correspond with Pierre, photographed him from all angles.

'Will you write in English or French?' Joanna asked.

'English. I shall. I might put the odd sentence in French.'

'Doesn't Margot mind?' Father, interfering.

'Why should she?' Ginny answered. 'He wouldn't write to me if it wasn't for her.'

The last-night farewells were cheerful; Joanna drank just a little too much and this made her giggle, and her laughter was infectious. The girls seemed to approve, to be protective of this slightly unusual mother; the parents made love, forgetful of thin walls.

They spent a day at Rouen on their way to Dieppe, where Richardson indulged his fantasy that he'd take up watercolour painting.

Margot offered advice; Joanna dubbed him Bonington for half a day; Virginia crossly confessed she hated art, and Fay said she liked a picture of apples on a plate they had at school. The holiday, in retrospect, seemed jam-packed with these family conversations, slightly cultural, part-confessional and yet artificial, as if they were all actors put up on a stage and told to improvise. Sometimes they aimed near truth, or sometimes showed off, prevaricated, rid themselves of the melancholy of the moment or reflected the bright sunshine. They were not, Richardson decided, to his eyes, the wife and family he observed in term-time.

'Will you be glad to be back?' he asked Fay, on the ferry.
'No.'

'Would you like to live in France, then?'

'For a little bit longer.'

'You like it when you get home,' Virginia told him. 'You've a great big pile of fascinating letters to read.'

'Mostly adverts, or demands. I'll be lucky to find one that's anything like interesting.'

'I don't like the shut-up smell of the house,' Joanna said.

'We've seen you throwing the windows open,' Ginny, 'however cold it is.'

'You oughtn't to feel the cold at your age, m'girl.' The mother; the tone of the sentence demonstrated Joanna was not altogether pleased to return.

'I think it's cold now, on this ship,' Fay told them.

'Who didn't need a thick cardigan?'

'How about you, Margot?'

186

Marguerite, by the rail watching the churning wake, did not hear or answer.

'She's got Stephen waiting for her,' Ginny said.

'Is he home, then?'

'I expect so.'

Marguerite turned her head, smiled at them, unaware that they were talking about her, wrapped up in the moment, the knock-about winds, the heavy wash of churning water, the metallic call of the gulls. Richardson, camera at the ready, snapped her, found his safety-catch still on, had to ask her to smile again. She obliged, and the factitious matched the spontaneous in beauty.

17

Within twenty-four hours of arrival home they had put the holiday aside. Joanna's washing machine seemed switched on for two solid days; the girls disappeared to their rooms, or those of friends; meals were listless occasions for eating. It took a week for spirits to be restored to normal courtesy.

Richardson completed his chapter inside ten days and carted the completed work to London. He offered to make this a family outing, but his editor chose a day when Joanna was engaged, and the girls lacked keenness. In the end he took Fay, who sat wide-eyed while Laura Wykes drank a glass of wine with him, and talked, with her usual violence, but as if her mind fought elsewhere. She couldn't give him a date for publication, not at least until she had read it, since she'd probably have alterations to suggest. They might as well do it properly while they were about it.

She spoke with confidence, as if she had it in her power to force him to write a good book when he would himself have been satisfied with a mediocre. It was incredible. This young woman, the word 'upstart' presented itself, six or seven years younger than he, who had probably last been in a school when she said farewell to her ladies' college before she went up to Oxford, had the arrogance to believe, or, worse, the hypocrisy to suggest, that she could tell him where he went wrong. He sipped the sour white wine, and felt angry. Ms Wykes's room was piled with books and papers, her desk a chaos amongst which she rummaged with confidence, found what she searched for; she handled her two telephones, her secretary, an intruding smooth type from publicity, and the managing director, who looked in, was introduced, breezed out, with a laughing, first-name aplomb that impressed. Her office, he noticed, that of a part-time editor, in expensive London, in days when publishers thought of little beside economies, was larger than his study back in the Midlands. At least, he comforted himself, his was tidier. It was quite likely that she shared this place with one, two or three other people, and that was the cause of these tottering piles of bumf.

He put his lips to the cold wine, wondering why he had refused coffee. Fay sat, pert and at ease with her large glass of ersatz orangeade, watching him. She had answered la Wykes with conversational grace, and now, with her feet not touching the floor, sat waiting in interest for the next development.

Laura laid down the law.

Shrugging inwardly, Richardson saw that he was on the receiving end of what he handed out every day in school.

Like him, she had the authority, or the authoritative voice; she sat behind the desk; she was interrupted by important phone messages or callers and could immediately take up her harangue where she had left off. She knew what was best, because she had experience of the world of publishing as he had in education; she would listen, take account of his objections, but on the assured basis that she knew what she was talking about as he didn't.

So he paused here, before this young mandarin, like a sixth former who needed to be convinced that one course had more advantages than another, or a head of department who had to be argued out of a pet scheme which would put some favoured notion of his own at risk or antagonize the rest of the staff. Her voice rang, strong, far-back, assertive. 'The market for educational philosophy, any marginal academic ventures, is in a volatile state these days. We expect it of fiction, of course. Thank God that's not my pigeon. But the difference between a good, commercial success and an absolute flop, and I mean "absolute", may depend on the re-writing of a few pages here, the re-shuffling or deletion of perfectly acceptable material there. I don't want you to be disappointed, because this in its way is an important contribution to social thinking at a time when such writing, such thinking is rare . . .' She looked him straight in the eye. Simplify the language, he thought, and he could hear himself convincing some awkward parents that the headmaster's contrary suggestion was exactly what they had wanted from the beginning.

He took out a perfectly ironed square of handkerchief to blow his nose.

When they were dismissed they lunched in a trattoria before Fay chose, to his surprise, the Science Museum rather than the V. and A. He must have described the one with more enthusiasm than the other. They tramped about, enjoying knowledgeable fathers and excited serious sons inspecting gleaming and archaic machinery. Best of all were jam and cream pastries for high tea. Though Fay seemed imperturbable through the day, skipping only from an excess of physical energy, and serene on the train which arrived half an hour behind time, she slept next morning until eleven o'clock.

'Did you feel tired?' Joanna asked. Mother and daughter shared amazed delight at the lateness of the hour.

'No.'

'Did Daddy make you walk a lot?'

'A bit.'

Richardson presented himself at school for the 'A' level results.

He kept out of the way while the secretaries, the deputy in charge of examinations and a couple of departmental heads tore off the result slips, put them into prepared envelopes. He locked his door, sat still as a stone, listened to the comments through the thin wall of the office as he read the dull, holiday mail and a duller report on literature for ethnic minorities.

'If that bloody idiot can get an A and a special One . . .' That was the head of the history department, a man of high standards and low prejudices, who had resolutely set his face against the head's teaching any examination forms in this, Richardson's own, subject. The senior English master had on the other hand welcomed him, but he didn't care, one said, and would have given the caretaker an 'A' level set if it relieved him of work. He wasn't there this morning, of course; he'd be hitting a golf-ball round one of the local courses, taking 50p a hole off other good players. The senior mathematician was bleating; computer studies had come up trumps again. Stanley Smith descended late, took over the lists; results in chemistry bettered prognostications but only by four per cent. Smith quietened the others, seeming to inhabit a larger, more orderly world, where people and figures did as they were bid. Richardson guessed the majority would be relieved when Smith left them for the inspectorate. 'He hardly seemed a mortal like the rest.' Where was that gem from? Lord Nelson? One of those Stanford sea-things Herbert Hargreaves had dashed his college choir through given half a chance.

By the time the staff had dispersed for lunch, Richardson had commandeered a packet of results and begun the laborious job of making his own summary. He did not mind the chore; it kept his teachers up to scratch. By tomorrow morning, when pupils in need of advice appeared, the headmaster would know what he was talking about and would have written notes of congratulation to the departments who had excelled and polite invitations to discuss the results to those less fortunately placed. He believed in old-fashioned competition, and they knew it. 'Examinations test teaching.' His own 'A' level English set had done well.

He completed the work, asked Miss Taylor's department to check and then type the lists. On the way home, he had decided against the car in favour of a bus ride and a half-hour walk, a woman stopped him, mouth grimacing from an otherwise unexpressive face.

'Mrs Miller,' she said.

Once she named herself he placed her; the woman whose daughter had been going round with a West Indian boy.

'Samantha has done well in the terminal examinations,' he

said. He felt a small pride that he had remembered his promise to keep an eye on her work.

'Yes. She has,' said Mrs Miller. 'Will she get her "A" levels next year?'

Richardson spoke about the necessity of constant application and the parent appeared as pleased as her features allowed. He wondered how old she was, under forty in all probability, and how she could allow herself to look so unattractive while spending freely on her clothes and her hair. At seventeen she might have been as attractive as Samantha. What did her husband think? Was she counted a choice specimen amongst her age and class? He dismissed the unworthy thoughts.

'She's not having much to do with that black lad.'

'I see.'

'She's on about goin' to university.'

'That's a distinct possibility.'

'But what's the good? Her dad keeps asking me. When she's finished there she won't be able to find a job, will she? That's what the papers say.'

He offered her statistics, gently and repetitively, unsure whether she'd grasp or remember his argument. The woman listened, said dismissively, 'All that studyin', and then she'll like get married and start a family.'

'How old were you when you had Samantha, Mrs Miller?'

She blushed; under the dull make-up she reddened.

'Seventeen.' She brazened it out.

That made her thirty-four. Good God. He stood in the street ashamed of himself, but inviting her to consult him if difficulties arose. She thanked him, her composure as such recovered, swung her plastic carrier from the caring Co-op and elbowed off.

Back at home Fay ran around in the garden with an Indian boy of perhaps eight while in the house Joanna entertained a lady in a ruby-red sari, the wife of a well-known barrister. The son, polite but unshy, had spoken with an English upper-class correctness, but his mother, whose eyes avoided Richardson's affected a fluent chichi.

'Of course,' Mrs Mudgal was explaining, 'we are Hindus.'

Richardson back to his study after five minutes in the

visitor's company, wondered when he had last had to account for his upbringing, derivation or religious beliefs. He decided it was probably at Oxford, in earnest, drunken conversation with fellow-students. In Joanna's bracing company one might be bamboozled into confession. The Indian boy now expounded the procedure before a race. 'On your marks; get set; go. And the pistol will fire on the last word.'

Two days before school started Richardson had spent an hour in the Central Library reading Plato for an epigraph for his book: profitable time-wasting. He emerged straight on to the street; the library was now more of an emporium than an institution of culture, in a street which he recalled as violently jammed with traffic, tramcars, vans, trolleys in pictorial histories of the city but now barely disturbed by a bus or cautious motorist.

'Mr Richardson.'

The voice suggested uncertainty. Richardson turned.

In the September sunshine, a smartly dressed man called attention to himself. He wore no jacket, but a modern shirt and a beautifully knitted cardigan which fastened with three buttons on the left shoulder. His shoes shone; the edges of his shirt-cuffs seemed brand-new or starched.

'Yes.' Richardson did not recognize the speaker, who, balding, brushed strands over his scalp, grew a bristly beard which contrasted with the flatness, the thinness of the hair on his head. But his eyes were prominent in the putty colour of the face, large, deep-brown, liquid as if they would brim over into tears, vulnerable, almost too big for use.

'I heard you lecture last year at the Teachers' Centre.' The voice had strength, denying the weakness of the eyes. No more was said, as if the speaker needed encouragement to continue.

'Oh, yes.' A falling sound, with a smile; credentials established.

'My name is Towers, Henry Towers.'

That meant nothing either.

'I'm the headmaster of the Alderman Colin Rattenbury Primary School.'

The man spoke significantly, as if the name should convey a message. It did not. Richardson waited, his face professionally registering interest.

192

'It was . . . seriously affected by a fire three weeks ago.' Towers shied, after he had spoken, as if away from the words, his choice of language. 'It was in the papers. In the national press as well as the local.'

'I'm sorry. I've been abroad.'

'Eighty thousand pounds' worth of damage.'

'Good God.'

'It was deliberately started. Arson.'

'Will you be able to open? The new term?'

'Yes. The office has been very good. But three classrooms were gutted, and there'll be no staffroom. All the administration will have to be done in a corner of the hall. But they've provided us with a couple of temporary cabins, we've got the ground, thank God, so we'll make a start on time. It will mean inconvenience, but . . .'

'That's good. Have they found out who's responsible?'

Towers's face fell.

'Yes, they have. A group of nine-year-olds. Pupils of the school.' He looked away guiltily.

'Were they particularly bad?'

'One of them. He was from a wild family. Father, older brothers in prison, and borstal. But the rest were not. Ordinary children from a housing estate. They were looking for kicks, I suppose. We'd allowed them to use the playground and the field during the holiday. And that was after some heartsearching because we could expect broken windows and damage. But these little devils broke in, made a pile of papers and baskets by my desk and set it ablaze. There must have been a dozen or fifteen of them in at it.'

'And the parents?'

'They vary. Some are upset and ashamed. Some don't bother or don't know what to say. And a few, well, if the local authority took their children into care, they'd be relieved. One mouth less. It has shaken me. When you get these children in the nursery or infant classes they're keen, amenable, willing to learn. Three or four years later they're hooligans.'

'Not all of them?'

'No, but a sufficiently large number to make me wonder what we're supposed to have done for them.'

193

Towers's eyes gazed blindly, wetly towards the buildings opposite; he licked his lips; his skin had lost what little colour it had and his face seemed discomposed, plastic, the features featureless.

'Will these children be back in the school?' Richardson asked.

'Yes. They've appeared before a magistrate, but they're innocent until they're proved guilty.' A spiritless reply. Again Towers shied, as if he could only collect himself with this nerve-stricken motion. 'They'll be with us.' He suddenly turned, whirling the thick body to confront his listener. 'You'd be amazed, Mr Richardson, at the effect of this on me.'

A silence stretched between the two men, unbroken by the multifarious sounds of a distant city-centre.

'I can't sleep. I'm on tranquillizers. You talk about the Ancient Mariner syndrome; here I am stopping people in the street. I feel guilty. That's the heart and nub of it. To all intents and purposes I was a well-balanced, successful man, doing a worthwhile job. It wasn't easy. These housing-estate children need holding down. There's pretty well no parental support. We're lucky to get a twenty per cent attendance on an open evening. The mothers will turn up for a jumble sale, and so that's the way we have to drag them in. But I would have said at the end of term in July that we were making progress with these kids, that they were learning something, that we had chased up truantism, that we laid on sports for them, took them on free outings, and then a fortnight later this happens. And why to me? There's no staff I know of that has worked more conscientiously than mine, given more of their own time and this is how they're rewarded.'

'You don't blame yourself, Mr Towers,' Richardson said, judge over Israel, 'do you? Rationally now? You can't.'

'Rationally.' The word blocked his mouth like a big pebble. 'When I stood there and saw the blackened mess that had been my office or spick-and-span classrooms, there was no rationality about it. Metal girders twisted, gaping holes, great charred areas; it was like war. The blaze must have been ferocious; it's a marvel nobody was killed. And when I looked at it, it was as if my heart was ripped out of me. Some of my teachers wept, and I'm not surprised. This was a centre of order and cleanliness

194

and sense in a world where those things are at a premium, and there they lay in bloody cinders, in ashes.' The voice cracked hysterically; his breath stank; his hands clawed the air. The man came to himself, glanced at Richardson in apology. 'It makes me angry.'

'And rightly,' Richardson backed him.

'But the worse thing is, is . . . that I've lost my confidence. I keep asking myself, "Why me? What have I done wrong?" Oh, I've felt discouraged before, but now I shall never walk into a classroom again without wondering when it'll be a black and charred chaos. And that won't do. You have to look forward in hope, not despair. I can't. I tell you I can't.'

Richardson lifted his head.

'It's a tragedy,' he said. 'But the thing about education is that one never knows what the results will be. We might hope to. We might expect to. But it needs only one lunatic to do vast damage. Or one genius to do vast good. And for all we know, your wild boy might now be on the way to a cure . . .'

'But the others. The decent ones. They were there with their boxes of matches.'

'I know. I know.'

'We're all hooligans deep down. Vandals, arsonists, pollutionists.'

'That's why,' Richardson said, 'it needs the professionals like yourself to . . .'

'Professional?' Towers spread his arms. 'The Director sent for me, and the whole interview I could see him summing me up, deciding that I wasn't fit to be in charge of a school, that I'd been given the chance, and I'd failed.'

'That's not the truth, Mr Towers. That's your state of shock. We'd all feel like that. You and I may not always agree with the Director, but he's no fool. He could even feel he was in some degree responsible. No. You've got to go back there the day after tomorrow, teaching the little horrors to read and tot up and keep their noses clean. And give them their music and poetry and races and visits. Twice as hard, if need be.'

'But my staff? Will they trust me?'

'Of course they will. They'll be blaming themselves as you do. And they'll need your support.'

'You don't understand, Mr Richardson.'

'I think I do.'

'The staff on the whole were against allowing the children into the playground in the holidays. I overruled them. Now they'll blame me for what happened, say I encouraged it. They will. I know them.'

'It's an occupational hazard amongst teachers to think you're right after the event. That, and muttering behind the hand. But pay no attention. You did what you thought best. Those children would have been in the playground whether you gave permission or not, as well you know. No, Mr Towers. Pick the bits up.'

'I've been there this morning. It's awful. Still.'

'That's so.'

'And the staff will be in tomorrow. We'd arranged it.'

'Needing your help.'

A saturnine man, in raincoat and trilby hat, wandered down the street and as he passed them, they heard him singing, not loudly but with a startling clarity.

'It may be that Death's bright angel
Will speak in that chord again
It may be that only in heaven
I shall hear that grand Amen.'

He conducted his performance delicately with his right hand, noticing nobody, intent on his small ritual.

' "The Lost Chord",' Towers said. 'Sullivan. My father used to sing it.' He took two steps to his left across the pavement as if clumsily practising a dance movement. 'This holiday's been catastrophic. I went to see my brother in Yorkshire. He's dying with cancer. At least that's what it looks like. They're giving him chemotherapy, but the effect of that's terrible. He's barely fifty, married late, and so has young children.' He shook his head.

Richardson tutted his sorrow.

'He's an Anglican vicar,' Towers continued. 'He was really clever, scholarship to Cambridge in classics, did well there. We thought he'd go into business. It shook me, I'd just started college. It shook my father. He was a Co-op manager. We'd

196

always been church-going; Dad was a sidesman, but we'd no idea Barry would do that. We were pretty certain that he'd been looking into managerial training courses.'

Richardson thought of his own brother.

'Was your father pleased?' he asked.

'He tried to make out he was, but I think, I wasn't there at the time, that he was stunned. The clergy aren't well paid, are they? Barry did it properly, took a research B D at Cambridge, and all the rest of it. But my father was worried. That's bad to say that of a man who's religious, but he had to scrape to buy a house and educate us, so I think he took it for granted that Barry would end up with a substantial salary.'

Towers's voice became animated over his brother's career, his father's doubts, his face alight.

'And now it's come to this. He's sick all the time, his hair's dropping out, his face is drawn, and he was a big, fine-looking chap. He could give me three inches, and he'd a fine crop of wavy hair, not like mine. It's harrowing to see him. And he insists on carrying on as best he can.'

'Is your father still alive?'

'No. He died last year. My mother is. She's seventy-six and lives on her own.'

'How long have the doctors given your brother?'

'They don't seem to have said. Or haven't been asked. I suppose compared to him I've plenty to be thankful for. If I were in his shoes, I'd be like Job's comforters, I'd curse God.'

'You didn't know about, about the illness before the holiday?'

'No. We knew he hadn't been well. But I hadn't actually seen him for two years. With one thing and the other. We correspond, or our wives did, and phoned. And do you know the effect on me, Mr Richardson? First that, Barry's death warrant, and then this fire? I'm looking for the third. Third time pays for all. That's superstition, if you like, but that's the effect. Me, an educated man. God. I'm waiting to be mugged or run over, or God knows what horror next.'

'Absolutely understandable, Mr Towers. But tomorrow you'll have to appear there with your staff, straightening things out.'

'I suppose so.'

'You'll tackle it adequately because you know the worst.' Was he overdoing, hamming it? 'Will you let me know how things shape?' To add a footnote to his book?

'Thank you, thank you.' Towers rubbed his palm over his head, flattening the streaks of hair. 'It's done me good to talk to you. It really has. People don't understand failure; do they? They're kind, but they've no idea, no idea.'

Richardson held out his hand. The two men shook, strongly.

'You'll let me know how things are, won't you? In a day or two, when you've had the chance to set things going.'

'I will. I'm most grateful. Thank you.' Towers still held his hand, noticed, dropped it. 'Shall I ring you at home?'

'You're more likely to find me at school.'

'Yes. Thank you again.'

'We'll lose a battle or two, Mr Towers, but not the war.' Richardson moved off, almost bumped into the other, who had awkwardly shifted his pitch. Now Richardson had escaped without further cliché.

When he repeated the encounter to Joanna, he could not conceal his satisfaction.

'I honestly think the man went away more cheerful,' he said.

'Honestly?' She mocked him.

They laughed together.

'I'm looking forward to a continuation of the Tony Moore–Lesley Allbright saga,' she told him.

In the rush of the first week he had no chance to talk to the protagonists. He ran across Miss Allbright in the corridor and invited her into his office, providing her with a cup of coffee, an unusual procedure. After he questioned her about her holiday, she had been to Yugoslavia with another young teacher, he asked about Moore.

'That's finished, as far as I'm concerned,' she said.

'I see. So you don't know how he's shaping?'

'You ought to question him.' She spoke with a ladylike but undisguised aggression.

'I have to get hold of him first, and that's not easy at this time of term. But I wanted to make a few enquiries of you before I put my big foot in it.'

198

'His wife's left him. Again.'

They said nothing for a time, toying with their cups.

'It's tricky,' Richardson said.

'I don't know much about it,' Miss Allbright answered. 'He doesn't talk to me at all now. But from what I can make out, they quarrelled again for some reason or another, and she packed her traps.'

'Where's she living?'

'Don't know.'

'There isn't another man?'

'No. Well, that's what they say.'

'Is there anything,' Richardson asked, 'that I can do, do you think? I trust your judgement.'

'I'd leave him to stew in his own juice. He'll come running to you fast enough if he wants anything.'

'Yes. He's an unhappy young man, don't you think?'

'He gets what he deserves. He's thoroughly selfish. If something suits his whims, then he'll put himself out.'

'So you're not surprised his wife's gone?'

'She's a nobody if ever I saw one.'

Lesley Allbright combined anger with assumed unconcern. She spoke with a genteel confidence as if her own problems had been solved, though she could hardly forgive herself for tangling with Moore, and Richardson for knowing about it. She side-stepped away, deprecating his welter of thanks, leaving his office heavy with her scent. Two days later her head of department let it out that the Allbright had met some man, a civil servant from Preston, on the Yugoslavian jaunt, and when not occupied with reading and writing love letters was walking on cloud nine.

'Will it last?' he enquired.

'Will anything?' The woman's face was sour, though whether at her lack of success or his facetious curiosity he could not guess.

He finally ran Moore down in the science block. The man looked miserable enough, and shifty, his lab coat torn and stained, one pocket nearly off.

'Hello. How are things with you, then?'

'Uh-uh, thank you.'

199

'Have a good holiday?'

'So, so, thanks.' Pause while Moore squinted round for an escape route.

'Were you pleased with the chemistry results?'

'Yes.' Brighter voice. 'The As especially. But they were bright sets. They'd do well in any case.'

'Back to the grindstone again?'

'Yes.' He had interpreted that as the sentence of dismissal. Moore began to step away.

'Your wife keeping well?'

'Yes, thank you.'

He'd pushed the door of a lab open, darted inside, quick as a snake, and as slippery.

Richardson made an enquiry of Smith after lunch.

'Has Tony Moore's wife left him again?'

'That's it, is it? He's like a bear with a sore head. Do you think he's attractive? To women?'

'Frankly, no.'

'My wife says he is. It surprised me. Anyhow, I'll find out for you.'

Smith bestrode his narrow world like a cheerful colossus. His forthcoming promotion, the handing over of his department, the uprooting of his home, the shifting of his children to other schools, suited him. If he could not move others, he'd move himself.

When Richardson arrived home that evening his wife placed a large coffee-table volume before him. She and the girls had already looked it through. *Ancient Indian Civilizations*.

'What's it like?'

'Beautiful,' Virginia answered.

'It makes you want . . .' Margot, 'to go there.'

'They know how to produce these things in America,' Joanna told him. 'It looks good enough to eat.'

Richardson fingered the glossy dust-cover. He felt miserable because at four o'clock he had received a phone call from the principal of the largest College of Further Education enquiring about James Walters, who was trying to sign on there for a one-year 'A' level course.

'He was honest with me,' Mr Milner said, 'about his cheating. Brazenly so. I'll give him that. Of course, it would have to come out in any case.'

Richardson gave a report on the boy's academic achievements in his school.

'He could pass "A" level then, well enough for university?'

'Easily.'

'Why didn't he then?' Milner's voice was odious, sneering, his local accent stressed. The man did not conceal his envy of Richardson's successful school.

'I can't say. He lost confidence in himself just at the wrong time. I wouldn't like to guess why that was.'

'Isn't it likely to happen again?' Milner thought he had cornered Richardson.

'I don't see why. He'll get three good As.'

'In which case why don't you take him back yourself?'

'Because,' Richardson allowed himself a high-class sigh, 'he hasn't applied to us. That's probably wise on his part. A completely new beginning, away from the unpleasantness.'

'Did you advise him to come here?'

'No.'

'Would you recommend him to us?'

'Certainly. Strongly. He's a good candidate.'

'If that's so,' Milner said grudgingly, 'I suppose I shall have to have him. I'm not sure we're doing right. Either to himself or to us. It's what the forces call "LMF".' He waited, vainly, for Richardson's question. 'Lack of moral fibre. Once one has failed as badly as this boy has, that should be it. The end. Finis.'

'That's a gloomy view of humanity, Mr Milner.'

'I'm near retirement. Sixty-three. In two years I shall be out of it, and glad to go. I can't say that my dealings with either staff or students has made me sanguine about human perfectibility.'

'No?' Now he had his question.

'No.' No more. He played the word like an ace. 'Well, thank you, Mr Richardson. I suppose we shall always be your dustbin.' And he replaced the phone.

Richardson, slowly turning the pages, felt Fay stand close to him. He put an arm about her waist, and felt better.

'Has it come from America?'

'Yes. Your uncle Eric sent it.' They arrived at an article on

201

the literature of ancient India; he put his finger on the name: E. P. Richardson, MA, D.Phil., D.Litt., (Professor of Sanskrit Studies, Yale).

'He must be clever,' Fay said.

'Oh, yes.'

'Cleverer than you?'

'Much.'

'Mummy said today to somebody, over the phone, that you were as clever as a barrow-load of monkeys.'

'Eric's as clever as a lorry-load, then,' he said, delighted.

'She was talking to Mrs Howard,' Virginia informed him. She'd been listening in all round. He loved his daughters, feared for them.

'Netta Howard rang,' Joanna told him over the washing-up bowl. 'She really wanted to speak to you.'

'I'm surprised.'

'She was full of your praises.'

'So you put her right. "Clever as a barrow-load of monkeys." '

'Little ears,' Joanna said, laughing. 'And I thought I was keeping my voice down.'

'What did she want?'

'Us to go to dinner with them. I've fixed a provisional date. Thursday week. Nothing in your diary.'

'Good. Her husband's back?'

'Yes. And you seem to be the cause.' Joanna glanced towards the door, but her daughters were out of earshot. She mimicked the thin voice on the phone. ' "Your husband made me look at myself. I didn't like what I saw." '

'Well, go on. Don't stop now. Praise me up.'

'That made her decide to become reconciled with her Simon. She wrote him a letter, and he came running back straight away.' Again the ghost-voice. ' "Your husband just talked to me. He didn't lay down the law. He just made me see somehow what I was doing." She was very grateful.'

'That was the very opposite of what she told me. She said I was full of certainties where no certainties existed.'

'Ah, your effect on these ladies.'

'And what did you say?' Richardson asked.

'I said I was very glad, and that I knew you would be. And then we began a little competition to find the right description of you. The go-between. The catalyst. The fixer. And do you know what she came up with?'

'I hardly dare to ask.'

'I hardly dare to tell you. "An agent for good." How about that then?'

'I'm blushing,' he said.

'The factor. The nuncio. The middleman.'

'You sound like Roget.'

'And you sound embarrassed.' Joanna, grinning, splashing with the taps. 'Don't worry. The family'll cut you down to size.'

'Did she make a favourable impression on you?'

'Yes. In a way. Not just because she praised you, though I liked that. She seemed, oh, enthusiastic somehow. Keen to get on with life. What do you think?'

'About her? She made a favourable impression until she turned on me. And that, perhaps, worked her bad temper off.' He stacked plates and dishes in a distant cupboard. 'I'm lucky. The problems I'm involved in aren't too tricky.'

Again, the third time in as many days, he brought up the subject of Henry Towers and his burnt-out school.

'Have you heard from him?'

'No. I expect he's finding it just about manageable, and so there's no need to talk to me.'

'I know you won't like this,' Joanna said. 'You'll write me off as superstitious, but I think your Towerses and, oh, that boy who cheated have got the mark on them. They're bound to fail. It's inbuilt.'

'That's a non-verifiable hypothesis, if you like,' he told her. 'Why can't we see the mark? Young Walters was a thoroughly satisfactory student for nearly seven years. Towers looks the part. Articulate, persuasive, well dressed in a much more up to date fashion than I am.'

'Still . . .'

'What about my father and James?'

'He recovered. To some extent.'

'There are some people . . .'

'Who can't cope with simple difficulties,' she interrupted.

203

'That's what I mean. And they seem to attract more problems. Towers is right to expect a third catastrophe. And a fourth, and more.'

They argued, without heat, since he did not believe Joanna believed her own theory, except in moments of exasperation.

About a week later, Towers made the telephone call. All shaped well; he was keeping his fingers crossed; the arsonists had not yet been to court, because of some snag or other. It was ridiculous. But, but, but his school prospered.

Richardson walked out from his office immediately after this conversation to keep an appointment with the City Architect's Department, which wanted his advice, they said, about school-building. He'd never been invited there before and was glad to take the opportunity; his new book would have a section on the foolishness of much traditional educational architecture. In the meeting he enjoyed himself; the occasion was a visit from a dozen young architects in training and together they discussed an urban comprehensive school one of them had designed for his finals. Richardson had a field-day; the headmaster's office was as far from the classrooms as it could be, instead of separate but near. The storage space was inadequate; lavatories were wrongly placed; changing rooms were far too large for the numbers, while the hall precluded even a half-full seated assembly. Would the laboratories, sited as they were, be adequately warm? How many textbooks, photocopies or pianos would such an establishment be expected to house? Had any attempt been made to find out? Would the kitchens and dining areas be suitable for quick change should the pattern of demand for school meals alter, as seemed likely? The chief architect, the deputy director, the education officer, the chairman of the education committee were forced back to reliance on the English schoolteachers' genius for improvisation, and such sentences as 'Money doesn't grow on trees' or 'In a kinder financial climate . . .' to cover their real lack of understanding. Richardson frightened them, brow-beat them, and the young men looked on baffled, convinced.

The meeting over, Richardson left, elated but certain he'd done himself no good with people who mattered. He stood for a moment outside the architect's place, which was situated in two beautiful eighteenth-century houses in a cul-de-sac cobbled and paved, planted with trees in character.

'Good afternoon.'

A voice startled him as he was still mentally running rings round the experts.

Felicity Brooks. He wondered, briefly, whether she had been waiting for him here, not putting it past her. They exchanged greetings and she explained that this old corner of the city pleased her, especially on a bright September afternoon. Her face was puffy, multi-coloured, her eyes darkly shadowed, lips thin and pallid; in an expensive dark two-piece she looked sick, ill at ease. These politenesses over, he prepared to move on, but she blocked his way, though whether this was deliberate he could not guess.

'Mrs Howard was in touch with us,' he tried again. 'Her husband's back with her.'

'And you're putting that down to your skill as a negotiator.'

The tone struck both rude and quiet. She looked old, the blotchy face unsuitable for the elegant clothes.

'Not at all.'

'It's nothing to do with you and the sooner you realize it the better.'

He did not reply; she railed against the preposterous claim he had not made. She swayed from the hips, feet still. The street closed deserted about them.

'The sooner you realize that the better.'

'I see.'

'God knows who you think you are, giving your orders. Just because you can lay down the law to schoolchildren and teachers . . .'

'I can't even do that, Mrs Brooks.'

She paid no attention.

'You go telling Netta and Veronica what they should do, or not do.'

'Both at your invitation.'

'Do you know what Conrad said about you? "Who's this prick Richardson? He wrote me a bloody great epistle, you never read such pompous, poncing cock." That's what he thought.'

'I'm sorry.'

'Sorry. You're not sorry. You're only too pleased with yourself. My father would have called you a stuffed shirt.'

'Mrs Brooks, you seem determined to pick a quarrel with me. I honestly don't know why. Did you come here deliberately, find out where I was?' His voice sounded weak to himself; though there was no one about, he could not be sure who was listening behind the curtained windows a yard or two away.

'Who in hell do you think you are? Why should I put myself out to find you? My God, you've got a good opinion of yourself. I wouldn't walk across the street to see you.'

'Mrs Brooks, how have I upset you?'

'Upset you?' She echoed his words, perhaps mocking. 'You couldn't upset a doll's tea-cup. With your blown-up opinion of yourself.'

She spoke no more loudly, maintained the accent of her class so that he could barely believe his ears.

'Mrs Brooks, I see something has annoyed you. If I am in any way to blame, I apologize. I cannot think . . .' He stopped. 'But this is no place to conduct an argument. I'm willing to listen to you, but not at the street corner.'

'No, because you don't want people to know what a bastard you are.'

'Perhaps so.'

He prepared to push past her; she raised her hands to defend herself.

'You came and talked to Veronica.'

He didn't answer.

'She died. I don't say it's your fault. But what do you know about people dying. I will tell you something.'

At this moment, the deputy director of education and the local education officer walked out and down the cobbled street. Mrs Brooks stopped; the two men both raised trilby hats, simultaneously, comically. The woman raised a tactful, social smile, allowed them to reach the end of the street.

'Between Veronica and Stephen,' she whispered, 'I lost two children. Both stillborn; both at the full term. And abroad. In foreign hospitals.'

206

The door opened again and a group of the young architects sauntered out, chattering. They looked towards Richardson, acknowledged him shyly, dropping their voices. The street seemed suddenly full. He looked at his watch in preparation for escape.

'You don't know what that means. You can't know, for all your pretensions. Two perfectly formed sons. I saw them. And now Vernie. And then I come on you, with your instructions.'

He touched her forearm. She recoiled, almost snarling.

'I'm sorry, Mrs Brooks. You're not . . .'

'You're not. Wait till your children break your heart. Is that Marguerite on the pill?' The demonstrative adjective was inhuman. 'Is she?'

'I don't know. I shouldn't think so.'

'Find out, then. Bloody find out.'

The door opened again; two girl secretaries emerged, high heels confidently clattering.

'Can I offer you a lift home,' he asked her. 'My car's just up the road.'

'I've got my own fucking car.'

That made his mind up for him. He wished her good afternoon and pushed curtly past. She made no attempt to obstruct him.

At the end of the short street, he glanced back. Felicity Brooks had turned and was fiddling in her handbag. He should face about, make tracks towards her, but could not; he shuddered, remembering her illness and Joanna's account of tears, of strange singing. Two youths carrying a length of new timber marched past on the main highway; the first, with an upstanding cock's comb, was yawning; the second, slightly younger, in overalls, suddenly let go of his end of the plank, out of devilment.

'Pick it up, you useless spunk-stain,' the leader ordered. Both laughed out loud, trotted off, swaggering.

Richardson shivered, stood still. Mrs Brooks came towards him, dangling her car keys. She turned along the main road flatly ignoring him, her expression privately pleased. He watched her; she was in no hurry but neither did she loiter. He clutched his briefcase to his chest desperately with both arms.

He could not remember the drive home, sat breathless in his car outside his house for twenty minutes.

Finally he forced himself indoors, where Marguerite handed him a letter from her headmistress inviting him to judge their festival of poetry.

'What do you think?' he asked, trying to keep his voice normal.

'You'll do it well,' she said, 'but as there are more losers than winners, you're bound to be unpopular.'

'You do it, Daddy,' Virginia said. 'And show old Dandruff up.'

The family sat down together and he began to recover. Joanna put a hand on his shoulder, showing she'd noticed something amiss; he'd soon be able to complain, explain. In a few minutes.

Confidence grew as he carved the chicken, serving his wife first.